Beneath the Pleasure Zones

THE RUPTURE

Paul Green

Mandrake of Oxford
© Paul A. Green & Mandrake 2014

Cover by Richard Coles

First Print Edition

All rights reserved. No part of this work may be reproduced, stored in a retrieval system. or transmitted in any form or any means, electronic, mechanical, photocopying, recording or otherwise without the prior permission of the publisher. Paul Andrew Green asserts all legal rights of paternity, integrity and intellectual property under the 1988 Copyright Act.

Published by Mandrake of Oxford PO Box 250, Oxford OX1 1AP (UK)

The author would like to thank Peter Carroll and Mandrake for permission to quote from *The Apophenion* (Mandrake 2008)

Contents

1 Lucas: the Post-Qliphothic Aeon 5
2 William: Atomised in the Rupture 43
3 Pleasure Centres PLC 61
4 The Polyverse 79
5 The Burrough 111
6 The Establishment 131
7 The Zone 142
8 Intervoid 155
9 The Anarchy Business 182
10 Time to Seize the Time 194
11 The Psychic National Gridlock 199
12 Dark Stuff 218
13 The Rapture of Rupture 231
14 Feast of Smoke 252
15 Serious Business in the Polyverse 274

For Cathy - and for Jez Welsh who first evoked the Quantum Brothers...

1
Lucas: the Post-Qliphothic Aeon

Special Effects of the Rupture

'The post-Qliphothic Aeon.' As time passed, the phrase seemed increasingly cryptic each time Lucas wrote it. This time he was using a cracked biro on the back of some old spreadsheets salvaged from a ruined tax office. He hoped that this latest attempt at a memoir would finally create an explanation, an exegesis that made sense of the Qliphothic Intrusion, the Yesodic Leakage, or as the authorities now termed it, desperate to sanitise its terrors, 'The Rupture.'

Over a decade now since that brief aperture in the consensus of what then passed for reality, the daily time-line. A sudden blinding fissure in the sky; an eruption of darkness across the cities; a crack in the shell of Malkuth, our root-world, according to the wandering street-prophets, that admitted the dark side of the Yesodic zones. The dark energies of the Qliphoth broke in and out. Everyone had a pet creed, a broken pot of theory that didn't quite hold up. 'No-one can develop a workable practice to cope fully with the afterbirths of the Rupture,' wrote Lucas, cautiously. And paused, yet again.

For this was personal history. His dead parents, Nick and Pauline, became vessels and he had been an agent, blundering into forbidden zones, who had 'let something fly in,' as the Lore of the Rupture had it. That's all he could tell himself.

Rain drummed on the roof of his shelter, a ramshackle extension to an old Carbon-Age observation post dug out of the wooded hillside in those far-off years when our defence mechanisms were launch-keys in plutonic silos. Now everyone was into psychic self-defence. He sensed a remote inner-ear distant babble, perhaps from the squabbling sages of nearby Leynebridge - and the moment of self-recollection was gone.

He pushed the precious paper to one side of the table. So much for his Neuro-Saxon Chronicle. His left temple ached. Focus on language had become difficult after the Rupture; and now it was impossible to concoct a narrative that he could live in comfortably.

Comforts in general were in short supply, especially here in the Borderlands, where the followers of the Lore had congregated, to live close to the Earth. He was lucky to have found this obscure squat outside Leynebridge. He surveyed his improvised living space, his bunk, his books leaning on the rusty shelves that would have housed a short-wave radio console or a geiger counter. His late mother's imported Chairman Mao alarm clock told him it was approximately eight-thirty. Simple tinplate mechanisms usually worked. So he peered out under the heavy concrete lintel into his extension, a crazy parody of a suburban conservatory cobbled together from plastic sheeting, corrugated iron and discarded pallets. It was raining steadily, as Vivienne had predicted. He'd overheard her reading the cards for a stout farmer in the Red Hag. He must try not to think too hard about dreamy Vivienne. But it stopped him thinking about his sex goddess Carla. Or Leila. Or Robyn. All his lost girls.

Time to work if he was going to eat today, to go to Leynebridge and share the battered ornaments of his knowledge at the Learning Repository. With the kids. Damned kids.

He still couldn't believe he'd fallen into his late mother's vocation as an educator, albeit in modes she never anticipated in her Age of Ideology (Marxist-Leninist). But in the chaos of the immediate post-Rupture period, it was his best chance of keeping his head down. Someone had to deal with the thousands of young persons traumatised by their new-found powers and the bombardments of a para-psychic society. *Flash-back: the ghost of himself barely out of his teens, helping his mother instill some simple left-brain skills into moaning semi-children huddled in the shell of Westway Community School.* The least he could do. All he could do. His encounters in the alt.worlds of the Polyverse, which still tried to entrap him in dream-frames, had given him some immunity against the Special Effects of the Rupture. He had survived. If only to talk it through.

Problem was that he was still talking it through (or its voices were talking through him) years later in the Borderlands, with nowhere to go but round and round. Except on his solitary shift at the 'community' radio station. Leynebridge 930 AM - which would inevitably close soon. It looked as if the community didn't want his communications.

He pulled the plastic sheeting off his trike and checked the battery. It might just last another season. Perhaps he could charge it up covertly at the studio, after his teaching session. The motor whined fitfully. With his bag of books over his shoulder and his greatcoat flapping in the drizzle, he bumped down the grass-fissured track towards the Leynebridge road.

The route curved down through a copse, passed an abandoned pub, its picnic tables chopped up for firewood, and crossed sloping pasture lands where huddles of sheep ruminated. As he cycled, he noticed a faint tremor behind his right temple. *The glistening hedgerows are signalling, alive with biomorphic energy.* Then he controlled the reflex - it was surely a slight breeze. Or the animals simply stating their presence-in-itself. The dim murmur in his head merged with the hum of the motor as the trike gathered speed. The Undermind was getting to him again.

As he reached the fork between Leynebridge and Old Hallows, he overtook a dented pick-up truck carrying a sagging pyramid of potatoes. The driver was mouthing something, probably some mantra intended to keep him focused on the road, but his fuel trailer full of methane was swinging everywhere, so Lucas gave him a wide berth. As the truck receded in his rear-view mirror he caught the mushy whisper of the Undermind in his inner ear *all over the village bruising his fat potatoes black and bloody all over her...* He tried to shake it out of his head – a futile reflex. He could only grip the handle bars tighter and wait for the turrets of the Leynebridge Tower to appear through the haze.

The road skirted a burying ground, another mass grave from Rupture-times. Between the yew trees and the crooked wooden markers, he noticed three Harvesters and looked away quickly. Hooded in grey they slowly moved their snaking detectors along the overgrown paths. Refugees from the Urbs often assumed they were using metal detectors to salvage precious resources - a saw blade, a claw hammer, a lock-knife. But Lucas knew their modus operandi. Even now, they still claimed an ancient right to harvest souls; and on their vigils they claimed to see a bluish orgone-flicker of astral energy hovering over the grassy mounds, to be gathered as a life-feed in their secret ceremonies. The Leynebridge Elders discouraged the micro-sect and it was unusual to see them after sun-rise. Another sign that the precarious social order was collapsing?

The Lore

'No-one expected this - the Middle Ages with a hole in the middle...' His words died in the air. His proteges looked blankly around the dusty classroom. Old Sir Flukey Luke was off on one of his spiralling digressions, although he had been drafted to teach the craft of the linear sentence, the unglamorous grammar that nobody else at the Learning Repository wanted to do. The sheer nullity of these sixteen year olds had provoked him into yet another random outburst — as random as the burst of private chatter from the Undermind which probably underlay their diffused attention. He had spent years trying to forget the Rupture and its preliminary, his own crucial rite of passage between the Sephiroth - the qabalistic terms were as good as any for mapping the space-time of the Polyverse - but he couldn't keep silent. 'You don't understand what it was like before. You don't get what it is now...'

Tyler, a plump apprentice butcher, sprawled across an old typist's chair and fingered a small gold pendant in the likeness of a bulldog. He yawned.

'Is this another story?'

'Is it true Lore?' Joshua, skinny and fidgety, seemed anxious to test his credentials, as always.

'It's a truth.'

'Would the Elders say it was true?'

'The Elders don't own the Lore, you know. I'm not always sure they really understand it anyway…'

Joshua pursed his lips. 'I ought to report that, Master Lucas. Disrespecting the Elderseers…' His voice wobbled with anxiety. 'That's shocking…'

'Don't worry, Josh!' Lucas had to keep it light, keep the sermon moving. 'Just my little joke. I speak in riddles, as usual.'

Tyler grimaced. 'Give us another of your old stories then.'

Lucas was losing part of his plot already. 'Once upon a time…' Tyler was groaning but he had to continue. 'Once upon a time you could conduct repeatable experiments.'

'X-periments…?' Joshua slowly mouthed the unfamiliar word.

'Yes! Let's say you were firing a rocket - like the rockets in the Feast of Smoke.' Tyler grinned. He remembered last year's Feast of Smoke, the burning pyres, the riotous horns.

'Now, if you knew what sort of powder you were using, and the quantity and the weight of the rocket and the wind speed and direction, you could predict how the rocket might fly. And you could test it, again and again, and if you varied the weight or the charge, you'd get consistent results, according to simple laws of motion. But now there are so many anomalies. Space-time quirks. Too much all-at-onceness.'

'But that's good, isn't it? That's why we have the Lore and the Powers, yes?' Josh was desperate for reassurance. It would be futile to continue.

Tyler giggled. 'He wants to be a little Elder. Or maybe a Harvester. I just want to get on the Lobe. Or go to the cities - and one of them

Pleasure Centres...' He was doodling the squat figure of a fertility charm in a scrawl of red crayon. Lucas ignored the reference to the Lobe - *No Lobe in Leynebridge* was the official Elder-teaching - and tried another probe.

'Do you know how many died in the first days of the Rupture, in this new age of Yesodic trickery and illusion?'

They were blanking again, the history of the mystery didn't do it for these boys even though they were engulfed by it. Then the chime of the Leynebridge Tower clock signalled the end of the session. Wordlessly they drifted away as Lucas picked up his unopened books. Time for his other gig.

The Way of Leynebridge

Rain spattered the tree-lined bank of the River Leyne. According to the latest edict from the Leynebridge Council of Elderseers it was now the day after Lugfest, the festival of harvesting and trial marriages, derived from the Celtic Lugnasah. Aran Yarland knew his Lore.

The morning rain dribbled along the rusty creases in dumped car bodies. These automotive relics formed a roughly circular barricade around Aran's enclosure. But Aran remembered that Forgan had performed a hasty rite on the twisted shells, so that should have cleansed them of the Carbon Spirit.

Aran repeated this formula sub-vocally: *cleanse them of the Carbon Spirit cleanse them of the Carbon Spirit.* His heavy cracked lips kept moving around the words as he moved around his conical hut in widening circles, in a lurching spiral, leaning on his crooked staff. This was the approved way of winding up his lower chakric energies as he prepared for his meeting, (perhaps his Binding Mating) with Viv. It was part of the Way of Leynebridge. The New Way of the Serpent.

It was time to walk the Whole of the Way. For the discovery of a long crooked stone walkway, in the course of excavating a proposed road extension, way back in the days of the Carbonites, was one of the first signs vouchsafed to the Elders. The path was supposed to be 'Bronze Age' according to old Noah Dodd, and it was surely meant to trace the serpentine sexual energies of the human body. The story went that after weeks of riot and resistance, the construction of a direct road out of the Valley had to be abandoned right there at the outskirts of Leynebridge, to allow the Serpent Way to coil protectively around the town, following the trees overhanging the river. Noah had even traced its power-flow around the central streets, so its energies clustered around all the key landmarks in the town. Aran would sing that story to his brood, when he had bred.

Aran marched with a long stride under his green kilt, his battered war-boots slipping on the outcrops of muddy stone. He tried to sense the energies of the stones working upwards through his legs and thighs. The willows arching over from the slopes above him would surely form a protective green tunnel. He could hear the distant rush of the river. If he could only focus more clearly down this long nave of leaves, he could perhaps decipher the current's message and relate its whorls and eddyings to his feelings for Viv and the impulse behind his mission. He found it hard to explain himself. But this encounter had to work. Mating had to be binding. A man couldn't easily take his chances outside the Borderlands.

Aran the craft-worker shaped slivers of silver and scraps of bronze into neo-celtic divination tools for rich tourists. He also made rune-knives and pendants. It was intricate work and sales were slow. But he was sure that he could imbue each one of them with a tiny spasm of the serpentine life-force, especially if he tumbled with Viv for hours on end in the flickering light of her wood fire.

He passed under a low stone bridge. There were rusty rails up there long ago; coal-burning dragons of iron supposedly rumbled overhead. He tried to imagine such thunder – the insistent shouting of the old Carbon Spirits - then controlled the thought-form. Viv grew uneasy when he talked about angry noises in his head. Especially when they turned into voices. But Underminding was true understanding. It was a sign he knew the deep Lore…

Aran pushed through a wicket-gate and turned up a steep narrow alley beside the churchyard. St. Michael's had long been shut, its lead stripped, its lancet windows boarded over, anticipating invading squads of Christian Heavy Shepherds or urban Islamist gangs, the Wahibist Mo-Boys. But the dead were still waiting in the long grass, cramped in their earth-boxes. Aran wondered if Mrs Nixon would come out and do her naked dance for them, flitting between the crooked gravestones and skewed buttresses. She always danced to her voices in the summer. He'd strained to hear them. Why were they silenced? Why was she no longer seen in the village streets? *Perhaps she had entered the cursed hulk of the church itself, and was crucified.* He fought the horrible exciting thought-demon. It was his demon, not even an Underminding. He must focus harder on Viv. He tramped faster through the gravel towards the road for High Town.

Leynebridge was formed by a warped triangle of streets, overlooked by the dark brow of Leyston Hill and the Burrough to the west. The Burrough kept them safe, according to Noah. The jagged crenellations of the Castle Tower and its crooked radio mast rose above a jumble of slate roofs, many now turfed for winter warmth, overlaid by moss and clumps of grass.

Roof-turbines squeaked and clattered in the breeze but Aran didn't register them, any more than he noticed the dung of heavy horses smeared across the cobbles or the giggly rickshaw boys clustered outside The Red Hag waiting for trade. The dingy pub advertised 'Grand Ceilidh Battle Every Saturday' and there was a time when Aran might have been a contender on the war-pipes, but now he had other contests on his mind.

As he passed the pillars of the Book Market and the lop-sided wooden statue of its founder, he wondered how Viv would receive him. There had been other lovers but he had no worries about his prowess. No need for the techno-fakery of the Pleasure Centres. Had he not pleasured her deeply the night they met, when she was selling crystals in the Tower gardens? Any girl might have agreed to bond with him after Lugfest. Yet he was drawn again and again to this perverse young woman, a 'bitch witch' according to some of his fellow crafters, and granddaughter of an Incomer, albeit a Elder. It wasn't just the motion of her hips in the dark or the undercurve of her bosom or those full lips. Her powers might challenge him. You could see it in the eyes. But what an alliance they'd make...

He reached the side door of Buzzard Books, Gavin Wharton's shop, and strode up the creaking stairs to her eyrie on the top floor. He beat on her door three times with his staff, the staff for binding a mating as blessed by Noah. He struck thrice three times, as according to Lore. There was no reply.

The door swung open on an empty low ceilinged room. He stared at her jumble of books, pots and quilts, sniffed her thick balmy scent on the dusty air. Then he pushed aside a pile of corn dollies, and tore back the saffron curtain at the far end of the room, to find her crouching on the bed, sorting out a pile of ornaments.

'I'm working,' she muttered. 'I'm thinking... I'm in a channel. Don't disturb me.' Aran snorted. Girls always had an alibi, hiding behind their thought-forms...

In the realm of books, in barns she had visited in dreams, she heard voices. They sang bawdy limericks. They bounced with bawdy. White faces flickered like butterfly wings.

'I've come to sort things out, Viv. We need to have a Mating, scribed properly with Noah, the whole Way, according to the true Way... you know...' From his shoulder-bag he produced a tarnished goblet, gripped her hand and curled her fingers around the stem. 'Look at this... All it needs is a bit of polish...'

She stared at the cup in silence, before picking up a scrap of silk and rubbing it mechanically around the rim. He waited for her reaction, for joy, tears, in-drawn breath. She put the cup down.

'Supposing it's ...' She paused. 'Like - not a way for us ...' She was almost mumbling. 'Suppose it became - a game with pretty trinkets - just like this one...'

Aran swung round, appalled. 'This Mating Cup was made by old Gil Norwood and charged by Forgan's spell-craft — what shite you talk!'

'A joke, Aran...'

'You should show respect for the Lore.' He sensed, obscurely, her resistance, a ragged veil across her thoughts. He was waiting for an apology. But he would be patient. She was worth the struggle.

'Aran, do you really believe everything surrounding the Way? Like the Feast of Smoke...'

Aran felt a spasm of anger. After all the patient tuition he had given her in the Way of Leynebridge... He gripped her shoulder, dragged her to her feet, and spun her round, his dreadlocks whirling.

'You disrespect the Feast? You're trying to say that Forgan and Noah Dodd and the Elders are cheap tricksters? You talk like a city Carbonite. Or someone that's been fooling with the Lobe. What would your grandmother say? You should be ashamed...'

'No - but there could be a mistake... a misunderstanding of the Rupture...' She hadn't expected this vehemence; but she wouldn't let go of her past. 'After all, there wasn't a Feast of Smoke when I was a little girl.'

'You must trust the wisdom of the Elderseers! They truly found the Way Back for us after the Rupture... your own grandmother foremost among them...' Aran was gripping her shoulder, shouting in her ear. Viv was distracted by the tassels on his hood, swaying in the breeze from the broken window. He was so huge and desperate.

'Their teaching is rote, there's no pleasure in it,' she murmured. Aran was a compulsive ritualist. He was rooting for an earth-mother and once he'd done the Beast Dance in the twisting pathways around the Burrough, he'd just write his clumsy chromosomic script in her secret zones and beget his lineage.

'Because of the Elderseers, everyone has work, and there's clean air and water in Leynebridge. We're close to each other and the Earth. People respect the Lore, and learn their Crafts!' He wasn't going to let her get away with such a tainted kind of knowing. He picked up his staff and jabbed at an old prayer rug as if trying to dislodge a disobedient djinn from the fabric.

'Aran, you don't understand...' She sighed.

'A shell-demon's got you, isn't that right? You need my protection, you need a cleansing.' He'd see to her, take care of her narrow shoulders and gently fuck this nonsense out of her. She twisted out of his grip.

'Aran, you better go...'

Tribal Radio

Lucas leant across a cluttered radio console in a cramped attic and squared up to the microphone. He was using his smooth voice, modeled around ancient BBC tapes, but he couldn't disguise a quiet desperation.

'This is Leynebridge Tribal Radio 930 AM.'

He knew that many of the Elders didn't like this electronic pollution, emanating from the sacred Tower itself. The tatty community radio equipment had supposedly been part of a slick commercial network operation, a subsidiary of a big entertainment franchise based in London. A man in an office had once told him all about it back in his Urban day. Lucas wasn't quite clear how this fragment of it still hung on, post-Rupture, in Leynebridge. The signal faded and peaked unpredictably, so his links and segues were often obliterated in crackly static and he never fully understood the operation of the console and the transmitter. But the traders still needed him to read their prolix bulletins and catalogues, which paid him a tiny pittance, while the old women surely needed him as a tame bard, an extra gossip, a distraction from the subliminal jabberwocky of the Undermind.

Using a random collection of old CDs and vinyl LPs he'd unearthed in a cupboard, he purveyed a scrambled nostalgia. The young people yearned for immersion in the Lobe, of course. Even if they couldn't get it here, it's all they wanted now. No wonder so many were leaving, despite the dangers in the cities.

So it didn't really matter what he played. He slid a disc, any disc, into the player. Let them guess what it is. The sound of surprise.

Piano and vibraphone chimed gently in the crackly headphones, and the little silences between the notes slowly started getting to him, small silvery spheres of time where he could escape, without having to open his mouth. For his own failures, his farces, his weak lusts and rages that kept repeating on him like bad food in his gullet.

Perhaps this long track from the lost world of the Modern Jazz Quartet would allow him an aperture, a portal to finding a fulcrum of meaning so that he could swing around the centre of his dwindling self. He needed to get motivating. Action was required. To stay here in the torpor of the Borderlands? To return to the terror of the City? To return and try and rescue Carla from herself?

Suddenly, realising that he was still grunting, muttering, snorting non-verbal angst into an open mic, he turned down the fader. He couldn't even get the basic competences right. Let the CD play. Just segue again and again. Back to back, track to track. After all, who was listening? Sooner or later the Elders were going to close him down and/or the parent organisation in London was going to rumble his case and seize their kit back, national advertising revenues having long ceased.

Through the narrow slit of a double-glazed window he could glimpse a little segment of High Town. One of the local craft persons, the dread Aran Yarland, was running towards the Red Hag, angry mouth working furiously, probably after slender Vivienne Crowe again. The metal worker would hand-fast with her sooner or later and she'd spend her days mothering and crafting. Anyway, she was barely aware of Lucas. A huge wedge of cloud slid across the rooftops.

'Light thickens...' His borrowed bardic broodings. But electricity was still buzzing away out there - surely they'd not switch it off tonight. And the Tower had access to an ancient diesel generator, that the Elderseers pretended not to notice. There were still a few closet Carbonites in their ranks. But all national services, social and otherwise, were faltering. 'There was a time when you could go cap in hand to the authorities and they'd provide a rescue package, ' - a favourite saying of Herbie, one of the old Borderlands book runner crowd, probably a bag-person now. So many of his buddies on the road, but not in the way Saint Kerouac had taught them to expect, pre-Rupture. They were bag people now. They called him sometimes, ranting away on stolen mini-phones that suddenly died.

And now almost every other day the station went off air because of local power cuts or breakdown of the back-up dynamo. The saurian black guck of the Mezozoic was running low. The odour of the new biomass plant across the river was almost reassuring, the stench of a species confronting its own deep shit at last. But even that was prone to random failures.

Lucas had ruefully accepted it all from the beginning, even when the chaos of the Rupture had turned so many former urban dwellers – teachers, sales managers, accountants - into fractious infantile arsonists who rejoiced in hurling cans of blazing petrol at the Energy Management police. He'd had brief spasms of rejoicing himself at the punitive taxes on non-essential vehicles, the massive tariffs on imported foodstuffs. For a few weeks he'd felt a kind of relief at the prospect of ditching the whole cargo cult of brands and customer choice – the choice to be mesmerised and zombified by the aisles of packaging in the glaring hypermarkets. When he'd heard the first reports of a mall riot, he'd laughed. 'We needed a good purge,' he told his imaginary friends in rural radio land, before stumbling through an advert for Trader Price's Economy Boot Store or Happy Hour at the Red Hag.

And Lucas told himself he had grown to love disasters. Perhaps it was his way of dealing with his post-Rupture-trauma – revisiting comprehensible calamities that pre-dated this Qliphothic madness. He was fascinated by old war footage, scoured the black market boot sales in Old Hallows for video documentaries and a battered VCR to play them on. Night after night following a grim session in the studio or the classroom he gazed at silver-grey shivery frames of an exploding Messerschmitt over the North Sea; at the skeletal dome of Hiroshima; the airship Hindenburg burning at its moorings. His spectatorship was consuming him. Perhaps he now needed another outrage to goad his adrenalin, as his significance dwindled in the great signage of things.

Now he had exhausted the world. He had burned up, all over and out, back there in the City - and before that, in the blazing amnesia of the Rupture. Yes, blown himself inside out. He had exhausted all the topics for the show – reminiscences of the Rupture, tales of oil crisis, tall stories from the assymetrical warfare on the streets of the world, orgy-cult scandals on the Lobe – he'd chewed them to death.

Night after night, with the black gourd of the microphone hanging in front of him, he'd tongued his way through the repertoire, harassed by the thin voices, those deconstructors of conspiracy who were going to make him share their comforting paranoia. They were his puppeteers. This was their talking cure.

'You're listening to Luke Beardsley...' The phrases dropped sideways from his mouth as he entered the microphone zone. His space. To fill with vibrating molecules of air. His tiny angry molecules.

Parcel Man

The methane-fuelled bus lurched and burped between the bare hedgerows. Sebastian Hackett had just sprayed the floor with bilious raspberry vomit. 'What, indeed, should a gentleman do?' He coughed melodramatically. 'The red red wine, the red... What a spending! Spending, we lay waste our powers...' A rivulet of bile trickled down his scarf. He wiped the scarf with his hunting cap. 'Ad vomitorium mihi,' he announced throatily to the whole bus.

The huddled crones on their merry way to Old Hallows, nearest hamlet and source of mushrooms, stared, grimacing mournfully like ornamental gnome-matrons.

Viv looked away, caught between pity and a dull anger at the familiar scenario. Hackett's drinking was typical of the human wreckage adrift in Leynebridge. Indirectly, he was another victim of the Rupture and the partitioning of UK plc into 'corrupt directories.' That was the odd term her grandfather William Crowe was supposed to have used, long ago, in a brief visit to Leynebridge, a few years after her mother Dawn's early death. Viv was a tiny and could only remember a man with thick glasses and funny breath. But Grandmother Elaine must have thought they might rehabilitate the old techno-fuehrer as a patriarch. That was the story, anyway, as Viv heard it in her teens. Dawn's lover Baggy - allegedly Viv's dad - was long gone, back to the cities. Maybe Grandmother Elaine hoped to reunite some partial nucleus of family for child Vivienne, her ward.

Instead William had apparently ignored his toddling granddaughter, being diverted by meeting this antiquarian Hackett. People said Seb Hackett was dandified then, sporting an ivory-handled cane 'for beating street rogues' and a ready line of chatter about Dr. Johnson and/or discrete gentlemen's clubs. Curiously, the two men had got on, to the extent that her grandfather had spent most of a disastrous visit drunk in the Red Hag. Grandmother Elaine recounted the episode every year, with icy contempt.

The bus stopped in a wasteland of ruined dwarf apple trees. Two potato farmers and a fruit farmer tumbled out. Hackett recognised the thin red-nosed man who was boarding. This passenger always carried a grubby brown paper parcel. His presence was reassuring, a cyclical routine in these uncertain climes.

The Parcel Man tugged at the peak of his cap and simpered at the driver, as he wheedled his way up the step in the hope of a free ride. The driver nodded wearily. The parcel was leaking drops of reddish-brown fluid. Vivienne wondered if it contained a small dead animal or some vegetable substance. As she looked across the aisle the Parcel Man hugged his burden defensively and started one of his monologues in a high quavering tone of indignation: 'Last night that bunch of lads down by the Tower were giving me a hard time – trying to pinch things, like. Flat-Heads they were, throwing those long pointed sticks - '

'I expect they were the spawn of the Council House Men,' said Hackett loudly. 'If you call those moss-covered hovels houses. I hear they're burning their furniture these days…'

As Hackett and the Parcel Man continued their ritualized exchange, and the old women started grumbling about the stupid things that silly man said on the wireless which you couldn't hear half the time anyway because the electric kept stopping, Viv suddenly realized that the bus might travel on for eternity, looping between Leynebridge and Old Hallows, and she might never get off. And if she did, Aran Yarland was always waiting for her.

Last of the Gutenberg Men

All day Gavin Wharton sat behind the green baize desktop in the front of his shop. He'd piled volumes high around him in a protective barricade. He erased old prices and invented new ones. Then he'd interleaf paper and stencil-carbon into his old Remington and type another catalogue entry. Capitalism wasn't his invention but he knew how to cater for commodity fetishism ('foxed, broken hinge, o/w VG, author's neat inscr, first thus').

He often told himself he might be the last of the Gutenberg men. They would need his oldie skills as the techno-world faltered. The local fluctuations of the magnetosphere and the psychosphere doomed word processing. One typed a sentence, saved it in some antique collectable computer – and then overnight it changed. Maybe the word order, sometimes the spelling, and of course one couldn't remember exactly what one (or someone) had written, intermittent amnesia being a widespread effect of the changes in the mental climate. All the narratives were now unreliable. Prices likewise. He told customers as much when he wanted to get rid of them. 'You couldn't possibly afford it,' he would utter in a low growl, as he pulled down the shutters, at irregular intervals.

When Noah entered his gloom, around mid-afternoon, he put aside his typewriter, the ledgers and catalogues, pulled out a pen-knife and began whittling away at his new staff. Banter was also a good defence against Dodd's likely demands for allegiance in the latest magickal dispute.

'Have you ever seen such a wand, Noah? I gave up on the swords. You just can't get the metal now... Have you any idea where they're still forging high-grade steel?'

Noah, unusually, ignored the digression. He normally relished discussing the minutiae of arcane practice. He leaned over Wharton's desk, breathing heavily.

'We may need all the swords we can find. And young men with staffs - to split heads and spill blood.'

Wharton looked puzzled. 'What is this latest apocalypse, Noah?'

'Materialists, Carbonites, Techno-Nihilists, Urbists, Lobe-addicts - they'll be swarming all over Leynebridge if this Lombard and his crew from London have their way. They want to build a Pleasure Centre. Here!'

'Have you tried evoking defensive forces? Surely the Serpent will protect us?' Wharton remembered the long rites, Noah and the Elders chanting in the rain, when the Serpent Way had first been unearthed. Even then, he'd had private doubts.

'We've lacked faith, Gavin. Too many compromises with technology. Allowing that radio to transmit Urban trash, for a start. Not mentoring the young people properly. No control of incomers. Lombard and his Lobe-merchants are the quintessence of materialist evil. An obscene intrusion!'

'How will this affect the book trade?' Wharton, lighting another cigarette, deliberately affected a scholarly detachment. It helped to control old Noah's agitation, which was starting to seep through his skull.

'It will destroy the whole town. Everything we've created, all that we've preserved. There's a meeting at the Red Hag tonight.'

Another Lost Girl

Lucas pushed his mic fader open – and then thought better of it and muted himself. He cued up a CD at random on the other deck. Goth doom-jazz – *Vigilante Crusade* by Bohren and The Club of Gore, a precious pre-Rupture rarity. That sepulchral drone would either anaesthetize his hypothetical listeners or enrage them.

As the track slowly marched past him in a majestic sweep of synths, he reached across the console and rummaged among a pile of papers. He was supposed to read an announcement about some new edict of the Elderseers. *If they're so bloody mystic, why can't they transmit their messages by telepathic thought-forms?* He remembered his mother Pauline, hoarse with irradiated lungs, a defiant material girl to the end, laughing bitterly in her hospice bed. He'd tried to explain that you could never rely on receiving a coherent thought-form. Only this random leakage of mental static, which one never quite filtered out. *Useless old men scoffing the pies again...* Did he really think that? Where did it all come from? *Here comes Mr Green in his fucking stupid hat...* In his precarious position, dependent on hand-outs and donations, he had tried to appease everybody. Now it looked as if he was losing the balancing point.

A small black notebook fell open across the faders. He flipped through; and recognized his own scribble:

Days of the black snow, black as swarf; the slippery shit on the cobbles; the wind-chill factor. My heart is as cold as an implant. Aliens would be fuelled by despair at our spiritual depravities. Carla went frolicking on the dark side. The nature spirits rage at the rapes in the desert, on the ramparts, the whole wriggling sprawl of strained torsos.

Somehow the universe had opened and closed – and birthed us as the post-people of the Qliphothic Function. Scientists spoke of 'a great singularity' but now that experiments were increasingly unrepeatable, scientific method was disreputable. Recall London, decelerating fast.

The wind brings the bagmen out. Their papery hands wilt in the sleet but they have to come out some time, to forage with their woolly bags and ear-muff hats.

Lucas couldn't recall the exact day of committing that scrawl (it seemed a geological age ago) but he still remembered walking quickly through the iced-up streets in his tatty white mac, past the smashed windows of a synagogue, desperately seeking an orientation. To intercept Carla at a railway station. The maze of the estates kept diverting him from his target. Old men in tarbushes argued with huge despairing gestures over buckets of faded videos. They had started burning the plastics for warmth. He might catch the toxins in his throat. Walk on. The Mo-Boy Brigades controlled most entrances and exits to the Gardens of the Western Suburbs, but you could duck back in the alleys. He'd slunk onwards, towards his flame-haired love-object. She could move like a slim flame in the wind.

Meters flickered on the console and The Club of Gore reverberated slowly across the aether of Leynebridge as Lucas tried to evoke his lost city. He remembered finding trains, a suburban train platform. He was trying to make a big speech, a very serious speech to Carla, as trains rumbled past, corridors of light, cages of noise hurtling towards the centres of power. She nodded, even if she didn't hear, just to pacify his angst.

'We could still find a few pleasures to share. Before it all caves in.

There's no one else. I just wish you could stop working for the Centres, that Lobe-work you're doing- '

He broke the rhythm, broke off. Her face was taut. Perhaps she pictured herself on a wooden footbridge amid drifting clouds of steam, years ago in a silver-grey movie. He'd loved her acting out those old films. She could manage that cut-glass accent he'd loved in Robyn. Another lost girl.

Maybe she had wondered how he could get away with this filibustering, how he could go on justifying his consumption of petrol, oxygen, protein. But all she could say, almost inaudibly, was 'How's things? How's …' Language was a bridge that burnt away even as you were standing on it.

'I have to move,' she said, wrapping an arm awkwardly around him in a haze of perfume, 'so no snogging now…' It was the kind of incongruous ancient slang that he found endearing, even as it defined the boundaries. He'd still been thinking about it as she disengaged and turned away towards the flickering sign for EXIT ZONE.

The Club of Gore had been silent now for thirty seconds. He was into dead air, he didn't exist for listeners, past or present, so he had to assert the eternal present, the presence of radio, and speak words, any words. He was going to let the words out.

'Doom jazz from the Club of Gore. Well, we all knew the doom was coming home to roost in our drugged puddings of bodies, even as we clamoured for our zimmer frames. We knew perfectly well about the shit-bombs hanging from the rectum of Moloch. But we had a delusion of golden electric harps rasping out the mucous music of the spheres and we couldn't concentrate, such was our famine for fame. Isn't that right? Fragments of old media take on a half-life of their own, don't they? The heads of the po-faced populace were infiltrated. Sub-texts sub-vocalise all the time. Talk about that talk. Non-stop hot chat. Trouble in the head, man. Dead radio vibrations across the nation. Old news leaks through all eyes....'

Lucas wished the young people would listen to him. Somebody had to call in.

Keeping Vigil

Aran's fury drove him through the day as he staggered between the inns of Leynebridge, fuelled by local liquors, bitter distillations of fruit and fungi that flooded his senses with tides of euphoria and nausea, in increasingly frequent reversals.

Circling back past the Red Hag he swung a punch at some wavering incomer who just happened to blunder into his path. The owlish person flinched and ran, clutching at a bloodied mouth. Aran knew there would be no retribution, the nearest community watch-person was at least five miles away riding an electric tricycle. They were more concerned with pacing the Borderland checkpoints and trying to keep the raff from the Urbs out.

As he wandered the steep streets, Aran pondered about becoming a stern Border guardian, keeping vigil to beat the shit out of treacherous incomers, those orc-men of the cities that Noah Dodd preached against in the weekly meetings at the Red Hag. Only last week he'd spotted a man in unfamiliar urban dress sneaking behind a pillar in the Book Market, trying to capture images of folk on some cunning digi-photo, or whatever they called them. He'd chased the image-thief as far as Sheep Street, before losing him in the alleys around Redlight Close.

The whole town needed a proper purge. He'd be especially hard on devious young orc-women.

Council of Elderseers

Viv was wanderlusting, but couldn't escape the gravity of Leynebridge. Here she was, back in the Market Square at twilight, having wasted most of the day on that futile trip to Old Hallows, a village created from a single crooked street with a pub and a junk shop. She realised that she'd been deluding herself : that somewhere in those dusty shelves she might find a talismanic object - a crumpled book, a crystal on a tarnished silver ring, a chipped clay figurine - that would help to resolve her dilemma over Aran.

The strategy had surely worked last year, when she'd discovered that little iron cauldron in the terrible week when Grandmother Elaine was so ill with the ague, and she'd boiled up special roots in it, like Noah Dodd had told her, to make a sticky black viscous mess that smelt the whole house out. Somehow her grandmother had managed to keep it down and the next day the fever abated. But then Viv believed in the Way of the Lore. Now she was undermined by doubts. Perhaps it served her right. She felt unsteady, as if there was a tiny split at the periphery of her vision, admitting a sudden glimpse of dark voids behind the membrane of appearances. Perhaps a second Rupture was looming.

Rain spattered against the pitted stonework of the Book Market. She shivered in her thin smock but she couldn't face returning immediately to her narrow attic over Wharton's shop. So she strode past his window display of bardic journals and scrying manuals, and headed up High Town towards the Red Hag. She needed hot food.

Aran might be there, of course, but hopefully he would be too drunk by now to be more than a nuisance. Perhaps she could improvise some spell-craft to keep him at arm's length. Perhaps she was a fool, resisting her own intermittent pangs of desire. And Aran was the strongest young man in Leynebridge. As things declined and the Incoming increased, there might come a time when she needed his protection.

As she crossed the cobbles in front of the Red Hag, she noticed the Castle Tower was dark. That Urbanite voice was no longer up there, talking itself to death with no-one listening, playing cold electrical music, disseminating dangerous radiation that penetrated soft tissues and delicate cells. *They should freeze his lightning.* She couldn't understand how the Elderseers still allowed it.

The front bar was packed. Her head was suddenly flooded with muddied thought streams and she had to pause and steady herself against a doorframe. Through the candle-light, the haze of hash fumes and between the talking heads, she caught sight of Aran, sprawled in a settle at the far end. He was gripping Gavin Wharton's sleeve, probably trying to pump the book dealer on her whereabouts. Wharton nodded and tugged his beard, as if his gestures were a semaphore that would resolve the mystery. Sebastian Hackett swayed behind them, sympathetically.

She recognised another figure on a stool near the door, narrow shoulders hunched over a notebook, high forehead, beakish nose. That man who sometimes taught in the Repository, who eyed her up the other day when she was trying to do a reading for a poor hill-farmer. It was rumoured he was the alien Urban voice that broadcast from the Tower. Some even said that as a teenager he'd played a big part in bringing the Rupture down upon the people. She couldn't understand how but there was something devious, dubious there. He called himself Lucas Beardsley. Lucas = Lucifer, Light-Bearer. But their Enlightenment gave birth to the Darkness. *His black light.* That's what Grandmother Elaine would say.

He was focusing on her. Not with his eyes, but she could feel it in her solar plexus, a slight but persistent pressure, even as his long fingers glided across the page. Was he writing sigils, like wave-forms, to intrude on her body...?

She turned quickly and pushed through towards the stairs. Perhaps she could get some veggy soup from the servery in the upper room. On the landing, a gnarled man in the white hooded robe of the Elderseers blocked her path.

'Closed for a meeting...'

Viv gestured at her drenched clothes. 'I'm just a poor half-drowned nymph,' she whispered, 'and I'm very discreet.' Her fey projections, that hint of naughtiness, seemed to work with these old fellows. He let her through.

The Council of Elderseers was in full cry. Standing room only around the long oak table, no chance of reaching the counter, as the chamber had already been invaded by traders, farmers, book runners, guildsmen of all the Leynebridge crafts. The Elders in their high-backed chairs were shouting over each other, while their audience drunkenly cheered or jeered. Forgan the Anointed Arch-Fool of Leynebridge leaped up, wavered unsteadily on his chair, waved his long beaded sleeves and pursed his lips.

He swelled his cheeks; and spouted a jet of flame across the table. The room filled with harsh cries and the smell of paraffin. Then, in a sudden silence, he began his rant, in that curious nasal drawl he used when the prankster spirits were about to speak through him.

'Fight fire with fire, my little old Elderbruvvers. Time to burn out this latest incursion, Lombard the Londoner, with our curses and dances. We must purge him out of Leynebridge with cosmic comedy, with a dance of flame-serpents. Let there be arson for his arse, incinerate his dream-hutches, burn his money, burn his play-house down and piss in the smoking ruins...'

Some Elders roared their approval and beat their tankards on the table. Raucous cries from a group of sheep-herds: 'Piss yourself, Forgan...'

A thin voice suddenly cut through the buzz. The cadaverous Trader Price in his wide-brimmed black hat. As a toddler she'd bought stale sweets at his shop, in those dim old days.

'Forgan, have you ever used rational thought? Have you considered the potential benefits of Mr Lombard's project for our winter economy?'

Noah Dodd flushed angrily. No wonder the kids called him 'Doddy Pork Face'. But her grandmother Elaine said Noah had saved Leynebridge. He'd see off the Trader.

'Sordid finance is not our ultimate concern, Trader Price - although it might be yours. We are sworn to protect the spirit of place, our Way, the ancient life-stream that flows in and around us as we walk the Serpent Path on our daily rites. We have already conceded much to Lombard - too much perhaps- but Leyston Burrough is sacred ground.'

Leyston Burrough: that squat overgrown grassy mound at the top of Leyston Hill, on the wrong side of the river. Cluttered with derelict tin shacks and rubbish, a gathering place for outcasts like Mrs Nixon. Not sacred but scary. How could anyone - the Elders, the shadowy Mr

Lombard in distant terrible London - care about Leyston Burrough? Right now she cared about food.

But now they were all yammering away in this stifling enclosure of smoke and damp wool. Her head throbbed with competing indignations. The Trader repeatedly recited phrases from some document he brandished, presumably from the mysterious Lombard, as if repetition would force the project into being. He pronounced the ugly jargon as if it were an incantation.

'Mr Lombard is offering to develop Leynebridge in a post-industrial strategy action plan by enhancing its unique cultural identity... it will be state-of-the-art, a state-of-the-art Virtual Reality Complex...'

'Lombard has no art,' growled Forgan, 'he's all state and no art.' Noah nodded. 'He's quango'd his way into a lost pot of state money to bankroll a fun fair for Carbonites.'

'What about fun for us?' yelled a plump butcher's lad. ' Anything's better while we're stuck in this dump. With you lot and your old processions and rituals. I bet they're not even old. I bet you made them up!'

Viv suddenly felt a spasm of anger, an icy spike of rage intruding. She realised her grandmother was in the room. Elaine threw back her hood, rose in her long white robe and glared at the fat boy who fell silent.

'Where would you be, young man, if you were not protected by our Ways? Selling your vital organs on the streets of a city, ever frightened of being kidnapped for forcible conversion, or helplessly addicted to synthetic pleasures? This gross proposition epitomises the crass mass culture that has destroyed the young people of our cities. It is rooted in the Grey silicon techno-worship, alien to real human needs, driven by the profit motive and the urge to destroy. We have raised you in a green life-affirming Way, to revere the Mysteries of the Earth. This aberration must be totally resisted - whatever it costs!'

Viv was exhilarated, and yet curiously embarrassed by her grandmother's fervour. She had heard these homilies so many times in the kitchen at home that she'd almost forgotten Elaine was a public figure in Leynebridge. She was right, of course, but this display of zeal seemed excessive, strident in its righteousness.

And suddenly, to her own surprise, despite her hunger, she found herself slowly backing away, as discretely as possible, towards the door, even as Grand Earth Mother Elaine rounded on another of Trader Price's supporters.

Viv realised she needed silence. A white empty room, with a single focus of attention. A naked sword on an oak table. A copper disc, a silver disc, a battered coin - some focal point to centre and slow down the centrifugal spin of voices with their messages, agendas, plots and plans. Let her grandmother take care of these babblers. Let her go.

Writing Amid the Tumult

Lucas knew his signals were too weak for Viv. She was escaping this fug. He had no chance. Perhaps his lust was too diffuse, he couldn't erase the burning icon of Carla. Aran would rule Vivienne's loins, that would be the way. But he kept his head down, kept writing amid the tumult. In a way the noise helped. He was isolated by the mushy noise of voices who would never read him aloud, which was as well for he was writing heresies.

They're plotting to dethrone Noah the Elderking. Off with his head. Public execution in the Tower Square. They'll bring creaky wooden machinery. A retroactive sacrifice, to re-write the Lore and revive the land, that's how they'll proclaim it. Poor old Noah in his smock dragged to the scaffold as the samba band plays and the crowd yelps. I can see it now, and if I can see it, that fangles a form in the astral places, that's what they say. I know, I've been there. Or there will be a burning. They'll burn him amid the books, thousands of bat-like fragments of ash swirling in the air... I must stop before it occurs...

The distractions of a psychenaut amid the fumes of cider and weed: as he crossed the room towards corridor leading to the toilets, the doors blurred and through them he glimpsed a squat naked man crawling on all fours across the wet tiles, gristle hanging from his chin. The creature crawled mechanically towards the end of the passage and reversed.

Horribly, Lucas realised he was studying some random projection of himself, a grainy psychogram. Then the creation collapsed in a puff of cloud. The room was roaring with laughter but the apparition was exclusive to him.

Lucas recognised the symptoms. His liquor had probably been strangely enriched, as the landlord of the Red Hag was given to random mushroom gathering at dawn, and such troves were often added to the local microbrew. He felt a rivulet of nausea trickling through him, but he knew if he kept walking steadily towards the door, into the cold air he could control his reflexes. But could he control his trike? As his shoulder blundered into the door frame, he realised his limbs were operating by remote control.

The surface of the earth rotated like a giant drum beneath him. A skein of brownish tissue appeared to drift from the side of his mouth and then dissolve, as he crawled across the cobblestones. The tramp of his feet reverberated through his skull, which was becoming a dome of doom, a chalice of ancient sickness, a receptacle for a sour fluid exuded from his brain. Somehow he was going to arrive at the town square.

After a sickly interval, the tricycle finally trembled in the lamplight. He gripped the railings as he inspected it, very slowly. It appeared intact but now registered as a skeletal assemblage of tubing with no clear function. He groped for the handlebar and toggled a switch, an impulse that might prove useful. The voltage needle didn't flicker. The lights were dead. After repeating this procedure several times, he thought of inspecting the battery compartment - and lifted the lid to find that both cables had been cut and the terminals had been crudely chopped away.

He peered across the square; and noticed a crude scrawl in red paint across the base of the Tower wall : *Make it go by magick?* On cue, he heard brawling voices and heavy boots...

He staggered back quickly, via a side alley to the rear of the Tower, where there was a unobtrusive service door that he sometimes used as a discreet entrance. For a few seconds the rusty lock jammed. Then, mercifully, it opened and he ducked inside as a large group of the local Flatheads spilled out across the square, obviously seeking validation in bloodied hands and feet. He hauled himself up the stairs to the dark cramped studio.

Five of Discs

Vivienne walked quickly through the colonnade of the old Book Market. The lanterns were flickering again. She glanced up at the fungi seeping through the crevices of the ancient stonework. Were they exuded from some alien pocket of space-time trapped in the masonry?

Would the past drug her with ripe delusions? 'Live in the fakery of the moment,' said the Urbanites, but they'd given up believing in anything, *only lived for a flying fuck in the dark*, or so it was whispered.

She needed to get to her secret space, the White Room. Her tiny bedsit over Wharton's shop was too stuffed with memorabilia. Her favourite toys, like Augustus the fatty-cat and Mr Monster Mole, would hypnotise her with their glassy eyes and keep her locked into the rites of her Leynebridge day, handicrafts in the morning, uneasy lunches with Grandmother Elaine, nightly rebuttals of poor old Aran. She should never have let him take her that crazy night. Only a few weeks ago she wanted Aran and his children, to be as full and rounded as Modron the Mother Goddess. But now she'd discovered something lean and wild in herself.

She quickened her pace. Flatheads, those disenfranchised rural youths who'd never quite bought into the Way, would be on the prowl. She'd always managed to project a protective zone around her and turn their threats into banter, but she'd been drained by the frustrations of the day, and this time of night they'd be well brewed up. The White Room was way down beyond High Town, a tiny disused chapel hidden at the back of a derelict garage. Gavin Wharton once had used it as a store room but he couldn't face hauling his stock through town on a barrow, so he gave her a key, probably in the hope that she'd move out of the bedsit, and then forgot about it.

She picked her way through rusting fuel pumps on the darkened garage forecourt and turned past a shuttered workshop, to the nettle-strewn porch of the Full Gospel Hall, a brick hutch that had once housed a gaggle of hymn-singing matrons in pre-Rupture days, although even then their numbers were dwindling. Now it was a dusty whitewashed space, lit by tiny windows.

The chill hit her as she entered. She groped for candles from her stock in an old chest of drawers and spaced them at the corners of a rickety table. After a struggle with matches they were lit. She had the wavering illusion of warmth.

Then in the depths of the drawer, she felt for the silk wrapping of her pack. She'd always kept her Tarot there, rather than the bedsit. The silence and emptiness of the room preserved the purity of the cards. How so? She knew so.

She spread another square of purple silk in the centre of the scarred table. Then, carefully, she extracted the pack, and faced the question. Until now she'd been focussed on escaping the fuggy collectivity of the Red Hag, the specific gravity of Grandmother Elaine's stern presence. Now she had to identify the true source of her malaise and divine an action. But what was the question? If she was the question, what was the answer?

Viv had been taught all the traditional modes of reading the Tarot. Elaine had expected her to memorise all the different spreads, by astrological houses, by zodiacal signs, by the Qabalistic Tree of Life. But tonight she felt overwhelmed by the complexity of the operations, with their elaborate sequences of shuffling and dealing. She still couldn't articulate the question.

In the distance, a sound of gunfire. Probably a Flathead on a shotgun rampage. They rejoiced in their shotguns like they rejoiced in their stubbly haircuts. 'Leynebridge born and Leynebridge bred, strong in arm and thick in head…' But the creatures of the cities could be worse. She had to locate her true will, quickly. Suppose her lust of result skewed the answer?

Suddenly, she opted for crude simplicity, shuffling and cutting the cards into four stacks, plus a signifier card for herself. Work, Love, Strife, Money. And she'd drawn the Princess of Wands for her signifier. Earth and Fire, a creature of extremes. She felt too weary for the role. Maybe this smoldering energy she felt was burning out already.

But, once started it was important not to delay the process through distraction so she drew her first card. For Work - the Five of Discs, Worry; for Love - The Four of Wands, Completion; for Strife - The Ten of Discs, Wealth; for Money - the Seven of Swords, Futility. She'd dealt herself a heavy hand.

Five of Discs was all too apt. Conflicting pressures result in inertia, a pentagonal geometry of stress that was ultimately unstable. The reading for Love was absurd - Completion. Her affair with Aran had never really started after that first wild night. Perhaps it was over before it started. The Four Wands interlocked, motionless. The reading for Strife was even more perverse. She had the strife but never the wealth. Perhaps accumulated wealth. A secret bequest from her grandmother? Unlikely. More likely, the weight of material possessions - the tenth cards were aligned most closely to the Earth. Perhaps the risk of becoming bogged down in matter, the toil and soil of Leynebridge in the long winters. And the Wealth card itself was feeble, a card of compromise and appeasement, her awkward relationship with Elaine, her vacillation over Aran. Futility indeed.

She peered at images in the flickering candlelight: four dove-headed wands locked in a circle ; a crescent moon at the tip of the seventh sword. Where was her story, the narrative that had always emerged under Elaine's guidance? Why were there no major trumps like the Priestess, the Lovers, Lust leaning back ecstatically astride her golden Beast? Yet somehow the meanness and mediocrity of the reading was right. It fitted the cold drab room, the vague unfocussed belligerence on the village streets.

Time to go. To let the candles smoke out the dead chapel. Back to her attic. To pack bags.

Thelema Riff

Lucas was off-air now. The room had stopped shaking and his metabolism had settled. He had programmed the CD players to repeat a sequence of *Daniel O'Donnell's Country Hits* for the next two hours. It was all his audience deserved. But he was going to pre-record his testimony, a final message to the denizens of Leynebridge. He warmed up by faking a public service information announcement.

'Tonight's factoids: the so-called "Way of Leynebridge" is, in practice, a complex synthesis of earth magic, shamanism, geomancy and fertility ritual. The name "Leynebridge" is actually a neologism, invented by the Elders, to replace the Pre-Rupture name. It is intended to symbolise the importance of the town as a confluence of energies and a bridge into new realms...'

The words came easily as he watched the big spools turning on the tape recorder. He began his Thelema riff, as a good way to start driving out his submerged daemons:

'Uncle Aleister's Aeon of Horus. That old slap-head Crowley saw it all coming. "The Crowned and Conquering Child." Ladies and gentlemen, I saw it panning out , years back, before the Qliphothic Rupture: the collapse of masculine authority; death of the author;

merging polymorphic perversities of the Lobe; the infantilism of pottymouth telly; tantrums of reality TV celebs; the mountains of wet teddies and rotting lilies at funerals, especially old Saintly Auntie Diana's; the fat bald dads in playsuits who have to get it all now, the latest glitzy toys; nursery food under the Golden Arches - all collapsed now; nursery rhyme pickney music; the lost arts of spelling and syntax; the androgynous child-men; the extended neoteny of modern yoof; separation of sex from procreation; baby mothers of the ghetto going it alone; the fascination with child molesters and paedos; children's books – anyone remember Harry Potty ?; childish embraces on the footy field ; on the curriculum all the rants and rages of the inner child…'

He pushed up the fader on the microphone. He wanted his signal to distort and crackle. Now he was on auto-pilot. The prophecies kept on coming...

'The key to the highway was lost on the rubber-smeared freeway. The young malcontents will have to burn there, there is no escape not even behind the palisade of electrified crucifixes, even behind a whole plantation of bodies shackled to rubber trees. The landlocked seas will bubble over whole suburbs. Moon-strikes are a distraction now, even as King Charlie's holy bowels strain while he receives well-wishers clustered around his commode. The best use for tubes and subways is to hide our bodies from inspection, using the tunnels as dark refrigeration pits…'

He'd walked the streets of Deptford, Oxford, Hereford, some kind of 'ford. The pavements were always strewn with sleepy people in dirty robes.

'The world picture is like a globe you stick over your head, so that you can't see it. All Chinamen are wearing them. Their flow of chi will be warped by so much internal heat. This is the origin of spontaneous human combustion. The torture cells of Venusberg are multiplied now by telepathy. Fiery wires are inserted into the flesh pots.'

He had the knowledge, the ley of the land, but no hot living body wanted to know.

'This is how we do the business now, at light speed. Surrogate lovers cry their agony across the townships of Earth. The whole of the unconscious crawls out of its hole. Our exoskeletons are fluted into branching cocks, hollowed into pearly orifices.'

He stopped and watched the tape spools slowly revolving. Once the world had been a continuum, a thin skin crawling with parasites maybe, but it went on, and went round and round. The fault lines may have been jagged but the datelines were international and the phone lines usually worked. The world-lines held steady. 'This planet has a beginning, a middle and an end,' according to the nasal intonations of some crazy old poet he remembered from the days of scratched vinyl. But the guts had somehow fallen out of the middle of England - to splatter all over him.

'Perhaps there's an enormous unconscious yearning for sharia law or bible-beating. Perhaps our cultural masochism and self-doubt is merely a prelude to guided submission. Even before the Rupture the Wahibo Mo-Boys and Heavy Shepherds already ruled in the vacuum of post-modernism. Anyone remember post-modernism? You lads rampaging in city centres and splattering the concrete with your vomit were crying out loud for conversion. Now you're over-ripe for the harvest, eager for huge simplicities, a safe-house heaven.'

Lucas had talked himself into dead air. The phones were still silent.

His tongue was bungled up. The words kept coming but they were all gobble and gargle. His news-belt was a collective fantasy. His actuality was in an under-state. All the links defined themselves ultimately as holes. He was a taped loop of folly bumping around broken capstan wheels. The long passages of memoire took him past a cast-iron antique street lamp. The light ghosted Carla's cheekbones. His perpetual adolescence was still scrolling down, down.

The mic lights on the console blinked faintly, to the rhythms of his breathing. He was just about live. He had to keep filling the silence.

'I'm in the middle. Mid-spectrum. Mid-life. Middle class. Muddled farce. I'm a myopic wailer. A failer. As you become an oldie, the possibility of infinity collapses around your arse. The light-slits of Time only admit one. But I'm still pop-eyed with intertextuality. Help me, somebody. I'm on a deadline...'

He cued another track from Bohren and the Club of Gore.

2
William: Atomised in the Rupture

Head Hunted

William was in a hollow chamber. The dream narrator said so. Light flickered. Perhaps he emitted this flickering light. Sometimes the curving walls were formed of impacted earth, and fungal stones densely inscribed with lines and whorls, ones and zeros, but when he looked more closely he couldn't read those codes; and filaments of wire, or dusty webbing, or tangled fibrous roots drifted across his face like insect limbs, and the walls became bony, slippery with secreted fluid, and white matter puffed into everything.

And there was a pillar at the centre, and she was tied to it, her flow of fine hair falling across bare back, pale buttocks, and she turned, smiling, and released her wrists, and took off her head with a single motion, and offered it, eyes gleaming - The dream rarely went further these days, and William, sweating in his sleeping bag on the lumpy mattress, had been saved by the bleeping digits of the clock, and now as he stumped about in the tiny bathroom, was determined to take a grip on the physical world, the worn plastic cistern handle, the mottled mirror displaying his face.

Dr. William Crowe had never been tempted to change his face by some magical procedure or change his ID by playing games with the collapsing bureaucracy, even by hacking through networks and infiltrating his corrupted files. None of that would have convinced him, in the lower levels of his being. For the defensive languages encoded in his po-face had somehow irradiated his entire infrastructure. Crowe hated the image of his balding head, as he urinated in the bleary light.

But this was smoggy summer in the outlands of London. Forget your forgettable face, nightmares about brains and sex. Go for bathroom gropes and pangs. A cratered tooth sang of corruption as cold bacterial water surged under dentine. Bowel shakes would wobble him later. He was always a worried organism.

Who had forwarded his CV to Pleasure Centres? Some smart head-hunter? It was a diabolical liberty, as South Londoners used to say. He hadn't applied for a job for months. Did he really have to find all his certificates in time for this interview? They'd be on a database, somewhere in the silicate wrinkles of the Lobe, almost certainly corrupted, cyphers lost in hyperspace, his lost competences... Hurry up, William, stop dreaming, get a move on...

His mother's imperious voice, over fifty years ago, squally with lungfuls of refined indignation - *William!* - down that little hall, across the brown linoleum patterned by golden lozenges of afternoon light... No, he never wanted to hurry off to piano lessons, he wanted to sit and finish his Meccano aeroplane. He dreaded most human interfaces, interviews, intercourse, but if he failed to attend his meagre benefits would erase themselves, wouldn't they?

He'd meant to scan the morning's multimedia, catch the 8.00 Lobe update. Too much retrospection already. Always scanning for memories that weren't quite there. He shuffled across the bed-sit room, trying to ignore the skeins of mould on the walls, sidestepping those damned fluffed-up clumps of carpet. He rummaged through the identikit of his possessions.

The name on his old ID pass was the authentic Dr. William Arthur Crowe MSc. PhD. High security had to be exact in these matters. Surely the guard at the Research Establishment used to smirk as he checked William through the gate and raised the boom to admit the Rover to the reserved parking place. William may have been a top-drawer boffin. But he had this moony loon-face which once made a girl at a sixth-form dance giggle into her handkerchief. He blamed his mother back then.

He tried the Lobe Newsnet again as he munched and slurped. Toast, coffee and a big shot of Dawn Surprise, the budget-priced North Korean vodka. Breakfast of champions. He had to learn which were the morning's relatively safe routes into the Central London sector. To the Head Offices of Pleasure Centres plc. His old monitor blipped and flickered, the mouse was grease-encrusted, but there was something happening...

The screen filled with the quivering monochrome image of a monitor. This wasn't the Newsnet logo. And on this screen-within-a-screen William could see two identical grey faces, Caucasian male, clean-shaven, forty-plus. Sober square-headed men in suits and ties, anyway. Solid no-nonsense men, with shiny well-parted hair. Like old 1950s publicity photos of bandleaders, movie gangsters, radio announcers. Each stared formally out of a flickering oval halo. Their graphite-coloured lips moved jerkily in unison.

Another viral infestation by those damned cyber-fibre pirates! No point in turning up the sound. He hadn't time to sort it out. When he had that flatlet in North London it was just the same, except he kept getting endless loops of a sermon from the Westminster Mosque when all he sought was a little diversion on the Fast Fun Action Line. No wonder the poor and/or technically disadvantaged gave up altogether on the cybernautic complexities of accessing the Lobe and still preferred to totally immerse themselves in pseudo-tactility at their neighbourhood Pleasure Centre. It used the Lobe but it was a user-friendly interface, a smiley face, so much consumer choice, all touchy-feely. 'You can get Virtually anything you want at Pleasure Centres.' Corny, but it worked. Perhaps Pleasure Centres really had work for an old cornball prof like him. But he had to stop getting lost in this somnambulistic drift, and get on with it.

He turned away, to delve for his CV; and there, under a precious, irreplaceable back issue of *Scientific American*, was the last uncrumpled copy.

Approaching seventy William was still attempting to rescript his life. But the standard version, the bit he couldn't get out of his head, always went like this: he was born in Tooting, South London. An end-of-terrace - but featuring leaded panes, and a privet hedge, in Saunders Road. The only son of Norah and Lionel. His sister Charlotte had somehow died in the War, she wasn't discussed. Lionel was a clerk for London Transport. The Underground, safe as houses, everybody said so. Despite that bomb down the lift shaft at Clapham South. Thin Norah had post-war nerves, couldn't stand the noise of machines, while sour Aunt Doris lurked in the spare bedroom. Everyone listened to the wireless. No-one had any spare change. But Uncle Doug round the corner had a motor-cycle and sidecar.

He ate horrible cod-liver-oil pills in jam at St. Cosmo's Primary and kids stole his macintosh, then broke his Coronation Mug. But he pulled himself together, mastered long-division, mental arithmetic, decimals, fractions. 'Quite the little professor, aren't we?' coo'd Mrs. Tulse, nervously, as he started playing with algebra months before taking the eleven-plus.

That was probably the year Uncle Doug took him to see the bouncing bomb in *The Dam Busters*, maybe the year he saw British Gaumont newsreels of mushrooming fireballs in the Maralinga outback, and stared for hours at the battered cone of a V2 rocket-motor in the War Museum at Lambeth. SCIENTISTS WARN, said all the papers. ATOM MEN'S DEADLY SECRETS. He realised big sums created powerfully corrective spells. They were his equalisers, they evoked a stunning revenge on the boring, bullying world.

That's what he needed right now. A triumphal bloody scenario, for a change. It's all he deserved. A dose of the right destiny, for once. To escape this deep gravity-well, with all its litter and dirty vests. He could not find clean socks. This biopic narration in his head would not stop. It was consuming time, his real-time life. He couldn't help it. He'd become a mechanical dreamer.

Yes, William had enjoyed his technicolour vision, long ago, on the night before his eleven-plus exam. He dreamed of the UK Secret Space Rocket. The cramped interior of the domed cabin was painted pastel green, walled with panels of round dials, racks of bakelite toggle switches, calibrated pointers, rows of buttons and solid well-machined levers, like the controls on Uncle Doug's bike, that Ariel Square Four. Secret formulae flashed across the tele-data screen of the electro-computer as he fed in the punched cards. Purple and amber warning lights glowed softly. With rising excitement, using his entire body weight, he'd pressed the central red switch on the Command Pedestal. Then smoke had filled the cabin of the UK Rocket, he could smell gunpowder and hot metal. The solid-fuel rockets were firing in clusters. This was his finest hour. This rocket would be his burning bush. He was about to ascend vertically into the future! And between his wet legs he felt the swelling curvature of the British Bomb...

At grammar school William's dreams had gone totally nuclear - he was going to control British Atoms for World Peace, he planned to design the first UK atomic space rocket, he was going to turn the launch key and see a finned cylinder rise from Woomera on a pyramid of fire.

For he knew, he damned well knew that Maths and Physics had created his sanity at the Grammar School, had given him a secret enfolded space, a realm of hidden dimensions where he could retreat from the Teddy Boy Years and the Big Beat Boom. Their dirty menace throbbed distantly, on the far side of a glassy wall, the steamed-up windows of coffee bars and youth clubs where girls laughed dangerously.

He'd paid a passing tribute to his youth by trying out some hobbies - archeology, home electronics - but all that really mattered was earning the stingy approval of Mr. Lawson, Head of Physics - who'd actually smiled when he won the Oxford Scholarship to read Maths. He was a little too early for the permissive society but no matter, there was work to be done, so he got a Double First. And then there was that groundbreaking doctoral dissertation on artificial intelligence. Once upon a time, he'd been a brilliant flash. It said so, right here on the CV.

No wonder the Ministry of Defence had head-hunted him; and tasked him to the Establishment. To work on our own truly British warheads. Admittedly he was working most of the time with computers, which were rapidly becoming his specialism, and there were no all-British space battleships to design, for even the Blue Streak missile had been cancelled. But those years were still his glory days. He'd show those idiots on the Pleasure Centres panel - or as much as the Official Secrets Act would allow. Whatever had happened he was still a loyal Servant of the Crown. A guardian of the Heritage.

Sadly he'd arrived too late to serve Blue Danube and Red Beard, those mighty fifteen-foot one-megaton monsters. He had missed the dawn splendours of Yellow Sun and Orange Herald. But he contributed to key projects - the 950 MC, the Chevaline warhead modernisation programme, the A 277 free-fall weapon, and the elaborate preparations for Trident - and then he had a little department of his own, surely, until...

Until the Blackout. He'd lost his mathematical cutting edge after the Blackout and all those tranquillisers and the ECT and Elaine walking out all over him in her scruffy boots before walking out with the damned kid. But Personnel were very kind (at least he thought so then) and they'd taken off him the serious hard stuff, to fool about with 'telepresence' gimmicks for remote-control weapons assembly and servicing. For a while, anyway.

There was such a bloody amnesiac haze shrouding that whole episode. How the hell could he gloss it over with Pleasure Centres? That sneak Denis Weekes alleged he was incompetent, too much of a maverick generalist, who could no longer cope with focussing on the specifics of his job - even when he was constantly being diverted by his manager's perverse priorities. But he was convinced that his demotion - no, redeployment - might have occurred because of his involvement in something else, some other project under the Establishment umbrella, something big. Which he couldn't deliver.

That was the worst of it. He couldn't deliver it, and now he wasn't clear what it was. His ROM had been sabotaged, his hard drive had been buried under a ton of shit. Electro-convulsive-therapy, for God's sake. Across his precious lobes. And amenotrophylene, they must have given him some of that, he's certain of it. Sleepy-juice for double-agents, to make them dozy. When he'd only been a hyper-alert patriot, playing his long game for Britain. No wonder his ancient night brain was deeply fucked, no wonder he needed these big shots of Korean vodka.

But as he recovered from the Blackout, he found the whole country was buggered up by this accursed so-called Rupture, declining into terminal lunacy and New Age psycho-burble. Nobody could give him a coherent account of how or why. There was a lot of rhetoric about incursions from an alternate reality but nobody seemed to able to do the maths properly and prove it.

Now Christian and Islamic fundamentalist militia battled for control of the inner cities, while that New Age brain-fungus, fed and watered by hallucinogens, spread throughout the countryside. After the Blackout Elaine tripped off to some strange neo-pagan community at Leynebridge on the Anglo-Welsh Borderlands. They'd only met once since, after Dawn died. There was somehow a grand-daughter, bawling away. A Viveca, a Vera? Marriage to Elaine had been a cold war from the start, and the Blackout plus the Rupture not long afterwards provided good opportunities to divorce him. Then it was downhill all the way to redundancy.

For the end of the world came, when suddenly we couldn't even afford our miracle bomb, when everything was cut, and cancelled, and decommissioned, and nothing and nobody worked properly any more and the redundancy notices went out for everybody, even creeps like Denis Weekes, and now the grass was growing around the guard-huts and the barbed-wire was corroding in the drizzle...

No, stress the good times in the interview. Pure work. Sixteen hours on a peak day. Balls to the rest of the silly sixties and seventies and eighties and their lazing and prancing, their obsession with the appearances of mere being, hazy crazy clothes and music. So he'd worn Aertex shirts and Hush Puppies and practical plastic Pakamaks all the way. So bloody what...

Anyway, so many of those public-school radicals had become street-walking bundles of rag and bone. Everyone looked as if they wore charity-shop rejects these days. Some young people even aped his style of haircut. At least he had decent old brogues for his interview.

Unlike most people under thirty he could handle the physics and maths behind the computing. At least he'd burnt out with real flair. But the clock was ticking. He really ought to make up his mind to go.

Unlike some of his colleagues - Ebdon, O'Dwyer, Weekes - who sold their supposed talents (and who knows what else) to the Caliphate or the Pacific Rim, William was a true patriot. So they could call him cranky, so there was this problem with his CV and of course they'd say he was too old to find a niche in what little remained of UK industry. But surely the nation needed some glittering fragment of his shattered expertise. He glanced at a week-old print-out of *The Times* business news: *Pleasure Centres is Britain's only home-grown Virtual Reality group, and one of its few remaining high-tech hopes. As our environment becomes increasingly threatened by post-Rupture malaise, overpopulation, crime and pollution there's a world wide demand for cheap interactive fantasy systems that can function reliably in our new unpredictable environment.*

It was no good. Time was a one-way runway, there was no escape from a descent into the nearing, narrowing future world: a dangerous journey, a futile interview. It might take him hours to get there. For nothing. Empty waiting rooms, null promises. A crash landing at ground zero.

He might be lucky, there could be more minor urban panic attacks, a Heavy Shepherd bomb scare perhaps, nothing too bad, just enough to prevent him from playing out some damning foolery at Pleasure Centres plc. They would probe. And there were areas where his life didn't add up, he couldn't integrate the data or differentiate the right answers.

Flinching at phantom memory traces, he jabbed awkwardly at the monitor, inadvertently punching up the audio button. One of the grey faces went on announcing its continuity. But their script was scarcely hard news any more, it had been around since the nineteen-twenties.

...Einstein never accepted that the universe was governed by chance. But most other scientists were willing to accept quantum mechanics because it agreed with experiment. This theory underlies nearly all modern science and technology. Indeed, it governs the behaviour of integrated circuits which are the essential components of computers...

The voice was metallic, the cadences were mechanical but William was almost moved. Perhaps a little fraternity of dedicated amateur science-freaks were trying to continue Reithian traditions of public service broadcasting. His Quantum Brothers, as it were, popping their heads over the parapet to cheer him up. Simple populist stuff, of course, eccentrically presented, but the lecturette might reach some lost bodies out there, take their minds out of the slow-burning urban inferno.

So much mindlessness in our terminal zones. A megaton SS-4 airburst over West Drayton would have been kinder, quicker, nobler even, than these slow-decay processes which were destroying the city he'd once defended. And at least Polaris might have had its moments of glorious purpose. He tried to control a barking laugh. It might upset Mrs. Kalyoubi downstairs. He turned up the monitor again. These brotherly clones were still teaching into the void, intoning in solemn unison.

Now we're about to enter a twilight zone - between sub-atomic events in the realm of the micro-processor and ghostly tremors troubling the left-brain, between microcosmic flutters of the heart and macrocosmic implosion of stock markets or neutron stars...

Macrocosm. He once acted on the macrocosm. He had to go out there in a few minutes. This attempt to jazz up the talking head format was well-meaning but confusing. The commentary had become virtually meaningless. That's what happened when arts people got their hands on science. But why had Pleasure Centres plc laid its sticky claw on him? Time to turn off the computer, kill the monitor and collect various bits of himself. Somewhere there was a long dark coat without holes. Perhaps even the briefcase. He had after all, been a Servant of the Crown.

For a moment he closed his eyes, tried to block out this dingy scenario that had crept up inexorably around him over fifty years. He stopped scanning the broken mattress and its bowels of disintegrating foam. Most personal items had long been sold or bartered, except books and discs and files, large tumbling heaps of them.

But absolute reality was all in his head, glittering like space dust. Mass, Energy, Space, Time, neutrons, protons, electrons, muons, pions, gluons, quarks, every single bloody charming particle, he knew them all, didn't he? And the languages: COBOL, FORTRAN, C, and their proliferating successors, he'd mastered them all, once upon a time.

So he just had to breathe carefully and face the mirror again. He scrutinised that mooning cranium, his untidy wisps of thinning sandy hair, his honking great stupid snotty nose, as Elaine had called it, as she'd smashed his spectacles in one of their late-period sessions of mutually achieved destruction. In the spasm of the recollection, he hit the panel of the monitor again. The graphite-coloured faces talked right back in level tones.

Einstein never accepted that the universe was governed by chance. But most other scientists were willing to accept quantum mechanics because...

Just another viral loop blatting away in its eternal recurrence. William pressed the power switch decisively and headed for his crooked doorway. He tussled abstractly with that damned warped door. He knew Einstein was right. Quantum mechanics were grubby nuisances, useful, even essential in some small scale applications. But in his brain of brains William was a Unified Field man. The cosmos should make sense, damn it. He didn't believe this magick nonsense that people were talking about.

And even now, setting his padlocks, glancing warily down the stairwell into Mrs. Kalyoubi's dusty bare-bulb hallway, he remained a High Frontier enthusiast, still yearning for the abandoned high ground of British Big Science. 'Our lost horizon, where we might have had a radiant dawn to brighten the abandoned campfires of England's youth...' Years ago they'd all laughed knowingly on the only occasion he'd raised his voice in a Junior Common Room Debate. No-one had taken any notice of him back then, he was: a thin grey man disjointed in greasy specs, spawn of sad Moloch, *war dwarf*

Who pushed away demo leaflets thrust in his hand by eager denim girls outside the Labs of Death

Who walked blank-faced through throngs of eager bards chanting holy sex on the banks of Isis

Who crushed flowers in the burning wheels of his brain and fried in the electric chair of Big Science

That's how Elaine's ex-boyfriend Larry had written about him, in the days when students reading English had poetic pretensions, their 'Beatnik' phase, he supposed; and Elaine kept reciting it years later in the terminal phase. William may have lost key data; but he couldn't erase those old words.

And he had kept recycling it, along with the whole soiled intimate matter, his marital material, his past-life regression, its inane music was going round and round and round. He struggled to locate the mortice key, somewhere in the smelly flaps and tents of his bog-awful coat, he had to make a move, for Time was firing its non-stop silver bullets...

He concentrated on crossing Mrs. Kalyoubi's territory in silence; and paused before opening the door to the street. No-one should see him. He had to wait just a moment, to psych up his defence mechanisms.

Imagery wouldn't stop infiltrating his head. Bullets splitting into smaller bullets, like a MIRV warhead re-entering the atmosphere, delivering its warheads to Moscow, Novosibirsk, Krasnoyarsk, the great forgotten badlands of history... He shook his head vigorously. He used to be much healthier, dealing with the equations, they were pure form, such abstract elegance. He did his best work when he went beyond words. And he'd been having curiously strong images this morning.

He didn't normally get such vivid eidetic images until he was on the verge of a new idea. Perhaps it could be today's bright notion, his lucky potion. But then maybe all this imagery was a hang-over, an aftermath, consequent upon an over-dose of certain *plaisirs* at a Pleasure Centre. That had been long long ago. But every day there were new rumours of long-term dangers – not that he believed the latest nonsense about Chronoclasms, whatever they were. However, if he stayed penniless in the city he could sink without trace in the Panic Zones or face the jolly mercies of the fundamentalists, undergo a forced conversion or worse.

And he faced other hazards. Horrid humiliations could lurk in an interview room. Room 932, Personnel Department, Pleasure Centres plc, The Complex, W2. 'Have you ever used one of our Centres, Dr. Crowe?' Yes. No. Honestly can't remember. But most of us have... He gripped the stub of the mortice key.

He could hear Mrs. Kalyoubi's TV booming through the wall as he stumbled down the stairs. The quantum physics lecturers were still droning on, at full volume. What was this suspicious Egyptian female dumpling going to make of Heisenberg's Uncertainty Principle? He suddenly realised that he'd been looking at his watch for seven minutes, that it was eight twenty-three, the Pleasure Centres would not stay on hold indefinitely, and he was standing on one leg in front of the doorway, the hatch to hell, there was no escape, and his arm had been twitching involuntarily, making his raised fist clench and unclench, until it ached.

Across the hallway Mrs. Kalyoubi's battered door started its habitual rattling. It might well take her several minutes to unlock, he had time to escape if only he could control these

pulses of random access memory which kept over-riding his logic circuits, inhibiting a successful launch.

Outside it was enemy territory, but he'd mapped it often enough on previous missions, and this trip to Pleasure Centres could be life-and-death, his whole money supply depended on it, so all he had to do was cruise carefully at the correct depth, keep safe distances, remember rules of engagement, avoid eye contact...

He was trembling. But, controlling his sphincter very carefully, he managed to insert the key; and opened the door to the street.

A Faulty Machine in the Ghost

Perhaps St. Damian's Avenue wasn't so bad now that he was actually walking up and down and along it. Light refreshing drizzle now dispelled the smog. Only a few battered women in headscarves on the way to work in the service industries and no scabby young males jerking around to the jagged beat of their hormones, they were the dangerous ones. Weak sunlight, gusts of wind, not a bagpuss in sight.

Bagpuss... That was Mrs. Kalyoubi's name for the whispering wheedling neighbourhood beggars who kept constant watch on all entrances and exits. Mrs. K must have acquired most of her English from recycled children's TV. That was perhaps typical of current English usage. No sign yet of family tepees built from black bags and shopping trolleys. This remained a quiet suburban community.

But as he hurried towards the station he was still depressed at viewing all these nice nineteen-thirties fake-timbered semis (three bedrooms, two reception rooms, garage, central heating). These were the properties that poor old Lionel and purse-lipped Norah would have aspired to, the next slippery rung.

Now the houses had become dowdy bedsit empires for the disadvantaged middle classes, for creatures like himself, proletarianised by the implosion of the UK economy. Mrs. Kalyoubi might be half-crazed, incoherent, a malevolent hump in dark shawls cursing her tenants for thought-crimes, but she was better news than some of the big absentee landlords, at least she provided basic facilities. William had lived in his own home once, but he didn't want to go on grinding his teeth about it.

The big house on the tree-sheltered corner, near the station, was still used as a family home. A young Korean executive, Mr. Kim, sales manager for the prestigious Fast Fun Electrics Co., had bought it for his wife and children. He was in the UK for a year or two, to promote such domestic products, including *Kwaidan Warriors*, a new children's big budget vidgame which could be accessed at home, sales steadily rising in the sarari-man sector, well ahead of Pleasure Centre's obsolescent *Dub Demons*, which one could only access in those sleazy high street PC outlets. William knew this from studying company correspondence, after Mr. Kim, who obviously had a priority energy allowance, had dropped some envelopes while unlocking his new electric Hyundai. He could quote it in the Pleasure Centres interview.

This morning Mr. Kim was moving fast, to dodge a cluster of beggars on the corner of the Avenue. These were several strata above the bagpuss level, for they lived in a portakabin in the playground of the old school. Perhaps they'd been teachers or worked for the Council or even the old-time police. William knew one of them had trained an Alsatian to catch briefcases. Another had clocked up the latest cultural crazes of the Pacific Rim and would appear every morning with old greenback Penguin thrillers, or cheap souvenirs of Queen Camilla's accession and brief reign, all much prized by sarari-men.

But as William entered the blank cube of the station hall, a protective autopilot took over, to create space for his highly specialised dreamtime. Buying his ticket from a vending machine, he ignored the handful of fellow consumers and the faded peeling collages of advertisement hoardings, grimy palimpsests of Britain's final boom industry. Finally the rusty train rumbled into the station and he slumped into a vacant seat.

He was looking at the screen of the rain-mottled window, at the sliding cityscape beyond. But he was already deciphering deep topologies, recursive geometries, an abstract dance of spatio-temporal relationships, patterns of light, mass and gravity which branched out into equations that interlocked, almost... He switched off words. It was all number from here. This was his Zen of the Aleph Null, a pure Zen of Quantities. He was always trying to bootstrap his own thinking. Elaine used to call it his Goofy Number Chewing Sessions Up In the

Loo, but he'd already forgotten that time period, it had only a secondary reality.

He'd been getting closer to the edge for months. Despite the pet food diet and the vodka and the noise at nights and the itching and his deplorable bouts of geriatric sex mania, he was fighting the legacy of his Blackout. There had been plateaux like this where he had floated in pure abstraction above the phenomenal world, when he had almost grasped the relationship between the performance of his brain's 'consciousness' programme, (as a series of wave/particle transactions at the sub-atomic level) and the general operation of the universe, cosmos, whatever that portion of his brain 'thought' it observed. And he was pretty certain that he knew how things were the way they were. The very fact of his Blackout proved his point. Perhaps even this alleged Rupture. All things were parts of a great machine that was running down. It was almost reassuring. Even God had black holes in his head.

William had been playing with these thought-experiments for years. The game had started as a relaxation. He'd been using computers for modelling blast and radiation yields and this had got him interested in the whole field of artificial intelligence, the controversies about the nature of 'consciousness' and its interaction with matter. Later, of course, they'd said he was weak minded, lacked discipline, threw their stupid book at him.

But William was always a hard numbers man, he wasn't going to be fooled by any hippy rubbish about magick mindstuff, no mellow spiritual bananas for William. The disgusting spongy brain was a future-shock absorber, that was all, and/or a black box that existed to replicate itself ad nauseam.

If you could only get enough of the right equations in place, and suitable algorithms, and an infinitely powerful computer, you could devise a credible model of 'consciousness' beyond the neuro-chemical level, at the level of sub-atomic interactions. You could build in random-probability elements if you liked that sort of thing.

Then you could compare/contrast the entire gimcrack gismo with major laws governing gravity, space-time, light, electromagnetism, the strong and weak forces, and all the rest of the palaver. You might not learn why the whole ramshackle construct of reality stood up in the way it did. But you'd know how the brain made such a spectacular mess of construing it.

As the train rumbled over the warped tracks outside Waterloo, William didn't pretend to have conclusively solved the mind/body problem. But he sure as hell suspected there was only a faulty machine in the ghost.

3
Pleasure Centres PLC

Escape from the Borderlands

A grey dawn. Viv sprawled across the narrow bed and thought about masturbating but decided against it. She sensed a residu of Elaine's warnings during her adolescent years about the dangers of inviting a hostile incubus through unstructured fantasising. Maybe it was the sheer drabness of this hotel room in the outer suburbs, its un-erotic grey sheets, dusty curtains and peeling pink wallpaper. Or maybe it was simply her exhaustion after that journey - and shock about the decision she seemed to have made.

Escape from the Borderlands had been unexpectedly easy. She'd been afraid that her discontent might have had some aetheric resonance with Elaine, but her grandmother's immersion in that debate at the Red Hag must have blocked any awareness of her impending departure, while Aran had already blotted himself out with booze.

She'd packed a rucksack with clothes, her cards, some sketches and samples of her craft work, with the vague rationalisation that she might 'go to London to promote her art'. She had walked to the edge of Leynebridge where she'd picked up the last bus to Old Hallows. Then a hitch on a taciturn farmer's lorry to the rail terminal at Worcester, where she'd slipped through the barrier to board the night train - the only train - to London.

It was a slow journey, a steam-hauled private operation on ancient corridor coaches. There was a nasty moment when a gang of Heavy Shepherds boarded the train at Reading and swarmed down the corridors demanding tithes. 'Don't steal from Jesus!' they shouted, brandishing their vicious cross-headed clubs as they burst into her compartment. She'd flashed the pentagram around her neck and mouthed a random curse. The nearest Shepherd paused, raised his club in a protective gesture and fled. The mob were finally herded off the train, which arrived hours late under the darkened arches of Paddington. She'd somehow got a bus, a 777, chosen as a promising number, which had terminated here, somewhere in the south western suburbs, outside this Budget Inn. As it had no free Lobe connection it was double-discount.

But her money would only last a few weeks and the chances of selling artwork were minimal without connections or a base. Divination skills were in demand in some zones but if you announced yourself as a Tarot reader or scryer in the wrong neighbourhood you'd be harassed (or worse) by local religious vigilantes, maybe even Techno-Nihilists.

She went over to the window and surveyed the almost empty high street two storeys below. Two hooded boys on bikes circled aimlessly around the mini-roundabout. The supermarket opposite was boarded up, but further down there were the usual 'bootshops', as they'd become known, selling everything and nothing, broken furniture, tinned food, old clothes, increasingly on a barter basis. One was just opening. A withered man in a long brown coat whistled tunelessly as he rolled up the shutters.

The rumour-mills in Leynebridge were right. It was even worse in the cities. At least they had fresh bread in the Borderlands. And the air here tasted of dirt. For a moment she felt faint and sick.

This had been an absurd crazy decision. Perhaps some entity was driving her into it. A Qliphothic hangover from the Rupture. They were alleged to infest people, mind-worming in the right brain, whispering away...

She stretched her arms and moved them around the points of the compass, mentally intoning the Tetragrammaton, as she'd been taught, to still the whispering, and began to feel calmer after a few minutes. She would trust to sleep and the redemption of dreams.

Monster Mash

William walked shoulder to shoulder with the hurrying hooded pedestrians of the West London zone. The crowd filled the whole width of the street. There were no buses or tubes in this sector today.

A rocket-firing contest was underway in the new stadium. Some event called 'The Feast of Smoke', apparently copying some ridiculous festivity of the Borderlands. As William crossed the street he could hear the garble of the tannoy announcements and glimpse the bulbous rockets with their retro fins roaring away on pillars of flame into the overcast.

He paused at the stadium entrance, trying to peer through the chain-link fencing. He was surprised at the bulk of the rockets, at least twenty feet high. Perhaps they were based on old Eurasian missiles. The crowds cheered them onwards and upwards. William wondered where they would land.

Then a special attraction was announced. The excited commentator seemed to be gabbling about something called 'The Monster Mash.' It was even squatter than the fin-tail rockets, an oversize conical bin-like device on rusty stilts.

It rose unsteadily amid billowing smoke, just clearing the roof of the stadium and the fluttering pennants – then veered over and toppled into the street, crashing down into a pedestrian subway on the central traffic island. And exploded in a great blot of flame.

Pedestrians screamed and scattered. A few with blazing cloaks and headscarves rolled through the gutters. But those at the edges of the crowd moved relentlessly forward, some not even turning their heads. William, shaking, realized that he no longer understood the urban rhythms.

In the Space Behind the Wall

Viv had tried to rest but she became convinced there was a space behind the wall where crystalline creatures were growing. These 'alien sex fiends' murmured at the edge of sleep. The synthetic succubi used to live in a rival dimension. They were elaborately polyhedral. Now here they were - in the space behind the wall, between the bricks and the plasterboard. They were silver or bluish green, covered in brick dust and spider webs, but growing day by day with a faint high ringing sound that you'd mistake for an appliance in the apartment next door. At intervals she swore she could hear a harsh crack - as the crystals expanded, putting greater pressure on the beams and joists. She had to get up and get out, fast.

Dream of Carla

Dreams used to help. Used to dream of Carla, my queen, flickering in the early morning daze, licking my ear, whispering her dreams, her journeys across a blue landscape where flying animals looped lazily overhead and the glitter of fountains carried a complex high frequency code which if interpreted correctly would give everyone a second crack at immortality. Her sweet tongue flickering in my ear. Those were training sessions where I would try to reprogramme the reality schedule, even while my mouth was opening and shutting like an old lizard's...

Lucas could not stop repeating the details of this lucid dream over and over, as if repetition would actualise the phantasm. *I am addicted* he wrote, before erasing it.

A Bit of Nurdle

The slate-glass tower of Pleasure Centres PLC was located in a muddy triangle of waste ground beneath the shadow of a flyover. The site was surrounded by barbed wire and electric fences. William, still trembling after the stadium incident, had to follow a circuitous route around the perimeter, searching with increasing anxiety for an entrance.

At last he found a blockhouse and barrier, obscured by a clutter of kebab stalls, where a mob of off-duty security guards gathered, muttering morosely in some polyglot jargon. 'Lobeshitters…' one announced, to the world at large. 'Lobeshitters and fraggles, is all.' He shrugged and spat absent-mindedly on William's brogues.

William pretended to ignore the gesture, although he could not help comparing it with his reception at the gates of a great Research Establishment in that other lost life. He elbowed his way towards the gatehouse window, clutching his letter. A small brown man peered uneasily through cracked perspex and mouthed some unintelligible phoneme through the intercom. William took this as an invitation to approach the gate, but a guard gripped his elbow. Another snatched the letter and passed it through a slot in the window. The small man glanced at it briefly; and crumpled it in his fist. William exploded.

'What is the meaning – I have an interview - '

'No worries,' said the guard, gripping his elbow tighter. 'You just got to fill in the proper form, that's all.'

The man behind the grubby perspex slid a pen and a pink form through his slot and adjusted his intercom mic. 'You fill it in nicely. Then everything all right.' The voice was croaky and anxious.

'He means,' said the guard, 'that you write your name on it and then slip a bit of nurdle in. You know… nurdle?' He winked and rubbed his finger and thumb together. 'Some like porno, some like dope, but he likes the old nurdle.'

William was beginning to understand the new economics. This was the only way now. He scribbled his name on the form and folded it around his last twenty-pound note. The guard smiled as the gatekeeper took it. The boom of the barrier was rising already. 'Good luck with your meeting, sir…'

Plutonic Realms

Later Viv found herself walking carefully in a shopping precinct somewhere. Her bag was unexpectedly heavy. The sound of many footsteps but no background chatter. Everything was domed under glass. Upscale urban women in cloaks and masks, goggled for air purity (or fetish chic?) floated up escalators. The shops were full of incomprehensible clothes.

She had sneaked past the hotel checkout while the clerk was Lobed into a gambling site. She had to quit, she couldn't trust those presences in the walls. They didn't correspond with anything she'd been taught. Mineral entities perhaps, malignant gnomings generated by the repressed demons of the city. She had stumbled over to the nearby railway station, boarded the next train and slipped off at a random stop before the ticket-master reached her carriage.

This would appear to be a high-income zone, heavily guarded by its own militia. She tried to project a veil of invisibility over her faded skirt and crooked green hat. For she was penetrating Saturnine or Plutonic realms. The ubiquitous right-angles and vertical planes of smoked glass might form an entrapment for her spirit so she had to keep moving right along.

The streets were half-empty. It had to be the seductive pull of the Lobe. People allegedly queued for hours at underground Pleasure Centres, legitimized by a government desperate for order at any price. The city was obviously populated by PC acolytes screaming in solitude towards their latest consummation.

She tried not to be irradiated by the huge illuminated advert scrolling across the middle storeys of the tower in front of her. *NIGHT OF THE QUANTUM BROTHERS - Coming Soon from Pleasure Centres.*

Those bland grey moustachiod faces, like old film actors, stared through the canyons of ferrocrete. The eyes seemed to be following her. Perhaps she should be following them. She might pick up an alignment, some channel of guidance...

Starting From Ground Zero

Dominic Pullman, Creative Manager of Pleasure Centres plc, leaned back in a black rubber doughnut-shaped chair, fiddling with his ear-piercing. His long stubbly face was impassive. William couldn't read the modern dress codes - the elegant mohair jacket with a t-shirt and torn denims. Was this man the real creative director or merely a flunkey weeding out the no-hopers? William surely was a hopeless old man, in the wrong clothes, perched on a plastic chair with a warped leg, already anxious to urinate.

'Tell us what you know about us,' murmured Pullman, 'from a consumer perspective.'

'You mean – have I ever used –'

'We know that. If you hadn't we wouldn't have invited you here. I mean – what's your awareness of the mission? What's your unique selling point?'

'Well...' William could only extrapolate from what he'd glimpsed on the Lobe and from that letter Mr Kim had dropped. 'You're now competing for the world market in virtual reality entertainment with multi-national corporations like Korea's Fast Fun Electrics Co. Not to mention all the standard video and audio material people can consume via the Web...'

Pullman pursed his lips, and William realised he'd made a near-fatal error of nomenclature. 'I mean, of course, the Lobe...' He'd never understood that curious after-effect of the Rupture, the verbal slippage and compulsive re-naming of everything. He stumbled on.

'Fast Fun is concentrating its efforts on miniaturizing the existing VR technology for the domestic user. Soon its cheap compact home VR sets could rival the immersion packages currently on offer at the average Pleasure Centre, and will overtake them - a replay of TV versus the old-style cinema.'

Pullman rummaged in his pockets and extracted a packet of cigarette papers. He started rolling up. William was startled by this criminal anachronism, but kept up his fabulation.

'If Pleasure Centres plc is to survive, the company has to set new standards not only of quality but format, innovations that are as superior to existing VR as digital video was to analogue.'

'So?' Pullman's tongue flickered along the damp seam of his roll-up. William's presence was obviously a distracting irritant.

'So you must create more convincing illusions of total sensory immersion - with a special emphasis on vision and inter-active tactility. This demands a whole new level of information processing capacity.'

Pullman nodded wearily and opened a bottle of Italian lager. The tobacco smoke was nagging at William's throat but he managed to splutter on.

'I expect you already employ specialists in optics, and neurology. As well as writers, researchers and graphic artists, and - ah - performers - to provide the content. However you will inevitably require more persons with expertise in computer architecture, distributive computing, and computer modeling of complex processes which is where I can offer some specialist experience. In my defence work, I was personally responsible for - ' He hesitated. There was still that black hole at the end of his CV...

Pullman raised a hand to cut him off. 'Don't worry yourself any further, Dr Crowe. I'm afraid you're hired.' He pointed to the door. 'Our Human Resources Officer Tom Liggett will show you around and then take you through to your living quarters. And Security will arrange for the collection of your personal effects. I'm sure you'll understand the importance of starting from ground zero...'

Straggle of Transients

Vivienne was queueing outside a black hole at the base of a large building. She couldn't see exactly where the queue was heading but all those in the cluster, a mob of at least fifty people, seemed to be equally disoriented by the data-storm of the city. Her training should have surely equipped her to transcend it, but her sense of divination, that easy channeling of the friendly elements which kept her balanced with the rhythms of Leynebridge had atrophied already, so she was stuck on the pavement in this straggle of transients seeking work and shelter. She listened numbly to fragments of dialogue:

'Hope it's not Shepherds...'

'Shepherds are OK, man. They got burgers with real hot meat. And ice cream on Sundays...'

'But they make you work. For a lousy bunk and a burger.'

'All you have to do is ship Bibles. Heft a few pallets of Bibles, that's all there is to it, keeps them happy. Just sing along with it.'

'Maybe it's Mo Boys...'

'They make you Submit. Right there on the door. Before you get a fucking sniff...'

Viv tried to get a closer look at the speakers, older beardy men huddling in ponchos against the wind, with its curious chemical taint. They didn't sound like Borderlanders, more urban, nasally-accented, but they'd obviously fallen through the interstices of the city's economy. Then the queue suddenly spilled forwards towards the black archway, nudging her along with its knees and patched elbows. She was in the throng of it, like it or not.

Back-projected Phantasm

Lucas was exploring limbo. He wrote: *The thick fog tastes of butter. The zero state is a terror state. I had a dream of being stuck in a bookshop, too fat to get out. Wharton was haranguing me again. I could smell food burning on the night wind. I am a back-projected phantasm of the living dead. Carla posed naked for me once in her peaked hat. It was pretty epiphanic. But for my cruddy genome I would have conquered her for ever. That was my karmic fudge. I shall become an old man writing in bed.*

He put down the leaky fountain pen that he'd stolen from Trader Price. Outside he could hear the distant throb of drums. Probably Forgan leading one of his parades along the Serpent Path. It was impossible to concentrate.

Induction

The induction had taken hours. The biometric sampling and profiling, painfully conducted by a large awkward woman in a lab coat, had been followed by a tour of the complex. As they walked his escort, the ruddy-faced Tom Liggett, talked constantly about the latest phase-end corporate targets and quality management systems. At first William tried to pick out key words relating to his new role but soon just let the jargon chatter past him. He was still wondering if some mistake had been made. Best not to ask any questions.

Most of the tour was underground. The glass tower contained the admin and financial offices of Pleasure Centres, but the research directorates and the huge chambers housing the servers supplying content for the various Pleasure Centres franchises were situated in a network of deep bunkers, an ex-government command facility sold off by the ever-dwindling State.

As he trudged down the bare yellow-painted tunnels, William reflected that if history had taken a different time-line some beleaguered commander down here might well have sent the command to deploy one of his masterpieces from the nuclear glory years. The notion gave him a sense of validation, a flicker of almost sexual potency. Perhaps he could bluff this out.

Liggett was now talking about somebody called Keith Lombard. His tone was reverential, even nervous. 'Mr Lombard is the new Chief Executive. He has great plans for us. Plans for expansion. Pleasure Centre franchises across the country. Everywhere from big leisure hubs like Torbeach to rural development areas like Leynebridge. Reaching new customers. With the new upgrades that we're going to develop. It's an exciting time...' Leynebridge? That Borderland enclave of mystic mediaevalists and hash-candy fools? His ex-wife Elaine's bolt-hole. Bolted with the doomed daughter. He hoped Liggett hadn't noticed his grimace.

They arrived at a kind of canteen, with a small snack bar and a coffee machine. Its scattering of brightly coloured plastic chairs and low tables reminded William of a children's play area, those boisterous combat zones he'd so carefully avoided, as a child - and absent father.

But Liggett was studying him anxiously. 'Time to meet the team, Dr. Crowe.' A red-haired young woman in a black trouser-suit was already extending a hand to him. He was struck by the elegant ellipses of her jaw and cheekbones, the sensual mouth, the full breasts under the black tunic. 'This is Carla Leppard, who's responsible for researching new ideas for our virtual experiences.'

William nodded, absently.

'She used to be producer for Jouissance Productions,' said Liggett, looking worried. The team bonding was not going according to in-house policy.

Carla Leppard smiled. 'It was just a little art-house VR outfit, Tom. Artisan erotica for the critics. I'm not surprised if Dr Crowe hasn't heard of it. Stop talking everything up. Just because we have visitors.'

'Dr Crowe isn't visiting, Carla. He's joining the team.' The woman glanced suspiciously at William and swung to face Liggett.

'That anus-on-legs Dominic is keeping me out of the loop again, isn't he?' Liggett flushed and tried to interrupt but she over-rode him.

'I'm sorry, Doctor, but this does seem a little unexpected. We're supposed to be developing new concepts for the youth market. And you're not exactly - '

'He's an AI programming specialist, Carla!' They had been joined by a young man in denims with an aquiline face and old-style pony-tail. 'With special credentials. Someone who might be able to help us with our Dub Demons bug, for a start.' A flicker of worry - and perhaps apology - crossed Carla Leppard's face. 'And I'm your project officer, Doctor - Mark Rinehart.'

'Dub Demons bug? I didn't know there was an issue. Does

Dominic know?' Liggett clutched his clipboard and prepared to make notes.

'There are no issues to concern you, Tom,' interjected Carla. 'You just better leave us to get acquainted with this miracle-working doctor.'

People to People Skills

'We believe that working for Pleasure Centres should be fun, ' said the Assessor. This large blonde woman in a yellow trouser suit snapped her ring-binder shut and smiled, smiled dangerously. The hessian walls were closing in around Vivienne and her will began leaking away. 'You might have thought you were queueing for dead-end chores in a dormitory with one of those sad faith-based Workfare Hostels but I can tell you, Vanessa…'

'Vivienne…' A weak murmur.

'I can assure you're in the right space at the right time. You're going to love it to bits here. We're recruiting Customer Hospitality Officers Level 1 right now for our re-vamped Centres and young women with people-to-people skills have top profile. You'll have on-site en suite accommodation, no dangerous walks to work, you're right there at the heart of what we do, with everything you need.'

She swung her desktop monitor round. It showed a tiny but neat pale peach bedroom, complete with Lobe screen and potted cheese-plant.

'What do I do?' The enfeebled words seemed to hover by her left ear. She felt disembodied, ghosted. 'Do I have to take part… in the… performances?'

'No way!' The woman looked slightly shocked at this presumption. 'We have our professionals for that. You just deal with Phase 1 Customer

Service. We'll train you up.' She clicked into a bleached still of a young women at a work station, smiling at a Korean salary man in a bowler hat and plus-fours. 'You check the booking, the payment protocol and read him the safety disclaimer. Then…'

She keyed into a jerky movie. The girl in her smart maroon PC overalls was escorting the man to a padded cubicle. A heavy immersion suit, glossy black body armour with a web of cables trailing from the helmet, hung in an alcove. Cyber-spider… Viv felt faintly sick. This was the acme of the Carbonite techcraft she'd been warned about so often. And now she was in the claws of the robot.

'Don't look so worried, Veronica. Not all the Playzones are adult-themed. Anyway, you don't have to perform. Just watch…'

As the pudgy salary man stripped, struggling with the plus-fours, and fed himself awkwardly through the zips and flaps of the thick-limbed suit - like a swollen corpse - the girl turned away to study a touch-screen wall panel. When he was suited, she guided him towards a long gurney, where he reclined, shifting uneasily as she plugged some more cables into the neck of the spherical helmet. Then, glancing at notes on a clipboard, she keyed in a code. Checking quickly over her shoulder, she dimmed the lights as she left the cell. The screen blanked.

'Easy-peasy, isn't it? That code looks as if she's set him up for an Edwardian Chorus Girl Romp with Beef Supper, it was one of the Korean focus-group faves. Naughty but nice for your man from Pusan…' The Assessor laughed throatily. 'He'll be out in an hour, a bit dazed. Just take him to the post-leisure zone to chill out, one of the medics will give him a quick check. That's all there is. Take the money, make them comfy, strap 'em in and everybody's chilled. The perfect post-Rupture fun time. Are you signing up, or what?'

Flagship Products

William was the first to arrive in the office. He'd slept well in the bland motel-like cubicle that he'd been allotted and served himself a basic breakfast in the empty canteen area. He'd discovered his few belongings neatly boxed up beside the bed, including certain crucial notebooks and memory units. The old photos were burned years ago, their data only distracted him. How had Dawn really died? It certainly wasn't his fault. He would have stopped her getting impregnated by a vanishing hippy. He had a blurred recall of Elaine hectoring him outside a pub, a wailing child clutching her skirts. Was that grandchild a Vera, a Veronica or a Vivienne? These had become mere rhetorical questions, with muffled answers, garbled voices on a flaking tape.

And he felt equally detached now from the detritus of his life at Mrs Kalyoubi's. He imagined her muttering with bewilderment as his effects were removed, but knew that another wrecked professional male would soon take his place in the tatty bed-sit and share her TV bellowing up through the floorboards.

Using a password that Carla had reluctantly supplied, he logged on to the Pleasure Centres internal network, to discover a mailbox already filling up with corporate messages about his new job description, his generous salary, the in-house target-management system and his new contractual obligations.

He glanced briefly at these but his real need to was to explore the databases for Pleasure Centres flagship products, the labyrinths of code that supported the user experience. He needed to investigate combat games like Dub Demons, Wargasm, the old favourite Megaton Command - and possibly the adult titles, that whole slew of retro-porn that Pleasure Centres had acquired for redevelopment in Virtual Reality on the Lobe. He was aware of those urges, still aching dimly, that had driven towards this software as a consumer; yet, for the moment he had to research the area objectively. His cursor hovered over the link to Dungeons of Venusberg.

'We're still working on the upgrade to that,' said Carla, leaning over his shoulder, hair flipping across her brow, 'but I'm glad to see you picked out the tough ones. Still, best to get back into form with something easy... I may have a little job for you...'

William felt uneasy.

Elysium

'It's part of your training, dear. You have to try a little taste of the customer experience. At the heart of what we do, remember?' Georgia was gentle but firm as she slid Vivienne's arms into the oily sleeves of the tactility suit. Resistance was futile. As Georgia lowered the helmet over her skull, she found herself flat and empty, colluding with her own passivity. She was *tabula rasa*, a sheet of blankness and they could scribble all over her, now that she was masked in darkness. The suit smelt of lavender air-freshener and she wondered vaguely if Georgia took unofficial surreptitious VR trips of her own.

'Now let's see if we can find you something appropriate for a nice country girl. We're not all raw sex and violence, you know.' She could hear Georgia's fingers pecking at a keyboard.

There was a sudden fugue of nausea and neural pain. As it faded an inscape stabilised around her. But she was still giddy, fighting for breath. A dark hollow space. Earth, stone and clay enclosing her. Light throbbed around the head of a stone pillar. Its rotating beam swept across her forehead and paused. Then, moving on, it traced a doorway through the stonework. Which slid aside, to reveal a square of daylight.

'Welcome to Elysium, the Otherworld...' A Druid-like figure stood silhouetted against the sun. She half-recognised him as a younger version of Noah Dodd, somehow coiffeured and airbrushed in his dazzling white robe. His voice was un-naturally sonorous.

'Taste the delights of immortality, my child, exploring realms of triumphal combat, or fufilled desire, or secret knowledge revealed.' His outline slowly faded, his hand still beckoning.

She was walking through a high lush pasture overlooking an orchard. The sky was crystalline blue and the fruit on the trees glittered in prismatic colours. A beautiful white stallion, saddled in shining leather, was grazing in a clearing. 'That is Fairfoot, your steed,' intoned the disembodied Druid voice. She mounted the docile animal and slowly rode him along a shining path beside a winding stream, down through forest glades towards a fork in the path under a great oak tree. Its foliage was saturated with colour and each leaf quivered in the breeze. She paused. Doves and butterflies fluttered around her.

Then, from the right hand fork in the path another rider galloped towards her, a tall warrior in the green kilt of the Leynebridge Clan. Yet she felt no fear. As he removed his helmet and sheathed his sword she recognised the heavy brow and braided hair of a typical Leynebridge craft-worker. His face seemed modeled on Aran's yet smoother and less defined. He smiled and gestured for her to follow down the steep path. She began to feel a pang of regret at her flight from Leynebridge – and renewed desire for this idealized 'Aran'. She wondered how she would feel as his hands tightened around her waist. The stream broadened and fell through mossy boulders into a small lake, overhung by willows.

On the shore an open pavilion had been pitched, where bearded nobles in white robes were feasting to the sound of lutes and fiddles. A silvery object sparkled on the flower-bedecked high table. She knew it was a vessel of some significance, a cup. Next to it was a pale object - a skull..?

The pseudo-Aran moved close, trying to tell her some secret about the cup. She felt his hand on her shoulder and his hot breath on her neck. But she needed to know about the skull. And now the enfolding reality-matrix was flawed by light-leaks and their words faltered and garbled like a badly dubbed soundtrack. The colours of trees, flesh, sky started bleaching, the violins rose inexorably in pitch. Then the whole scenario flared up in a slow dazzle around her - only to black out abruptly.

For at least a minute she hung in a void. She felt trapped in some alien nervous system, routing arbitrary signals of pain through her skull. Then suddenly she could breathe properly as her supervisor removed the headpiece. Georgia was grey faced with anxiety.

'I'm really sorry, dear. But I had to get you out quickly. I should never have hooked you up with that one. It's still in development, as they say. More than my job's worth if something went wrong. I think that's more than enough for today. You get the idea. Let's go and look at your new room...You won't tell anybody about my little cock up, will you?'

Viv realised she didn't have anyone to tell.

4
The Polyverse

Poetry Was Making a Comeback

Lucas wanted to be mad again, to ride his nutritious primal madness, but the madness just wouldn't come. He leaned against the porthole of his bunker scanning flat grey sky and drizzly fields. He couldn't focus any energy, dulled by those creeping neighbourly thought-clouds. A mental fog floating over the Borderlands kept seeping in: *got great bollocks on her / so I turned round and round and told him all our workings were robed no sky-clad fandangles thank you very much / get off my ground fat old mouldy bastard...* Concentration dribbled away. He was going robotic.

Once again, he surveyed his options. To muddle along in Leynebridge with bits of tutoring and talking to no-one on the wireless while the New Age drifted around him into premature senility and melt-down. To recycle bleary memories of Carla; to probe the trauma/delirium of his pre-Rupture story, still surfacing in dreams - *Leila's pale breasts flecked with his blood the Qliphothic egregore enfolding Robyn oh stupid gibbering dada dad mother screaming to the rescue.* Such an overload of his mind that action stalled, faced with the sliding membranes of the Polyverse. He'd lost his grip.

His old magickal staff leaned in the corner of the room, half-hidden by a tottering pile of stale clothes and smudged news sheets. He extracted it awkwardly, then slumped down with it across his knees. It had been a crude effort. He'd tried to carve the ibis of Thoth on the handle, but the bird-god's beak had broken off and the lunar head-dress had cracked when he'd hurled it across Carla's bedroom on the evening she'd announced her latest professional infidelity. That night he'd left London for good. So much for phallic weaponry. He picked at the peeling gold paint.

Yet grasping the staff restored a kind of clarity. He needed to focus on fast-forward, pick a path through the blur of shadow-realms. No point in looking back, although the past kept glaring back in unselected highlights: *Robyn smiling in the rain Leila grins placing his hand between her thighs Mum dragging him back through red-moon fog and leggy brains...* He had to keep running towards some epiphany, not away from it. He suddenly imagined the staff as an immense consecrated dildo, for the pleasuring (or punishing?) of those runaway ghost women, was shocked at his own grotesquerie, yet jerked it upright and raised it high, scraping the ceiling.

He staggered for a second - then found himself holding the staff with both hands as it twitched and bucked, shaping loops in the moist air. He was apparently dowsing for new letter-forms. The poetry was making a come-back. He knew it. He was going to have to write himself out of this damp corner.

The Ant Hills of Allah's Army

In the morning Omar Majid delivered vegetables, to subsidise his studies. He drove the stuttering mini-van through the maze of estates and terraces. Exhaustion made him crash the gears. He had to concentrate to remember the itinerary of restaurants and community centres. And he flinched as a kid, maybe eleven, dodged across the road, waving a crude sword. It could be a ruse to make him slow as the van passed over a Kaffir mine. No – just another lost scavenger putting on a territorial show.

But generally this area of West London was thriving. Orderly groups of young women in black jilbabs marched out of their enclaves everyday to tend their vegetable gardens in the public parks. In the rusty deserts of the city they were nurturing green shoots. Their menfolk with the crossbows watched from the green-flagged towers. These were their checkpoints. They built them from scaffolding discarded by feckless drunk Pinky builders.

'Our women will be the ant-hills of Allah's army,' said Uncle Abdul, years ago, as he walked child Omar home from the mosque. But Omar couldn't stop thinking of his infidel woman, with her red hair and pointed breasts. She was the woman who would deliver him to Hell. If only he could find some distraction, even another sin, a greater sin perhaps, just to burn that image out of his brain, her corona of flaming hair as she knelt over him.

Porno Madness

William knew that he should have remained at his workstation. It was a job that could easily be done via remote access to the server. Carla Leppard had implied that it was an easy assignment, suitable as an entry-level chore for a senior citizen. 'There's a little bug in the software for the Dub Demons real-time graphic rendering system. Some glitch in the codes that organise the pixels in the eyepiece display creates a distorted morphing image once the customer is suited up. It gets worse as they explore the gaming environment and encounter the avatars, and it also seems to trigger related problems with the tactility in the body-suit and glove-sets. Parents have complained their kids are scared and word's getting out on the Lobenet. I need you to sort it, William, ASAP.' And she'd gone to a meeting with Pullman, probably to complain about the deployment of an Alzheimer's person on her team.

But as a working scientist he believed in fieldwork, empirical observation, testing all hypotheses. That was why he was here, delivered by a corporate Pleasure Centres electro-buggy to the pavement outside the biggest PC franchise in the City. Surely it would be helpful if he first visited the arcade and inspected the actual equipment. Maybe there was an on-site hardware problem, a faulty headset processor, for example, a dubious connection downstream of the servers. He'd known how tiny problems could affect the most sophisticated systems, like a faulty keyboard membrane that could have sent a W177 megatonner to Leningrad, or that miscalculation by Denis Weekes that might have obliterated Berkshire. Perhaps he could even immerse himself in Dub Demons and see this alleged bug. He wouldn't put it past Ms Leppard to task him with the solution of a non-existent problem.

As he entered the grubby lobby with its flashing digital banners ('What's Your Pleasure?') and ravaged plastic sofas, he recognised, of course, the recurrent bug in his own system, his old addiction to PC's clumsy cyber-sleaze VR that he'd tasted in his twilight zone of divorce and unemployment. But as he approached reception and the skinny dark-haired girl at the desk started sizing him up, he repressed any reflex of anticipation and produced his ID. 'I'm a Senior Technical Officer,' he announced. 'I believe there's a problem.'

The girl looked at him uneasily. Then she peered into a screen as she scanned his card, fumbling with the card-reader. 'I was told by management all the trouble-shooting was done off-site. Out-sourced or something like it ... All off-site is management policy.' She appeared to be repeating a script that had been reluctantly learned and scarcely understood.

'I've been briefed by senior management, young lady. I need to check a reported issue with Dub Demons. Can you get me suited up, please?'

She nodded, seemingly abstracted, but remained sitting, as if hypnotised by the monitor. If this was the level of service customers were receiving, no wonder the help line was bombarded with complaints.

'This is a Grade 5 Priority call-out, you know...' Even for a civilian establishment the discipline here was sloppy. 'I report directly to Dominic Pullman.'

But she still looked vacant as she escorted him down the narrow corridors, past the winking red lights of cubicles. The Pleasure Centres budget packages were still packing them in. Dim bleached episodes from Wargasm and Titillation Island replayed over his nervous system as they located an empty cubicle and slid back the heavy door.

The polyfibre suit was even clumsier than he remembered. Or perhaps he was clumsier now, struggling with the gloves. For a second he recalled the glove-boxes for remotely handling plutonium in the Citadel at the Establishment. He was proud then. He had a grip. He had been chosen.

The sensors in the headpiece prodded painfully through his thinning hair, while the eyepieces, with their close proximity to the cornea, made him feel faintly sick. Although most of the stimuli were direct-injected into the cortex via magnetic resonance, the data gloves and motion trackers embedded in the suit, which smelt of sweat and aftershave, translated his reactions into action in the virtual environment. As he wrestled with the head-mounted display he noticed the small

CCTV camera in the cornice of the room and remembered that his grapplings and gropings with the ghosts of the digital world would be monitored - had always been monitored - and might survive for ever deep in the drives of the Pleasure Centre complex.

With the suit on, he was in darkness. He could only hear the girl through the earpieces of the helmet, clicking keys on the console that launched the programme. She paused. 'I'm afraid there's a problem with Dub Demons.' Her voice sounded thin and remote.

'I know there's a problem. That's why I'm here.' Surely Pleasure Centres could automate the whole boot-up process with AI and get rid of these incompetent wet-ware assistants.

'According to the system it's listed as unavailable.'

William felt a surge of annoyance - and anxiety. Was this assignment just a ruse by Carla Leppard, as he feared, a ploy to keep him busy while she plotted his removal? Was the Pleasure Centres data storage flawed at the most basic level? He asked the assistant to double-check the reference code. After a long interval while she struggled with the interface - she was surely a trainee - she confessed that PC3783256 Dub Demons seemed to have temporarily disappeared.

Yet if the issue with displays and playback was a local problem then perhaps it scarcely mattered which programme he engaged with. He wasn't going to wait around while she fiddled and fussed. Now that he was enmeshed in this suit, it would be futile to return to HQ with nothing to report. Dub Demons was an ancient shoot-em'up, recently refurbed for faster rendering and new FX. Giant dog-faced warriors biting each other's throats, according to the trailer. Too tame for today's kids perhaps. Or maybe there was simply a compatibility issue with whatever upgrade had been mis-installed. He could check out an old release that was contemporary with Dub Demons. A number flashed and winked in his memory. 'Try PC1562109...'

The girl sounded flustered when she found Porno Madness on the database, as if she was surprised that that a senior citizen with top management connections would want to voyeur a primitive interactive 3-D sexbot display. He was surprised himself - that libido still flickered, however long divorced from a usable object.

A guitar riff screeched in his earpiece and the musty darkness brightened as the virtual space fell, jerkily, into place around him. As he recalled, the action played out in an industrial zone like a warehouse, lit by fizzing floods, reverberating to the din of overdriven amplifiers. Some kind of band on a stage, spidery girls in spikes thrashing away at guitars and drums, a screaming vocal:

Pretend not to look when you're peeping in the shopfront
Seeking for relief in the hand-written ads
'Swedish momma give free french letters'
Can't find what you're groping for - just too bad!
It's PORNO MADNESS
PORNO MADNESS...

The music dipped, just as he remembered, getting really hungry for the replay now. In front of the stage, only virtual feet away from him, two pale girls appeared, in the latex sex-wear of a previous century.

They froze and posed defiantly, flaunting all the black lipstick and metal accessories of that period, those late seventies creatures that had passed him by, like alien visitors, 'punks', punkettes for the pleasuring of. He was certain he'd seen this before and tasted, briefly, the relief of their madness.

Abruptly the blonde in the ripped plastic skirt pouted and spat at him. Droplets glistened... he could swear his forehead felt the dribble impacting. She started sawing away at the zip between her rubber-sheathed breasts. Her black-haired companion was already fondling her waist, stroking torn fishnets, seeking an entry.

For the first time in years, his brain was triggering the mechanics of arousal. Soon he would be inter-acting, would be giving direct commands for posture, pressure, angle, expressive quotient. His golems would please him.

But something wasn't quite right. His field of vision trembled, freckled with blots of light. As the pseudo-Gothic brunette toyed with the studs on her companion's leather collar, that corona of blonde hair blurred and liquefied, to morph into an irregular brownish mass. The two bodies darkened and thickened into clumps of blackness on a bleached screen.

And sprouted new heads - identical grey faces, Caucasian male, clean-shaven, forty-plus. The kind he's seen on pirated breakfast Lobe-TV. Sober square-headed men in suits and ties, anyway. Solid no-nonsense men, with shiny well-parted hair. Like old 1950s publicity photos of bandleaders, movie gangsters, radio announcers.

Each now stared formally out of a flickering oval halo. The warehouse background faded away. Their graphite-coloured lips moved jerkily in unison. But this time their accents were glottal, nasal, estuarine: *what you looking at sir all nice girls sir best show in town sir now you see 'em now you don't something special for the weekend sir members only it can be arranged via action at a distance we can ghost you in a private club sir no extra charge for exit sign here nice motor nice set up you got here sir go round your house looking for business know what my bruvver don't think he likes you you like he's a bit of the old bit you know what I mean what you looking at sir all nice girls*

A huge burst of black noise - and total black-out. The virtual sex-club had folded into itself. He was sweating inside the suit, suddenly aware of aching eyes and needles of pain through his neck. Nowhere he wanted to go now except into a dark concavity between tawny thighs in 40-watt red lighting. Such a pert aperture into another's terrifying wriggly oddity. He'd been driven by the biology, like every other body sliding around on the wet surfaces of the city. Sex expertise was the product mix here in the Pleasure Zones. But he was not driving dynamic change, couldn't do the business. The technology had conned him. He was under panic attack, he needed a new action plan.

He pressed the escape button and began scrabbling at the base of his helmet, desperate to tear it off, maybe tear off his own head with it. He gasped as he twisted a ligament struggling with the legs of the suit. He was an archetypal old fool. As they shouted in the old movies - *let's get out of here...*

The grey walls of the cubicle fell into place around him. His hands drifted down to the lost spigot of his sex. Nothing doing down there, just a tassel of tissue, no rampant arc. He realised that the CCTV was panning slowly back and forth, archiving his onanistic mimesis.

'Are you going to file a report?' asked the receptionist as he shuffled past her desk. Was she trembling or was she merely staring? He didn't turn round.

Chronoclasm

Lucas was scribbling in his hole. The only game he had left. Yet, if he wrote enough, if he could write himself into the steady state of the lost art, if he could shimmy like a shaman and get outside his bloody body and rise to the over-view of an overman then maybe he could find a signpost to take him through the fug. With an application of will the distant telepathic drone of Leynebridge could be faded down and he could fly above the murk of local emotions, script himself into a new zone.

Space curdles around time, around the time I met Carla. There's a leakage of partially false memory, maybe swell of a breast in a darkened room, distant squabbly voices we decided to ignore; and later her hoarse whisper: 'You'll go to hell if you touch me...' What was her hell? How could hell erupt from her lifestyle-magazine hedonistics? I'd fingered more than a nerve. It was a complex of fears, as if all the real-time hells she feared, like the Penitence Hostels set up by the Heavy Shepherds had somehow migrated to an afterlife, and she was going to be fast-tracked there. So I got up and went over to the window. 'Looks like I came in through the wrong time-portal.' The arch joke didn't impress. 'Your love is just a syndrome, 'she said. 'It's all sex and mod clothes.'

Mod? I didn't get her latest anachronism. There'd been enough chronoclasms, it was only a year or two after the Rupture and while I was floundering along helping in my mother's Post-Trauma Centre using my alleged spiritual expertise, Carla, inoculated by her techno-scepticism, was riding the waves of chaos, ducking and diving through the wave-front that was breaking up the old consensus, documenting the fluctuations with a steadi-cam and desktop editing and selling the product to what was left of the TV networks. And then she got sub-contracted to Jouissance and started performing as a sex queen...

The pen faltered. This was all wrong, retrogressive, chewing the tired bits of language over and over - *Carla, Rupture, Trauma* - while around him the chaos of space-time was delivering new fraggings of fractals and reality was getting increasingly non-consensual.

The Elders of Leynebridge thought they had the Way, a muddy synthesis of old-tyme shamanism and earth-magick, all neatly hierarchical, but they were going round and round in sacred circles, which became secret spirals getting tighter and tighter, to disappear into the grand sphincter of death, because their world was contracting all around them as the techno-nihilists digitised it and the faith-based cults rampaged against it. He was reduced, yet again, to attempting poetry.

> *zap into the chaosphere*
> *stalk the dead talkers*
> *into a hypno dance slick*
> *spike dreams of a moon-maiden*
> *gravity sucks the riper colours*
> *into the bloodhead*
> *a new signature*

For a moment, he felt charged with a current of dark energy, a tiny incandescence in his brain. Then the murmur of the village began again. He had a sudden projection of himself walking the streets, grey-faced, haggard, head sunk on his chest, talking to his handful of bent coins. No more talking to microphones or adolescents. That seemed to be decided. It was written. But if he failed to support himself by next winter he'd be joining the out-people at Leyston Burrough, impaling their rats on coat hangers over a fire of burning tyres.

The Body of Soft Darkness

Omar tried to keep his eyes shut but the distant yelling in the streets wouldn't let him sleep. He couldn't look at the bedroom, his bedside shrine, the reproachful eyes of family photos. He was overcome with guilt and despair. He didn't like this heavy waking body any more. Somehow he'd acquired an aching head, a sore throat, and the light nausea of a summer virus. Of course: he'd slept naked with the window open, dreaming that Miss Carla's white shape was still shifting beside him in the gloom. She haunted him.

How had he allowed himself to get entangled with the flaming tresses of this Lilith? How could he explain things to Uncle Abdul? That a pretty kaffir woman had smiled at him across their market stall? And invited him to do some market research about new Lobe products - at her nearby flat? That now he was addicted to her?

He had to get up and wash. The rhythms of purification would cleanse his heart. He would soon forget this shameful sex episode. It would become a sequence from those illicit Fast Fun DVDs that vulgar Hisham used to steal from the corner shop, to be buried in the communal garbage next morning. But this was even worse, this Lady Carla was a Lobe-mistress, she boasted she made techno-magick sex scenes that you could get right inside, and worst off all that once again he had willingly entered her seductive trip, sipping wine that made him buzzy and there was no need to screen anything any more because soon her arms were opening wide, her shift tumbled to the carpet and he was rocking between her thighs... He would have to wash very thoroughly, he would have to find a sura to meditate and follow the precepts of Ramadan rigorously. That might absolve him, yet again.

They said the great battle of the new millenium was between young Islam and the Old West. Conspiracy theorists in various Moslem camps - and so many of Uncle Abdul's relatives throughout the London diaspora - had been tracing the pattern since the middle eighties of the last century, even before the so-called Rupture, that mass delusion of the Infidels that they tried to impose on everybody. Even nutty old Aunt Shahida out in the suburbs who watched kids' TV all day knew something was up. Uncle Abdul had argued with the local imam about the ancient fatwa against some apostate, a man called Rushdie. 'Why all that fuss about a silly writer? Ignore his made-up story and he will go away...' But his uncle was forced to admit that the bloody invasions and interferences across the Caliphate had been part of a huge persecution plot across the decades, Western liberal secularists taking a last grandstand against the People of the Book. Last week's sermon summed it all up. Now Allah was punishing the Kaffirs with collective madness. Out in the countryside, they believed in witchcraft and mind-reading. In the cities they were immersed in the filth of their Pleasure Centres. And out there in the big real world Jerusalem would fall to the Caliphate, according to short-wave radio and the Lobe.

Omar studied his face in the mirror. A lock of his hair, lush and ultra-black, coiled over his temple. She'd stroked it. With soft, soothing explanations. *Everything's going to be all right, Omar. Don't worry about me, or what I do. No need to ask too much. It's what I'm doing with you that matters.* Now he was terrified. What a foolish weakling he'd been, toying with this little transitory romance. He must not forget: his father Tariq murdered, as if by a djinn. It was worse. The charring of the flesh and the roasting of the limbs was done by a human being. A British helicopter pilot in his chariot of fire. Now those chariots were fallen.

His recollection was interrupted by sirens. The three-notes cadence signified it was a Neo-Christian patrol meddling in his neighbourhood. Fate was writing itself badly tonight. But two-note meant Kaffir and they were worse. They denied that common faith of all the books: *There is no God but God. God is Great.* He, praise His Name, was not an enfeebled blind watchmaker, a blundering force with a thousand faces, a mad monster mole bumping about under the hilly gardens of chaos

- He is That IS, fierce and unquenchable, the blazing well-head of eternal undying flame, bright against the murky infidel skies. And Mohammed was his Prophet. It was written.

Perhaps the seduction of Omar had been part of a conspiracy. To win hearts and minds. They always tried that. She was already turning him into an infidel with her wiles. Like last night, her lips tracing the contours of his pectorals, her mouth brushing his taut stomach, while she was whispering something indeterminate, whispering in a voice like perfumed smoke... 'What is it?' he murmured, suddenly anxious. Had his body disappointed her? Had she suddenly recalled a trace they had failed to cover, that indiscreet card she'd sent, one single ill-timed mini-phone call?

'There's no future in this, Omar. And no past. That's the truth about sex. Living for a moment... It's all in the present, isn't it? A deja vu, pour le voyeur, toi, cherie..'

He hadn't understood her Anglicised fake French. In the moment he could only focus on the swing of her breasts; and now he was hardening already, thanks for the memory, right here in Uncle Abdul's house, the shame of it, he couldn't help it —but he had to fight for control of this past self, with its transfusions of nostalgia and lust. 'You make my little heart pump iron...' She'd repeated it gleefully as they'd coupled on the bed, the floor, the sofa. But it was his heart surely that had jumped and convulsed. Not just in the deed, the act of penetration, entering the Body of Soft Darkness Herself. No, that was a dangerous sin of the senses, a mad spasm of his wild young lust. But Uncle Abdul, his kind protector, might forgive him. And Allah the All-Merciful would surely, in the Eternity of His Goodness, forgive - please...

No, what shocked him was something inexplicable a blasphemy

so vast and deep that he could scarcely understand it or articulate it to himself ; in the present. *No future. No past. No Time.* This crazy Kaffir woman didn't believe in Time itself, in Allah's great architecture of Past, Present, Future with Mohammed, His Prophet, placed at its centre as the guardian of History, controlling the Gates of Paradise. And for a Timeless interval, he'd allowed himself to share her inner chaos, to sport with her in the vortex of her delusions, her fool's paradise, all that slipping and sliding on the slopes of desire, along those infinite contours...

He fought for control. He was slipping and sliding. The boy couldn't help it. Bodies a-slipping and a-sliding, like that sinful oldie American jukebox song, leering old devil's music. Who knows what would have happened if he'd stayed the whole night, as she kept begging?

He recalled stepping silently into her living room. She'd pinned a tiny snapshot of him over her desk. He stared at her pictures, her bookshelves, the multiplicity of books, the alien curvature of an entangled wire sculpture on a coffee table, a lurid collage of bodies that covered an entire wall... Who was she really, what else had she done in her Pleasure Centres? He'd crept out as she breathed softly in the darkness.

In Goddess We Trust

Lucas had only eaten beans in the last twenty four hours. It was important to conserve resources. He'd lined the study area with crinkly silver foil, on an intuition that it might block the intrusions of neighbourly folk-thought, but it had made little difference. He wrote:

the huge huggy of a dread god

jellies the cosmos
in goddess we trust
across the abyss
meditations continue in spare rooms
the light is heavy a grain of photons
glimmer of bare legs at one end of a world
not a natter of plural worlds
surplus value becomes anti-alchemical
smears a nigredo in your face
I licked with my spite
how I lost your plot

It wouldn't call Carla home. But something must surely get through...

The Quantum Brothers Love You

Viv recognised, helplessly, that that she was being modified. For the first few days in her cell over the red-lit cubicles, she'd attempted her usual rites and readings but it was becoming more and more difficult to sustain the right kind of detached concentration. She had never been very systematic or disciplined in her deployment of the Tarot and now she was merely shuffling cards at random rather than attempting the elaborate spreads of the Tree of Life. The pack was no longer carefully wrapped but scattered across the narrow bed. She spent most evenings lying there.

Although the work at Pleasure Centres wasn't physically demanding - customers could be processed in a few minutes - and she had finally memorised all the buttons on the touch screens, the daily routine was numbing. The punters all mumbled in the same accents of desperation.

The only visitor that stood out was that gawky old technician who'd thoroughly confused her and managed to screw up the technology with his furtive fumblings.

When she finished her shift at the desk it was all she could do to pick up some packet from the corner boot-shop, hastily micro-wave its bland contents, and slump in front of the Lobe screen to watch a jerky re-run of the Best of Primeshop TV. Focus groups had shown that viewers were still nostalgic for those pre-Rupture parades of consumer desirables, even though most of them were no longer available.

It was partly the sheer blandness of the room, the placebo effect of its pastel peach decor, the blankness of the walls. The curious deodorant piped through the ventilators, a kind of anti-incense was subtly diluting her spirit. Yet there was little opportunity - or incentive - to leave her residential unit. Her wages mostly consisted of this subsidised accommodation plus a small cash hand-out. And the streets were dangerous. Even though she was dreaming and visioning less, fragmented images or indistinct mouthings still intruded via the hypnogogic route: *the middle-people huddle in their parish halls to become like little wooden toys with chipped paint, strung along on wires as they be dragged into some flames.* Best to keep a very low profile.

Tonight she was not going to surrender to the Lobe. She pulled out her bag and unrolled her pictures. Perhaps she could try to draw again. That had been her irrationale for this doomed expedition. To test her will as an artist. She studied her sketches of Samhain entities, ink and charcoal wraiths she'd sketched for Aran, to help him shape his vague foreshadowings into bronze or silver while he was apprenticed to Gil Norwood. Back in Leynebridge her quick nervous line, with its jagged spirals and swatches of black, seemed animated by the caprices of spirit night-walkers. The figures danced. In this sterile compartment, under the steady glare of the fluorescent ceiling, they'd become mere scratchings, smears and random marks. She was wasting her time to even try.

Yet Aran, great stolid Aran, had found meaning in them. They'd energised him, made him produce some of his most cunning amulets and figurines, too impish and phallic for the casual tourist but much prized by Forgan and his circle of pranksters as accessories for the Feast of Smoke.

In desperation, half-laughing at the irony of her situation, she attempted to focus on Aran, to find a resonance with him. He must be angry but she couldn't cope at that point with his sullen drunks, his raw possessive hunger for her. Perhaps he might understand in time, that she needed space. That was a form of words, who knew what she needed? Did Aran know? But he couldn't project clearly articulated thought forms, only swirling images at irregular intervals. The Rupture had bestowed its gifts with predictable randomness.

As she lay across the bed, she felt a sudden spasm of desperate nostalgia for the cobbled streets of Leynebridge, the din of the Red Hag on a Saturday night - and the huge hands of Aran sliding down her body as he'd taken her that midnight in the Castle Gardens.

For a second she felt a wariness about her rogue arousal but maybe the fantasy was a way back to her de-centred self, so she let herself drift with it, eyes closing, an inner space opening where Aran, stiff in outline, like a figure in an ancient Egyptian stele, rose over her as a vast god-form. An absurd voice-over echoed through her skull, in impeccable BBC accents - *here the god Set is depicted with erect phallus preparing to mount a hand-maiden of Isis* - but her laughter, weirdly internalised, only aggravated her excitement.

And Aran or at least his torso was twisting above her, the intimate burr of his voice blurring into a roar of pleasure/pain because the Serpent of Leynebridge had reticulated itself into a writhing net, whipping around his back and ribs, entangling her in knots of agony...

A deafening staccato bleep pierced the dreamscape. She was curled up half-naked on the bed. The noise, from the Lobe monitor, refused to stop. The screen flashed. And stabilised, into a monochrome image.

Those bland grey moustachiod faces, like old-time film directors, stared through the lobe-cam lens. A banner ran across the bottom of the screen, slowly repeating itself.

THE QUANTUM BROTHERS LOVE YOU THE QUANTUM BROTHERS LOVE YOU THE QUANTUM BROTHERS LOVE YOU THE QUANTUM BROTHERS LOVE YOU LOVE YOU LOVE YOU LOVE YOU LOVE YOU LOVE YOU

Dub Demons

Omar should have been in college, studying accountancy or on his way back to assist in Uncle Abdul's warehouse. He felt guilty, thinking of the gentle old man anxiously sucking at a tiny cup of sweet coffee, waiting for his strong nephew to help sort the fruits and heave the heavy boxes as they packed the van for the next delivery. Omar had been raised to respect his elders and serve the community. And now all he wanted to do was play. He told himself that it might help to expunge the flaming memory of that woman.

Yet going to a Pleasure Centres arcade was almost as bad. Every Friday at the mosque the imam preached against the idolatry of virtual reality gaming, its hideous parody of Paradise - it was yet another example of the infidel wizardry that had brought chaos upon the city. This blasphemous multiplication of human images in warped electronic fantasies was intended to further weaken the pure reality that brothers and sisters were fighting so hard to establish.

As Omar lingered at the entrance, he felt almost nauseous - but also light-headed with reckless exhilaration. For an hour he was going to escape the routines of his enclave - and maybe the afterburn of Carla. Pleasure Centres might be seedy down-market establishments with obsolescent gear and corny games, but Hisham had told him that the corporation sometimes used this place to surreptitiously beta-test new packages. In a sudden recurrent spasm of guilt-inflected desire, he recognised that it was highly likely he could access something that his temptress Carla had been involved in, even performed in... and perhaps this was his motivation for this little escapade. He struggled with the thought until he'd erased it. No, he could act out some manly adventure that tested his courage and skill - it could almost be a kind of jihad...

The slim girl at the desk noticed him, a lean brown boy in a scuffed leather jacket. Her routine was to ask the punter which service they'd like, take them through the options and disclaimers, before they had a chance to drift out again - but Viv paused. He seemed restless and agitated. A young Anglo Alliance suicide bomber had devastated a Pleasure Centre in Manchester only two months ago, according to her manager. Security procedures dictated that she should summon someone in a uniform to eject him. Instead she felt a sick apprehension and an overwhelming sense of protectiveness towards this young man.

'Are you alright?' He was twitching his fingers and rocking on the balls of his feet, clenching and unclenching his fist, as if already embroiled in a virtual conflict. Ignoring her, he strode across the lobby and began studying the wall display where brief 2-D preview clips were scrolling across a battery of flickering screens. A muffled megabass voice intoned: *Torture Cells of Venusberg - a World of Control.*

'I want Dub Demons…' A mumble rather than a command. He wasn't sure. But this looked promising- a shoot-out against giant semi-human dogs, partial clones of their lumpen pink-faced proletariat owners, an urban amphitheatre of purification and retribution. It might somehow redeem him.

'Dub Demons isn't available, I'm afraid…' It seemed the safest option. This boy was dangerously good-looking, but she wanted him out. For his own good. He stared at the display, hunching his shoulders - then stared at her.

'So why is it showing on there?' He pointed to the display.

'We had some intermittent technical problems. It's not very reliable. Honestly, you're better off with something else…'

A grinning paunchy salary-man staggered out of the cubicle area. 'You tell him try Venusberg. Quality girl-friend experience. Worth big nurdle!' Omar shook his head as the man tossed a coin in the gratuity tray on his way out.

'I want to fight the Demons. Now, please.' Viv could sense the dark energy coiling up inside him. He wouldn't be refused. It was scripted thus, she couldn't help it. She nodded and began to process his order.

Inside the suit, Omar heard the assistant keying in his programme and then the click of the door. His helmet suddenly seemed too tight and he nearly yelled for help, to escape from this torture chamber.

They were going to lock him into deep hell and he was going to have to fight his way out. But this was his virtual jihad and he had to embrace it.

Then the grey virtual space around him brightened and cleared, to reveal the intersection of two narrow streets, hemmed in by cavernous black glass towers.

The streets were empty, except for an antique finned automobile parked about fifty metres away to the west, where a red giant sun sank between the black silhouettes. A sign flashed high on one of the northern towers - *FAST FUN FINANCE- GET THAT NURDLE!*

The air tasted of distilled sewage. The nearest doorway, an entrance to some kind of bank, was smeared with excrement.

Something to the east was growling. The light strobed for a moment, hurting his eyeballs, and his hands went into spasm. When his field of vision stabilised again, he caught sight of two Dub Demons rounding the corner.

The bodies were upright, pale, humanoid. One gripped a hammer, another carried a thick stave. Their pot bellies swelled over heavy blue jeans from which massive cocks protruded. Their work boots were crusted with mud. From the neck upwards, they were canine, hugely jowled dribbling mastiffs, sniffing for blood.

A third dogman crawled out on all fours from behind the dented grey limousine. He/it clasped a human hand in his jaws and trailed it slowly along the gutter. Omar noticed that as soon as he tracked the movement, his viewpoint zoomed, uncontrollably, to the pale dead hand, its scabs and broken fingernails.

His own hands felt puffy and insubstantial. They looked quasi-transparent in contrast with that dogmeat limb. He was mere phantom tissue, trembling.

The two upright dog demons saw the crawler's bounty and gave chase, roaring in full strength. Their target tried to dodge and run. For a few seconds, Omar hoped that the pursuit would take them up the street, towards that bloody sun, but no such luck.

A screen display warned him about energising his olfactory barrier. He didn't react until it was too late. They turned back, sniffing and growling, bloodshot eyes staring at him. He moved back, fatally.

The sudden impact of their bodies felled him. Frontal canines tore at his cheek, ripped into his neck. They were chewing his fat and flesh, his throat flooded with blood, the pain and terror and dog-breath stench was hyper-real as they snarled and snapped, he was gargling a scream in the wrong dream, a horror-drome, no safe-words or exit signs, blinded with blood, his brain was going down...

Food of the Ghosts

The old man was being recycled in his sleep. For Child William fed the ghosts every dream-time. He had to pass through the corridors of his grandfather's house, over the brown linoleum, across the faded crimson carpet, past the huge statue of the Virgin Mary on the hall stand, past the flickering candles, doors banging in the night wind – but the ghosts had to be fed.

The food of the ghosts was left on small red plates at regular intervals along the carpet beside the stove. The food resembled chopped up rose petals or small glazed sweets. Yet they glowed like molten stones in the gloom. 'The shapes do not matter,' he told himself. He knew somehow that the ghosts would be conjured from his sweats and humours and bad smells. He had to creep back into the mahogany darkness before they came to feed....

Then he wrested control of the dream, fading out the hall of ghosts, placing himself on the empty avenue outside. There was no network of invisible rays beaming their codes behind his back. No ghosts in machines. He was a free agent in a bright flat world where all the streets ran one way, with beginnings, middle, ends. The bright world would wake him up.

Desperate Sigil

Some days Lucas believed that sex was a portal to divinity, a rending of the veil. At other times, he felt it was cellular madness, that he was being used by his own biology in a curious uncomfortable experiment. But despite the chill and the failing light, he wrote his desperate sigil . First the statement of intent: *It is my will to win back Carla as my lover.* Then the compression of the letters:

ITSMYWLNBACKROVE.

Then the randomisation: *YSTMROBANVEKTWIC*

He had to be careful about wanting it/her too much. The lust of result, the result of lust. Focus on the sign, not the signified. Let the unconscious do its work. Or its worst. He wrote the mantra out again. And again, this time on a bloodied scrap of paper. He took a deep breath and began to intone, again and again:

YSTMROBANVEKTWIC

Many minutes passed, as his voice slowly droned through the phonemes. The letters on the paper dimmed , glimpsed through half-closed eyes, and seemed to entangle with each other, into a twisted glyph, a graffito scrawled from another dimension, knotted together by the pressure of his will and the pain of his lungs. The mantra grew louder and filled all the space between his ears, while his tongue and throat became sore with the effort of enunciation. Eventually with the entangled glyph spinning before his eyes, he fell back, exhausted, and slept.

Inappropriate

'It all looks very inappropriate, William…' Tom Liggett looked worried. 'This could be a serious disciplinary matter.' He glanced across the table at Mark Rinehart, seeking further validation. Rinehart shook his head slowly.

'I can't believe that someone with a high-security background like yours could be so unprofessional. You were tasked to resolve the Dub Demons issue. And never even investigated the programme. Now a customer's died… A Mo-Boy, but a customer all the same.'

Liggett clutched a file and adjusted his tie. 'The PR fallout could be deadly. It's a very sensitive demographic. When Pullman hears this '

'I was told the dog-fighting game was unavailable.' William heard his voice as if from a distance, feeble and remote in this windowless room. Rinehart wasn't going to let go.

'You could have challenged the customer adviser and checked it out properly, run the code behind the front-end. After all, what do those check-in people know? Instead, for your own senile amusement you indulge in a bit of obsolescent adult entertainment. And then you complain that it doesn't work and it's infested by men with old-fashioned haircuts. It would be ridiculous if the outcome wasn't so bad.'

'You haven't had an autopsy yet. And I'm right, surely, to bring up the issue of those playback anomalies. Even for Porno Madness.' He was a very old and foolish man. Nevertheless, those stolid moustached faces still interposed themselves in his dreamscapes.

Liggett was all for looking on the positive side, seeking out the spin factor. 'I suppose we could tell the media that the customer failed to follow Pleasure Centres safety guidelines. That he ignored the Escape option, specially designed to allow our valued customers to switch out of an excessively frightening sequence - so the guy had a stroke.'

Rinehart grabbed the file from Liggett and flipped through it, grimacing. 'The kid never reached the escape button. He just had some kind of massive abnormal brain and CNS dysfunction. As if the neurons in his brain had been disrupted at the sub-molecular level. Cortex, amagdyla, thalamus - all systems blown out. We guessed that much from the look on his face and the state of the body. Not a pleasing sight. The check-in girl was off-sick for several days afterwards. As for your mystery men grafting their heads on to the sex artistes - the code's too ancient and corrupted now to reconstruct them - if they ever existed in the first place. As is the dog-fighting package. But if you'd followed through the assignment, that kid might be alive. Even if he was a renegade Mo-Boy."

Ligget got up and paced around the table. 'Does Carla know about this?' William felt benumbed now. His redundancy must be imminent. Back, so soon, to hostels, cubicles, streets. Or worse.

'I left a message last night but she hasn't responded.' Rinehart shrugged. 'Odd, really, given that she likes to have maximum input. But I understand she has a busy social life.' Liggett nodded and looked as if he was about to make a note on his clipboard, then paused mid-gesture.

William suddenly sensed an uneven triangulation of power here -

like the jockeying between Weekes, Ebdon and O'Dwyer when they were all ganging up on him decades ago in the meeting room at the Establishment. He couldn't hold his own back then, his head spinning with strings of equations. But now he had a desperate stratagem.

'I will make this matter my personal responsibility and speak directly with Ms. Leppard. I have a proposal.'

'For your clearing your desk?' Rinehart laughed bitterly. 'I wish you luck.'

Crisis

Lucas had fallen asleep, head resting on his notebook. The latest entry in the magickal journal was illegible. He dreamed that Carla had changed her name to Barbie-Lon and was demanding him to smear his hairy body in red clay. He was losing their shouting match...

And then two hands were gripping his shoulders and he inhaled stenches of nicotine, bad beer and old tweed, a beard prodded his cheek, and the room was full of beards - for both Wharton the bookseller and Dodd the Elder had somehow forced their way in and were shouting at him about awakening, help needed, a great crisis...

'Be careful, Gavin. His chants are dangerous. He might be controlled by contagious entities.' That was Noah Dodd alright, all fustian and bombast.

'I don't care. Leynebridge needs every practitioner we can find, anything to thwart Lombard and his Zoning of Leyston Burrough, you can't afford to be precious.'

'But he is an Incomer... They say he played a key part in the Rupture.'

'All the more reason to use him...'

Lucas sat dumbly as they explained and re-explained things. Pleasure Centres. Techno-Nihilist Incursions. Community Rites and Tactics of Collective Spellcraft. Their speeches bubbled and slowly burst around him, but the beards kept frothing away. He was marginal, out here in his hutch, a burned-out Qliphothic survivor of so many convulsive Ruptures, what could he do? He kept on trying to explain but they wouldn't listen.

Neural Network

Carla Leppard sat with her back to him as he entered. William stood, awaiting a directive. A huge flat-screen monitor on the windowless side wall was running Pleasure Centres promos, with the sound almost turned down, an endlessly dissolving montage of ray guns, buttocks, spaceships, swelling breasts, sex toys, blazing towers, narrated by the faintest husk of a baritone voice-over: 'In a World where Pleasure Rules...'

She suddenly swivelled in her high leather chair. He decided to remain standing.

'Well?' Her eyelids were puffy, her red hair straggly. William had been expecting a shout, but the interrogation was muted, a flat metallic syllable. 'There's no excuse, is there, for this level of incompetence...'

She paused, allowed a beat of silence, following her corporate script perhaps. She was obviously waiting for some blurt of self-justification. 'There's no option but to let you go. Our Mr. Liggett will probably take you through the formality of an appeal, for form's sake, but frankly there's no place for a drooling senior on my team. I think Pullman planted you to undermine me. You're not a professional any more, just a care in the community case. And I don't care any more...'

Her hand trembled slightly as she turned away, but William couldn't quite decode this. His alleged failure was somehow personalised. It was as if he had exhausted her.

'I have a proposal, Ms Leppard.'

'Don't delude yourself that old-fashioned formalities are going to make things all right. Don't we even get an apology?'

'I regret the fatality. And my oversight in not checking the system as originally tasked. But I am not convinced the two are linked. The boy's physiology and psychological profile might not have been sufficiently robust to cope with the levels of stress induced by Dub Demons, which might well have provoked a neural seizure. I didn't programme that platform, Ms Leppard. And there was no procedure in place to profile vulnerable customers.' He was determined to go down in flames.

'I think you better leave, Dr. Crowe. I can call Security if you like.' She was already reaching for the button.

'My proposal would prevent incidents like this recurring. It would address an underlying flaw in the Pleasure Centres customer interface.'

'Flaw? What flaw?' She leaned forward, glaring, sweeping papers aside.

'You're familiar with the whole process - the entire programme?'

'I don't know every single line of code, if that's what you mean. My input is creative rather than tech support.' He sensed an insecurity there, something he could nag and worry.

'Let's review the whole Pleasure Centres operation.'

She sighed. 'Don't lecture me. You've got sixty seconds to make your point.'

'We need to see my proposal in context. When consumers log on, they confront a multi-media, multi-user cyberspace, constructed from the interaction of various transputers and neural network processors, often geographically dispersed. Some of these processors are dedicated to generating, in real time, the graphical and sensory interface in which the consumer/participant is immersed. Certain processors monitor his reactions.'

'And?'

'Some programmes generate "user-friendly" interfaces in the form of virtual persons, who welcome the user to the system and guide him through his various options. Another sub-system contains a huge memory bank of multi-media samples - people, creatures, objects, backgrounds and for the consumer "virtual character" roles, often derived from popular figures in our post-Rupture media landscape... Self-modifying programmes - your "talent agents" - constantly scan the Lobe for the remnants of new audio-visual samples that could be added to the mix.' This didn't really explain the surprise emergence of the Quantum Brothers but he couldn't stop now. Probably rogue hackers having a bit of sport.

Carla was growing impatient again. 'You're forgetting the special material commissioned in-house from our performance artistes. It's the most requested content.' But she'd stopped looking at her watch. If only he could sustain this improvisation.

'A neural network coordinates the deployment of all these fantasy elements, either according to the rules of specific games, or following general rules (equivalent to dramatic conventions) of character development and narrative, which is a special innovation of Pleasure Centres - and of course your particular contribution.'

'Where is all this going?'

'The user can then select certain preferences, like the choice of avatars, in his virtual adventure while sensors monitor neural activity, eye-movement, heartbeat, skin conductivity, and body language, feeding back into the programme to modify the customer experience in real-time. And that's as far as it goes...'

'So? What exactly are you trying to say?' Her eyes blazed as her hand groped for the phone.

'What Pleasure Centres needs is total user feedback, which utilises all the information provided by the VR participant, consciously or otherwise.'

'This is total bullshit, Crowe. And in your heart you know it.'

'I'm not talking about the heart. I'm talking about exploiting the collective unconscious of the Lobe. And what it knows about you.' For a second she looked puzzled, even anxious. He pressed home his advantage.

'As you know, special programmes known as "confidential agents" used to scour the recesses of the Lobe in the old Web times, scanning networking sites, educational profiles, criminal records, career and credit records, consumption patterns and browsing habits for every byte of information about the user, however trivial. They supplied information to security and police databases, financial institutions, employers.'

'You're talking pre-Rupture here. Things are much more aleatory and corrupted these days, it's difficult to rely on agents.'

'My new agenting software would collate everything the Lobe knows about the subject and feed it automatically into the VR preferences as the subject logs in. Not only his previous consumer history with Pleasure Centres, his preferences for blondes or brunettes, swords or sorcery - but every file about him, globally. The expert system constructs a psychological profile; and VR interaction is modified accordingly to suit the customer's deepest needs. An ex-teacher might find himself drawn into a shoot-out in a class-room, a salary man checking out as obese in his health records would be offered sumo-girls. Potentially dangerous or vulnerable clients could be immediately deflected into some kind of counselling or therepeutic inter-action. This could have saved that unfortunate Moslem boy...'

'How on earth can you say that?' She'd turned away from him again. Her voice was smaller.

'Extreme guilt at participating in a forbidden infidel pleasure, perhaps. Extreme fear of white racist bestiality, even in virtual form. A massive overload of anxiety, leading to stroke or heart attack. If the system had known of his background, it might have blocked the game or slanted the action differently.'

'I don't believe you can do it.' She rose and began walking him towards the door, face still averted. He had to believe.

'I have devised something similar in my previous employment. A large self-modifying intelligent application creating an ever-expanding database across a whole platform.' As he spoke, a spongy cloud still obscured the detail of exactly how or why he'd done it. He was neurally fudged, suffering a memory block, lost addresses, a kernel flaw. The damnable Blackout was lurking yet again, the aftermath of that elite commission which had nearly burnt out his brain.

'You have a week to make it work.' The door slammed.

5
The Burrough

A Great Disturbance in the Earth

Noah Dodd looked up through the morning mist towards Leyston Hill and pointed towards the stony hump poking through the trees at the summit. 'Lombard wants to dig right into the Burrough. It's unnatural and dangerous. A great disturbance in the Earth - for their Carbonite greed. You would have thought the Rupture had never happened...'

Lucas recognised that Dodd would never accept his version of the Qliphothic Ruptures. The old man was convinced they were simply a punishment for humanity's environmental crimes. Best to say nothing. So, still suffering from the pseudo-tinnitus of Leynebridge psychochatter, he took the binoculars.

He found himself peering at a small shanty town of tents and corrugated iron shacks clustered around the summit. He zoomed in on a three-legged mongrel cocking its leg against a heap of crates, which must have been some kind of dwelling, because a statuesque woman in rags, flaunting bare blue-ringed nipples, emerged and began shouting. A white-haired man with a tape measure was planting a line of sticks between his tent and the woman's hovel. He yelled back, brandishing a hammer. Garbled obscenities drifted on the wind.

'You're being distracted by Mrs Nixon's on-going boundary dispute,' muttered Noah, grabbing the glasses.

'Maybe if Lombard's scheme cleared this miserable squalor, it might not be a bad thing.' Lucas hadn't realised the full extent of the social decay, even here in Leynebridge. Perhaps he had spent too long in his bunker, in his thwarted amorous rites.

'And where would the Hill people go - back down into the town again, to carry on their harassment and scandalising?' Noah looked anxious as if this beggarly invasion was imminent.

'They can't be more of a menace than the Flatheads.' Lucas recalled the stomping boots and guttural blood-cries that had pursued him through High Town.

'You have a point,' conceded Wharton grudgingly, sucking hard on his nicotine-pipe, a startling transgression that Noah seemed willing to ignore. 'Sebastian Hackett told me that the Parcel Man's body was found last Thursday in the toilets behind the Tower. Head crushed to pulp. Probably the "local juveniles", he said.' Wharton smiled grimly as he mimicked Hackett's patrician drawl. Noah nodded, as if the episode was only to be expected.

'Why the Parcel Man?' Lucas remembered Hackett musing about him, trying to divine the obsessive pattern of his daily routine. 'He was a harmless bag-person.'

'Hackett is certain they were after the wretched man's parcel. Hackett, moreover, alleges it contained a sheep's brain. He suspects the Parcel Man traded animal brains to the Harvesters.'

'Harvesters...?' Noah frowned.

'Did you know they believe that the tissue can be re-animated by the human souls they have supposedly harvested with their contraptions? They try to preserve it under small glass pyramids. Which they bombard with what they've stored in their House of Afterlife. A desperate strategy. The local youth didn't like it... They were afraid of becoming specimens.'

Dodd looked accusingly at Lucas. 'If our young people were properly educated in the Ways of Leynebridge and not distracted by alien techno-nihilist entertainment, perhaps these confrontations might not arise.'

Lucas turned away. He wasn't going to pursue these tired arguments. 'When's the Pleasure Centres deputation arriving?'

'In about three hours. At the old Book Market. They call it a consultation. We must raise our energies…'

Cultural Centre

The morning sunshine had turned to drizzle, despite Forgan the Clown waving his solar totem. Lucas sensed a queasiness in High Town, a dull ache of collective apprehension mixed with excitement. The white-hooded Elderseers clustered around Noah frowned at the large turnout. Surprisingly he couldn't see Viv's magisterial grandmother. His forehead throbbed, as the pulse of drums and the random chants of the impatient crowd gathering around the Book Market were drowned in the throbbing downdraft of a large twin-rotor helicopter, as it settled into the derelict car park nearby.

Almost immediately two girls in halter-top maroon jumpsuits appeared in the hatchway with small hand-trolleys blazoned with the PC Logo. They ducked under the spinning blades, dived across the road into the crowd and immediately began to distribute small plastic bags. Scuffling broke out at once between a few young men who grabbed at the offerings and those Elders who struggled to stop the gifting, lashing out with their carved staves. Big Neil, the acting town-warden, gestured with his shotgun and the fracas subsided.

Then, flanked by two fat minders in dark glasses carrying golf umbrellas, a stubbly Dominic Pullman stepped carefully through the porticos of the Book Market where the Elders had set up a small podium and provided a dented megaphone. Lucas, standing at the back of the mob, had been expecting a stone-faced man in a grey suit and was surprised at the effete stance and casual dress of the Pleasure Centres envoy. He'd creased his leather jacket and his pinkish jeans seemed torn.

Now Trader Price and a cluster of local farmers were shaking hands with the visitor and murmuring in his ear so Lucas presumed that some kind of protocol had been been arranged for this delicate encounter. With a muttered introduction for 'Our Distinguished Guest from Pleasure Centres,' Price nudged him towards the centre of the platform.

Pullman was nonplussed by the megaphone, examining it as if it contained an explosive device. He glanced anxiously across the swaying heads of a restive crowd, and launched into what had perhaps been intended as an intimately voiced charm offensive, a close-miked voice of authority. Lucas had briefly tasted the intoxicating power of the close-mic technique. Now Pullman's hoarse fragments echoed in the battered tin cone. Lucas tried, reluctantly, to de-code the tortured managerial jargon, distracted by the telepathic leakage from the scrum around him.

'The ongoing process of consultation...proud to be a guest of Leynebridge...outreach programme...important site in our national heritage...unique attractions...redevelopment of the Burrough in creative partnership with Pleasure Centres...this unique community with special needs...stakeholding with mutual benefits...the forthcoming Festival of Smoke...all about people...celebrating diversity... every person matters... we're all in this together...'

no man takes our beasting not lord snotty but you could have a lovely Rupture sorry season stop them fucking the earth i just want bigger eats you get him in the eyes with some old bottle in those centres you can do anything you wannabee do it all over all over the lobe what's a folk to do buggered in the red hag and they should have burned the tower another posh drone fight them with riddling and gnome-riddance and holy flame-grills...

'Pleasure Centres .... our dynamic strategy of rural regeneration... local economy...fusing age-old wisdoms with new technology...a generous offer for the land...guarantee sorely-needed local jobs... growing a tourist economy...unique local culture... improving security... feedback... sensitive landscaping ... jobs... housing.... state of the art Lobe provision...'

lovely bubbly job he says they'll stop the harvesting that posh man sick on the bus again they're all the same bring in more women for a good whipping forgan stop stop it he does the switcheroo for the midwinter lights coughing the witch-blood can't go on like this he does go on giss a bag then traders are a trick and treat can't trust any body I wish he'd stop waving that gun around his head pray to the snake force serpent save us bite his balls off

With a sudden surge of effort - although he could never conceptualise quite how he did it - Lucas at last managed to block most of the cackling static and tune more finely into Pullman's pitch.

'This new Centre ... not some crude concrete block full of hi-tech sex'n'violence games... envisage Leyston Burrough cleared of its recent accretions. This Cultural Centre, constructed of natural organic materials... landscaped carefully into the shape of the Burrough itself. Inside, visitors will experience a new kind of VR, superior not only in its technical quality but in its content. The installation will offer a series of structured interfaces with the unique culture of Leynebridge. The cyber-tourist will not only survey the history of the locality, but interact with Leynebridge's colourful tribal rites of birth, marriage, initiation and death, before undergoing an awesome encounter with virtual representations of your ancient Gods. Our high-tech Virtual Reality could even enhance events like the Festival of Smoke. The Centre will be an invaluable learning resource for their children, a way of reinforcing the unique Leynebridge way of life, its book-craft and hand-craft, for future generations...'

The mental babble around Lucas was oddly muted now and the murmurs of protest were fading. Leynebridge seemed suddenly passive, mesmerised by the flow of Pullman's alien corporate rhetoric, those cadences for doing the business that Lucas hadn't heard for years. He remembered Mr. Kraskolkyn, the Qliphothic entrepreneur, and shuddered.

Forgan lurched forward, fire-staff raised, dancing a mad morris on the spot to the beat of his phlegmy ranting. 'You've been sent here to snare us, haven't you? We know you're Lombard's creature. You're his shape-shifter, his shirt-lifter. You're a face-sitting shit-brainer. We can sniff into your buzzy words. And taste the fly-shit. You'd make us safe and healthy, geld our manhoods, soil our maidenheads, blind our minds, sell us to the Urbanites as a song-dancing sideshow, in a little zone of diversion. To act out your scriptings, your routines. And lose all the Force of our Lore..."

Pullman looked puzzled and hurt. 'The Pleasure Centres philosophy values preserving local customs... Our deep-core values...'

'...are customer service. And servitude. You'd stack us high and sell us cheap.'

Gavin Wharton's dry interjection somehow reduced the impact of Forgan's ranting. The shaman coughed and spluttered as the discourse slipped from spiritual battle to parish economics. Dodd tried to regain the psychic high ground. He was flushed, breathing heavily. 'As Elder of Leynebridge, I say this cannot be. Our true Lore... our way of living...' He faltered. The crowd murmured again. Lucas began to pick up the wrong vibe *long money better than the snake doctor nothing for kids round and round here* as the bookserfs and farmfolk shuffled uneasily from foot to foot, some daring to turn and glare at Elderseer Dodd, despite the brooding presence of his minder, Aran.

Trader Price capitalised on the new mood of anti-Elder truculence. 'I think it's time for the common townsfolk to have a voice.' A couple of crop-skulled youths cheered. 'Let's hear it for the Trader...'

Pullman smiled. 'This is your rainbow window of opportunity - to make Leynebridge a place of pilgrimage for visitors from all over the country. The new interfacing technologies exclusive to Pleasure Centres will ensure that the town will be a national landmark, a rich repository of this unique local culture you have evolved in response to the challenging events of recent years. Surely you would like to nominate a trusted local business person as an advocate...'

Lucas lost the drift. He knew what was coming. As the Trader was mobbed by by shouting supporters, he watched two children squabbling over one of the bags Pullman's entourage had scattered, tearing out lurid Pleasure Centres flyers of dinosaurs in gunships.

A few minutes later Pullman's helicopter rose over Leyston Burrough as the Elders scattered.

Memory Probe

William sat at his work station facing a blank scribbling pad. According to the team's official investigations there was no input that could be related to the irregular manifestations of those elusive digital poltergeists - whose flickering images emerged momentarily on the monitor screens every time there was a major disruption. Therefore, officially, they didn't exist. The phenomenon was unlike any virus that Mark and his clones had encountered before - indeed it appeared to leave no trace of code in the system. Yet he had seen the Quantum Brothers, in all their morphing glory.

He was glad Rinehart had left the office and couldn't voyeur his stasis, or report his apparent blockage to Liggett, who now smiled awkwardly as they passed in the corridors. He chewed his stylus. Despite the convenience of the screen, he still preferred to scrawl his way towards the core of an idea before elaborating the algorithms in lines of code. *Lies of code*. He'd written the phrase automatically. Curious.

Anyway, he couldn't totally trust digital memory - who could these days? The constant seizures on the Lobe disrupted life and *undermined the Undermind* - another stupid pun on auto-write... And now these random glitches at the Centres were worming away at the entertainment infrastructure.

The core of his memory of the Establishment blackout was hollowed, cored out, filled only by a cloudy mess of semi-reminiscence, dream drippage... How he'd berated Elaine when she'd taken up the New Age vogue of logging her dreams, waking him up at three AM as she fussed with her bedside notebook. Dreams were merely a side-effect of memory overload, the process of de-fragging the brain's hard drive. Dr. Christopher Evans had simulated it at the National Physical

Laboratory back in 1974, when you could still do proper science. Yet fragments might prompt recall.

He'd been given some assignment that involved collating a vast amount of data, storing it and searching it for deep levels of interconnection. But where were the witnesses? Elaine, fled to that huddle of Borderland cottages to delude her coven of old field-hippies, would surely have erased any memory of those convulsive months.

He tried to focus on the detail of this vast project. Perhaps evoking the people might help. Evoking faces and voices and the texture of live-in events - pre-Rupture - had always been one of his blind spots. 'This Ebdon you're always going on about - what does he look like?' It was just her way of distracting him from his tea-time rants after a bad day at the Establishment. 'He has a face,' William would mutter impatiently, ' just a bloody peasant-cunning sort of face.'

Get a retro-fix on that face. Purplish. Dark jowls. A lick of hair over a balding pate. A thick west-country burr. 'At-the-end-of-the-day.' His robotic expression. 'At the end of the day, it will really be a beginning for the end-times, Dr Crowe. You better get on with it.' The formality of the entitlement was a veiled insult. End-times seemed to be a recurrent theme. Ebdon had been an early adopter of the Heavy Shepherd creed. He probably spoke in tongues over his Sunday roast. 'This comes into play at the end of the day, you understand. A last resort...' A Doomsday weapon, UK's answer to the Soviet fifty megaton Tsar Bomba? But the skills were already in place for that, they just had to make one bigger and badder.

He tried another memory probe. Denis Weekes, prissy, silver-haired, always smiling, was surely the arch-plotter, double-booking rooms to lock him out of seminars, diverting his funding, cross-examining his expenses, reallocating his lab team to other jobs. But he could never prove it. In person, Weekes was all smiles, breathing pseudo-romantic guff all over the project. 'What you're doing, William, is saving the heritage of British civilisation from alien destruction, conserving its essence.'

That was the objective. But what were the targets? If only he could establish the context in more detail... He tried to visualise his old desk in the main block - was it the Citadel? Somewhere, in drawers or cabinets there might be a folder, a print-out, a notebook that had survived the wholesale shredding and burning of the panic decommissioning process. People like Elaine, of course, believed things could be viewed remotely - scrying, she called it - but all he saw was an empty void. As for digital data, either the amnesiac silicon of burnt-out processors or the scorched-earth policies of the old MOD would have taken care of that.

Perhaps there was only one way back. He shivered and felt queasy now, but there was no evading the huge question. He needed to go on a pilgrimage. His dark Haj.

Art

Vivienne knelt by the bed in her cubicle, staring at her cards. They lay where she'd scattered them weeks ago. Now she'd been depleted by the robotic routines of the Centre they looked like rectangles of coloured pasteboard, fast-fading icons from a lost cryptography.

She picked up the nearest one, half-obscured by her pillow. XIV. A Trump card. The words were playing with her again. She pondered these allusions and cross references like 'The Trumpet Sounds for Babalon!' - recurrent doom-speak of the Heavy Shepherd Newsletters that were pushed under her door every evening. The skirmishes between the Shepherds and the Wahibist Mo-Boys were louder these nights, you could sometimes hear small-arms fire ricocheting between the towers, the splintering of glass, raucous gang-chants. Her insomnia was reinforced by the frequent grind of an electric drill against her dividing wall. Perhaps her unseen neighbour was setting up a bedsit arms depot.

She was trying to hold the card steady, struggling to focus and to remember. A crowned woman in a flaring green robe was leaning over a great golden cauldron, holding a burning lance and a silver chalice. The woman was mingling droplets of flame and transparent fluid in the cauldron, which was supported, heraldically, by a White Lion and a Red Eagle.

A Latin motto was inscribed in a rainbow corona around the head of the robed figure. She ought to be able to translate it. Her grandmother Elaine had drummed the correspondences into her by rote. Even as an empty form of words it might help her. She muttered the formula: 'Visit the interior parts of the Earth: by rectification thou shalt find the hidden stone.'

The card was named ART.

Artistes

'You just can't find the artistes these days...' Mark Rinehart scrolled through clips of sex-work that had been salvaged from a burnt-out studio in Berwick Street. The flame-throwers of the Heavy Shepherds had missed these tape-loops on one of their recent Purity Drives through old Soho. Vintage analogue erotica were especially prized by Pleasure Centres as a recycled resource because so much digital material had been lost in the random file-corruption and system melt-down of the Ruptures.

Mark paused the bleached-out tape at a wavering image of a lace-gloved hand adjusting a nipple. 'That's a classic porno-trope. And such classy lighting...' He turned to Carla who was on the far side of the office, studying a storyboard. Most of the frames were blank. 'Have you ever thought of doing a VR version of those great sequences you directed for Jouissance? I know they'd be expensive and a bit niche for our average customer but we need to come up with something different pretty fast. Pullman's getting edgy. Especially after the Dub Demons business.'

She scribbled in one of the boxes and ignored him. He shrugged and resumed his playback.

The black-laced hand gripped a violet wand and flicked wearily at thighs. But focus was blurry now. He was meant to be taking notes, looking for material that could be sampled, re-modelled, and fed into a lo-cost entry-level VR porno. The punters liked the old franchises. The Centres had to keep overheads down, to allow funds for R&D. Liggett said that if Fast Fun Electric succeeded in miniaturizing the total immersion experience for the low-budget home user, then Pleasure Centres had no future. Pullman had gone off to plug some weird VR tourist attraction on the Borderlands but what was the point of that? Crowe, that old buzzard in the shabby suit, was supposed to be the artificial intelligence guru who was going to design a killer app, but all he'd done so far was to miss a system check that got a punter killed. Fortunately it was only a Mo-boy, so Liggett was doing a damage limitation exercise.

Meanwhile the alleged 'viral infestations' on the software

continued. Clients seeking solace with VR sexbots were rewarded with the smiling immobile face of a digitised Queen Camilla, while in the poorest areas of the conurbations there were reports of several clients being blinded - perhaps permanently - by sudden surges of light in the headsets. No point in asking Carla about the progress of this 'special project.' Ever since that Dub Demons incident, she'd gone monosyllabic.

As the tape started repeating itself, Carla tossed the storyboard aside, flicked back her hair impatiently, and strode out of the room, her face set rigid.

Total Recall

Lucas was in total recall. Total recall of those illuminated moments in the all-nite city. Moments that flared and smoldered and stank. 'The bright lights burned down the big city.' Line from an old movie. The flickering persistence of retro-vision. They'd had a big night, a very bad night, at the Gun and Chalice, returning deafened by a mediocre porn-metal band.

'I am not your private priestess, ' she screamed as they stumbled through the door. 'You're not a celebrity teenage warlock any more, Lucas. You're a person who works in washeterias and teaches adolescent proles and talks into dead microphones in your bedroom. You just can't face the nagging reality of making money. I've made money, my action plans got results. My dungeons are lit by lightning. Because I can use my assets. Everybody wants a body these days. But you gave up interacting with the material world a long time ago. You just mooch around re-running your magickal stagecraft like...'

He'd arranged his books on the table in blocks, to form hollow squares, like the defences for a gated housing scheme. The flat smelt of burnt rice. It was easier to buy rice in those early days.

She sighed. The gap between them was widening by the second, but he didn't know why.

' I have to go, Lucas. I'm going for good.'

He was sick with misery but kept on talking, any old rubbish about goods and chattels.

'What about your prayer rug? It's a valuable artefact. Don't you want it?'

'It was made by the bruised fingers of some kid in Stepney. You might as well keep it.' But she really was going, stuffing her white leather jacket and her sanitary towels and a CD by The Mighty Orgone Pirates into a holdall with a broken zip.

He fired at will. Random scattergun noise in his raw mouth.

"Do you want to know why I hate Rinehart?"

"Why?" She was still looking for her red striped socks, knocking a pyramid of paperbacks to the floor.

'He infected you...'

' That's so crass. Crass and cheap. I never know you could be so cheap and nasty.'

'Now you can't even recognize it. That's part of the problem.'

'You don't even know what you're trying to say.'

'He infected your soul.'

'That's soggy rhetoric...'

'Your innocence was your immunity. And he took it out of you. To fill you up with his words and pics. While you fucked the whole world.'

She had pushed past straight past him, off to create more urban pleasure domes for strangers. And he'd pushed off for Leynebridge 'to find a little space'. Which was now contracting around him.

Dungeon Girl

Vivienne soon discovered that the black mask was tacky. The last performer to wear it must have salivated excessively and the latex straps were worn. They kept telling her that this roll-on part was part of her training, that more important and lucrative roles would follow. Meanwhile they were going to follow the costumes and mise-en-scene of the original videos as far as possible. But they could only salvage so much for direct conversion to VR. Some of the footage had to be recreated by a special process but Mr. Rinehart was all techno-talk, she couldn't follow a word of it. The masks and basques weren't only decorative erotica, they were 'bio-wired', apparently. Her expressions, body language and every tiny bit of tactility were somehow scanned and mapped, so that they could be fed into the immersive matrix for the lone consumer, male or female.

She looked around the little studio with its grey-carpeted walls and flaking acoustic tiles. A set had been thrown together in the corner, to simulate a dungeon. Planking formed a wooden cell with fake metal bars where plastic manacles were tacked to a canvas flat, painted to resemble moss-covered masonry. The cameras and lights were still hooded in dust-covers, but she could hear Rinehart bickering with technicians and assistants in the gallery upstairs. Soon they'd be hunched over their monitors and computers, watching, always watching. It was her first shoot, or 'hyperreality enactment' as Mr Rinehart would call it. She just wanted it to be over quickly.

The horrible incident involving the Dub Demons had led to a

curious outcome, one that left her benumbed by her own fatalism yet strangely relieved. When Mr Rinehart had interviewed about her actions on that day, as part of Pleasure Centres on-going enquiry, his questions about her routine interaction with that odd elderly techie had been quite cursory. Rinehart seemed more interested in her background as a Borderlander, which he'd managed to tease out of her when he noticed her pentagram pendant. She usually concealed it but somehow she forgot that morning, she was so dazed after finding a corpse in the Centre. Soon Rinehart was talking about her artistic potential. When he made her an offer - some work as an extra to start with, but no more customer service (in the usual sense) she silenced faint murmurs in her head and, exhausted, sleep-walked right into it.

'Where's our other dungeon girl?' Rinehart strode in, waving his clipboard angrily. He turned to Vivienne, as if she knew. 'And take that stupid mask off! We have to interface your cute quiverings with reaction shots of the Commandant, which will also become the POV of the consumer, and also integrate the old set-piece of the burning Schloss Webelsburg, while dropping in another retake of the U-Boat orgy - AND keeping all the tactile feeds in sync...' He suddenly laughed, the hysteria of total exhaustion. 'Bloody Pullman doesn't have to do this every day. More fucking sequels to Space Virgins of the Third Reich!'

They were pulling the covers off the kit and fiddling with lights. Soon it would be time for action.

Party at Lombard's

Carla used to love parties. Lucas - poor sad mad Lucas - preferred to lock himself away and brood on his great Qliphothic Ruptures and his role therein, which was one of many reasons she had to let him go.

Tonight's party at Lombard's would have thrilled her once, the remnants of London's cultural/sexual elite meeting and greeting. Now it was a networking chore, a charade to blank out her image of Omar refrigerated in a morgue somewhere.

She tried to make an entrance in her black dress with the zips. But everyone had clustered at the far end of Lombard's long penthouse suite around a temporary stage where Duke Harold's Royal Metro-Tones, elderly Jamaicans in maroon tuxedos, were chugging away at a subdued ska beat. The drummer and bass player stared over swaying heads into some internalised space. A grey-haired trombonist - Duke Harold himself - took the vocal mic as saxes riffed solemnly behind him:

Sound system man talk all over the island
Dancing in the street outside the record shack

There was a high melancholy cadence in the vocal, an elegy for a lost mythic time and place that broke through Carla's armouring for a few seconds. 'Exiles' music' Lucas might have called it. He would have wondered dreamily how these entertainers from another era had arrived here, of all places, under the uneasy patronage of Lombard and Pullman.

At the edge of the crowd she took a foaming purple cocktail from Lombard's huge Samoan butler, who thrust his tray at her cleavage with a broad lascivious grin. 'Just take two, Miss. Nice, nice...' Why did Lombard employ a Samoan? Were they more grounded? Was it true that the further you were from the epicentre of the Ruptures (supposedly near London all those years ago) the less you felt their long-term effects? Did that explain the dominance of the Pacific Rim economies? Were those rumours themselves yet more examples of info-pollution and epistemological chaos, that alleged Qliphothic fall-out?

Then she was distracted by the shifting mix of voices. Lucas had claimed to receive telepathic cross-talk like so many of those lost losers on the Borderlands. She found it difficult enough just to focus on ordinary gossip.

Lombard was holding audience at the centre of a small group vying for his attentions. He had enthroned himself on a leather sofa designed to resemble a large shiny lump of liver. Acolytes clustered at his feet, kneeling, enthralled children around a favourite uncle, adoring every quiver of his jowls. Even through the rock-steady bass, Carla could hear his coarse edgy baritone.

'Pleasure Centres? That's a joke. Where have you been hiding, Vivienne, my little love? In the great chocolate-box of life? There's no fruity centre of consciousness. Just hard nuts... '

A slim dark-haired girl in a leather basque and fishnet stockings gazed up at him. She had that narcoleptic look which performance artists often cultivated. Dominic Pullman tugged gently on the long silver chain attached to her pentagram necklace, as if to cue a response, then interjected, with a quiet religious fervour: 'We are re-run, recycled, endless repeats in the loop of time.'

Lombard belched and laughed as he rang his jewelled fingers through the girl's hair. Pullman swigged his imported lager and smiled carefully. Carla noticed for the first time that he was balding. His lips seemed sorely inflamed. Perhaps he'd caught some random bug on his trip to the Borderlands, where all things lurked. He tried for another aphorism, as Lombard's resident philosopher.

'Maybe Time-flux compresses us, keeps us temporally unified according to a classical model of identity.' Then he mumbled some phrase that lost in the gabble around them.

Lombard shrugged. Then he leant across the sofa and gripped Pullman's ear, glaring indignantly. 'In the galleries of our Lobe, there must be no escape from yourself.'

Pullman, wincing at Lombard's grip, seemed to be fabulating desperately, as he so often did at the weekly meetings. 'But alternatively the drive of the cultures might be towards an electronic externalization of polymorphousness, multiple genders, iconic cloning... old Crowe's alleged vision of those Quantum Fathers...'

'The Quantum Brothers? Don't believe a word of it. They're just fake-liturgical gravy-trainers. It's just another hackers' cult, disguised as fat poppa science. They're playing-acting Techie Nihilists. With televised rituals... They come on like balding uber-babies - clawed their way through the City to clone its wealth and spent it all roasting little tattooed whores.' He cackled.

The glassy walls of the room trembled and shivered around her. Carla felt trapped in an overheated mirage, immersed now in a mush of voices. Cold sweat must be liquefying her mascara. The purple cocktails had been a mistake. She hovered unsteadily at the edge of the group, unsure whether to stand, sit or kneel. The protocol around Lombard was obscure and maybe all she wanted to do was lie in some soft dark cell, away from this spew of talk, talk, talk.

Then sudden nausea came from everywhere and nowhere, all at once. Her stomach lurched and she was slipping up, sliding to the marble floor on a spreading puddle of her own vomit. She crawled slowly in a small stinking circle as the room spectated; they were waiting to be cued by Lombard.

The Chief Executive rose, and glared. 'Painting the carpet, eh?' He'd adopted a bogus Australian accent. 'The posh art-bitch paints my virtual carpet. Soils my fucking marbles! After all my hospitality, my power-sharing. Is this her performance piece? Doggy-style shag-fest in her old sick? She's out of here this minute.' He snapped his fingers. 'Where are my drongos? I want her fired. Out of the biggest cannon you got.'

The Metro-Tones started playing again as the large Samoan butlers dragged her to the door. 'Disgusting… such slackness and nastiness…' they rumbled in her ear, as they threw her down the emergency stairwell.

6
The Establishment

Looking For Signage

William was afraid at first. He had almost forgotten how to drive; and he wasn't sure how he could obtain a vehicle via the labyrinths of the Pleasure Centres corporate bureaucracy. Carla might reluctantly authorise it - if he could devise a plausible justification - but she hadn't been at work for several days. Eventually he persuaded Tom Liggett that he needed to travel to the Borderlands and inspect the site that Pleasure Centres was developing - a follow-up to Pullman's recent visit.

Liggett was uneasy at first, as he understood that the Leyston Burrough complex was still in the very early planning stages. William implied that he had learned important lessons about safety from the Dub Demons experience which had to be embedded in any new project. He also managed to convince Liggett, who only had a vague grasp of technicalities, that equipment was already in place there. As he suspected,

Liggett knew less about the progress of this cutting-edge enterprise than he liked to pretend, while Rinehart was immersed in production work and wasn't likely to undermine William's claim.

It was raining as he collected the car from the gatehouse, where only weeks ago he'd been forced to bribe his way into the PC compound. The small uniformed Asian who'd taken his *nurdle* had been replaced by a flat-capped obese Caucasian who only grunted as he took the paperwork and handed William the keys.

He tugged on the door of the ancient olive-green Austin Cambridge, a vehicle that had survived the first wave of anti-Carbonite car-trashers, perhaps because its dumpy contours didn't incite them as much as a Porsche or a BMW. It had been converted to run on gas and the elegant leather-faced rear seats had been replaced by a large rusty tank. The engine burbled into life, after a few false starts. He slowly edged the car under the barrier, struggling with the unfamiliar steering wheel. Proceed with caution - his mantra. Large areas of the city were supposedly danger zones - Panic Zones - of perpetual carnival /riot. Its fashions were mostly derived from cheapo virtual reality routines. They said Meat Boys jousted with Ripper Girls in Dionysian rites of consumption/destruction and wild car chases. The Panic Police dispensed rough justice.

Flipping on creaky wipers, he peered down the dank street. Many traffic notices had been removed and some local militias had renamed roads, to suit the new ideology of the district. He was now apparently in Abdulfattah Parade, outside Bobby's Halal Meatland, but on the other side of the next intersection it became Ezekiel Street, the territorial boundary signified by a pink neon cross flashing intermittently over the corner storefront. Two thick-set men in the blue tabards of the Heavy Shepherds were waiting to flag him down.

William turned left instead, looking for signage that would take him to the Westway and point him towards Reading. Screw Leynebridge and the Borderlands, their spurious barrows and tumps. The Establishment was radiating its strong force, to pull him backwards into the dark sphere of his enigma.

Synchronicity

Lucas was running out of food. His entrancements, his secret raptures and terrors had deflected him from foraging. The notion of cycling into Leynebridge was unappealing, as he had no wish to be conscripted into Noah's psychic alliance against the Leyston Burrough development. Despite all his focusing exercises he could still sense the psycho-babble of the Elders and their sulky serfs at the back of his brainspace. His stock of various pre-Rupture currencies was depleted and none of the relics he'd salvaged from his mother's wrecked flat had much barter value in the Market Square. The idea of selling Pauline's faded socialist tracts or her collection of VHS industrial action documentaries was, in any case, an obscure betrayal. They were the last physical links he had with her. He'd refused to throw them out, even to appease Carla.

But the so-called material world was bringing him down again, as it always did. He checked his shelves again. A tinned pie and a flat bottle of the local brew. Perhaps he could sell off his small-press poetry collection for some fresh vegetables.

As he fumbled among his papers, he heard a thud at the door. Gavin Wharton pushed his way in.

'This is synchronicity, Gavin. I've got this box of poetry pamphlets, first-edition Charles Kennings, all signed -'

'Forget it, Lucas. Noah had a dream last night in which you urinated on the Serpent Path. He's convinced now you're an Urbanite agent and he's sending men with spiked clubs and torches. You need to leave Leynebridge immediately...'

Buried in the Depths of the Earth

Traffic was light on the M4 but it was a slow road, potholed and pitted. Sometimes William had to swerve to avoid saplings poking through the tarmac. He wasn't planning to stop. The few remaining service areas were faith-based, run by the Heavy Shepherds from their Roadside Pulpits, or the Wahibos, who could be spotted by their concrete minarets.

The slip road to Windsor was barricaded with the rusty hulks of old sports utility vehicles. Two redcoats in traditional bearskins watched him through binoculars as he puttered past their sentry box. His Britannic Majesty's kingdom, now administered from the Castle, had shrunk to the size of Vatican City, with ornamental guards.

William recalled Uncle Doug saluting the bakelite wireless as another monarch was anointed on that rainy day so many decades ago. He felt a faint urge to turn back and pay homage. He was still a servant of the Crown. Perhaps that was his ontological security, to have served in a matriarchy. For a second he let the car drift. Vegetable trucks in the adjacent lane beeped him, and he pulled back on course.

Once there were other grander convoys commanding the nation's motorways. He used to enjoy watching the mighty Foden transports leaving the base, each with two warheads bound for the submarine base up north, escorted by fire-engines, police vehicles, breakdown trucks - a royal progress sweeping past the pathetic huddle of protesters at the gates with their tatty rainbow placards. He never imagined then that Elaine would join their feeble ranks. That woman just turned her back on progress.

He was making good progress, despite the sluggish engine of his corporate transport and a confusing B-road diversion around Maidenhead, policed by local securi-men. A pall of oily smoke drifting over the town suggested some random arson episode had occurred. Out in the Borderlands they'd call it psycho-pyromania and put it down to the warped souls of techno-urbanites spontaneously combusting their habitat. He suspected a simpler explanation - maybe a supermarket riot gone wrong. Curious how these Borderlanders were so self-righteous and bombastic about our Bomb, which we'd never used. But their psycho-dabblings had unleashed a slow decay of the very mettle of society.

As he drove past Wokingham towards Reading, overtaken intermittently by fluorescent Fast Fun delivery trucks, he evoked himself in lecture mode holding forth to a youthful Elaine, now chastened and bound in a leather armchair. She might as well know all her utopias were doomed.

Fight or flight, nature or nurture, it didn't matter. Bombs ruled from the depths of the reptilian brain to the most arcane convolutions of the cerebral cortex. The nuclear bomb was the ultimate achievement of Western civilisation. It was a scientific and technological tour-de-force, releasing the binding forces of the universe in a controlled explosion, a Faustian fire-crack of the cosmic code.

But it also gave us existential gravitas, moral responsibility for preventing potential mass suicide. Despite the temptation to purify the planet by irradiating the bacteria of our filthy human presence, we had refrained from childish mayhem, we had shown iron restraint, the iron self-control of true patriarchs. Contrast this with the child-like irresponsibility of Elaine and her kind who tried to evade the consequences of knowledge and true will, who merely hoped the horrid thing would dis-invent itself so that they wouldn't have to carry the heavy metal burden. 'They ought to be all buried,' Elaine used to sob, mechanically, 'buried in the depths of the Earth...'

Buried in the depths of the Earth. Buried in the depths of the Earth. Buried in the depths of the Earth. He couldn't stop muttering her stock phrase as the wheels throbbed on the patchy tarmac. Her nuisance value was still troubling him, crazy after all these years. His head ached now with squinting through the rain, his brain was clouding up. *Depths of the Earth.* She was nagging again, the phrase nagged, it almost hurt. He had to stop the dread loop. He'd miss Junction 12 - Theale, Newbury, Aldermaston.

Hard Fun

Rinehart was kneeling against a sofa in the deserted studio, head in hands. The sagging Nazi dungeon set had been dismantled and replaced by gilded furnishings for an aristo drawing room ('The Hon. Mrs Veale's Academy of Female Correction III') but the sessions were still going badly. The camcorder feed to the VR mixer kept breaking down and the tactile pressure-capture wouldn't sync properly for the new girl (V-somebody) who seemed utterly spaced out and kept forgetting her rudimentary lines.

Perhaps tomorrow's shoot would go better and Pullman would

stop sending him sarcastic memos. Carla was a bitch sometimes but at least she protected him because of their shared past at Jouissance Productions. She'd been a regular at Mrs Veale's flogging parties in the old days, an inspired actor-director. But where was she when he needed him? If he lost this coveted job, there was nowhere else to go. Mark Rinehart would be futureless.

He tried to memorise some directorial spiel, notes to give his female conscripts. That might give him the heat he craved, some hotness to harden his core...

Time for the training, girls. You're such nice mute creatures, harnessed tight for some hard fun. Sonia, red hair, twenty-eight, will begin the training. She is training Veronica, nineteen, brunette, for customer service. She will play hard with the black rod on the customer preference for white flesh. She is leading Veronica towards guided satisfaction. The training will be recorded for training purposes. The target is floating in an agony of bliss. Not a word, not a sound. Not a tremble of a lip...

Abruptly he found he was crying, the release of semen coinciding with a rush of tears.

* * *

Later Viv was certain she was confined in a bare chamber, a cube with dark red plasterboard walls. These walls were punctuated at irregular intervals on all sides with circular apertures, wrist-size, at varying heights. A light flashed in the ceiling and she could hear dim music on the far side of the partition. She knelt facing the wall with the most holes.

The thick time-worms protruded through these openings. They were pale, either pinkish or yellowish, and they flexed towards her, like huge cilia or phototropic plants, seeking contact.

'You're in a deep Zone now,' intoned a voice through a grill high in the wall. ' You have to respond.'

The thickest worm extruded another few inches from its hole, elongating in front of her, then flapping and flipping around her like an air hose at excess pressure. 'It's heat-seeking. Or meat-seeking...' The thin twanging voice sounded like Rinehart. 'It can't tell the difference some days. The time-worms perforate everything in this locale.'

The time-worm curled slowly around her waist. 'It's seeking appeasement,' said the voice, sternly. 'Go to work...'

Deep Fun

The gatehouse was unmanned and the perimeter barbed wire was festooned with shreds of banners. One remnant flapped across his face. 'Nuke Doomfest!' There had been a few weeks of jubilation in the peace camps as chaotic 'post-Rupture conditions' forced the government to finally abandon the UK nuclear weapons programme. There had been less rejoicing, William recalled, when it was later revealed that stocks of plutonium might have been acquired by private entrepreneurs for resale to a triumphant Caliphate - or local militias.

He left the Austin on the overgrown grass verge and ducked under the barrier. The entrance concourse was cluttered with abandoned construction materials and equipment. He squeezed between huge pallets of bricks and roofing materials, past an overturned yellow digger and random piles of rusty scaffolding, towards the general direction of the Admin complex. It was hard to orient himself amid this chaos - and the wreckage of his memories.

He crunched over broken wine bottles. Had there been a

triumphalist carnival incursion by the peace-rioters? Perhaps instead there had been frenzied terminal office parties, support staff manically toasting their final redundancy. William hated parties, viscerally. A staff party had first revealed Elaine's libidinous truculence, the defiant thrust of her hip between a middle manager's thighs during some disco nonsense. But he wasn't revisiting that zone of shame. There was this deeper blockage...

A large building with a curved roof seemed to be unfinished and he ought to remember its name and function - maybe a replacement for the old Citadel, where materials for the core of the weapon were first manipulated - so carefully - in those clumsy robotic glove-boxes.

Soft rain trickled down his face as he scanned the rooftops, office blocks, silos, domes, the forest of masts and towers, the rusting crane that still swung over the incomplete building. Somewhere in this sprawling maze of concrete and glass was the key to arming his memory, fusing that dazzling burst of recall.

His target was clear enough - the Warhead Physics Department where he had worked for so many years devising algorithms to calculate the optimal shape for explosive lenses or predict the pattern of blast yields. But it was hard to find the co-ordinates. Signs had been torn down or painted over, while several buildings were partially demolished, virtually heaps of rubble. Maybe this had been a half-baked scorched earth policy, hurriedly executed as the possible consequences of decommissioning dawned too late on terrified managers. He struggled to control tears of rage. This abdication of responsibility - the squandering of so much hard-earned expertise - was evidenced in the upended filing cabinets, discarded laser goggles, broken keyboards and bulging sacks of shredded paper that littered the tarmac. He had a slim chance of finding the contents of his office.

He wandered randomly through the rain-swept avenues of the site, losing all sense of time. The doors on many buildings had been breached. He entered one long windowless hangar in the hope of finding some familiar trigger point. He recognised the enormous red-painted tubes of heavy-duty lasers and the monitor stations for studying plasma diffraction patterns. Here the destruction had been limited. Although the instrument panels were thick with dust he could almost believe that workers in their blue overalls were about to charge up the system and fire off another round of tests to mimic a nuclear detonation.

As he left the plasma physics lab he suddenly felt faint and nauseous. An old paranoia resurfaced, a psychic tic that Elaine used to exploit, his fear that he could be contaminated by the site's residual radiation. He squatted on the ground, shaking his head. 'That's utterly irrational. All precautions are taken,' he said, suddenly hearing his voice echo against steel shutters and blank walls, a replay of those marital teatime squabbles decades ago. His migraine had returned at full strength. Fragments of code which he couldn't quite decipher floated through his field of vision in a blurred greyish montage. He was edging up to the trauma zone. But the zone was exerting its own fatal attraction.

After trudging back and forth several times through the complex, with no sign of a security presence, he at last found the route to the Supercomputing facility. His feet ached, his head throbbed and he stumbled several times in haste and exhaustion before staggering into the lobby and down the familiar stairs. In these basement rooms he'd find the machines that had, in a sense, been his closest companions during his years at the Establishment, the clusters of IBMs, the giant arrays of the Cray. The pang in his skull had intensified and he now seemed afflicted with a steady drone in his inner ear.

As he entered the sub-basement computer facility, the drone thickened. He stared down the long narrow corridor of processor cabinets, rows of dark monoliths. It was stuffy in here and curiously warm.

Then he knew why. His aching brain had failed to register the flickering lights behind the cabinet grills.

The Establishment was derelict, wasted, abandoned. Yet somehow, despite the alleged 'Rupture', despite the pusillanimity of politicians and the fecklessness of the mob, these mighty machines were still powered up, capable of processing millions of calculations per second.

His rising excitement mingled with bewilderment and bitterness. Who was sustaining research here? Why was there zero security? Was there still a clandestine bomb development programme? Why hadn't William Crowe PhD been recruited? And, underlying all, the abyss of his amnesia. What had he done down here, in this digital cavern, that had led to his traumatic expulsion?

He started walking down the dark avenue between the drives and servers, under the dim glow of emergency strip-lights. If he could locate the main workstation he might understand whatever was happening here. Or who was supervising it. A glimmer of what he might have executed in his glory years was now seeping through. He couldn't stop the tremors.

He tried to take control. 'Dr. Crowe…' That's what they called him, whispering deferentially as he ticked off their tasks and targets. 'It's fully operational, Dr Crowe…' 'If you'd like to come this way, Dr Crowe…' Female voices, too. Professionally cool but respectful. Not

Elaine's scornful rants. Then he recognised the voices were externalising themselves, in and around the dark towers.

And his arms were gripped expertly behind him by two smiling young women in maroon jump-suits with holsters and truncheons. He struggled - and winced. 'Please remain stationary, Dr Crowe. I'm Emily, this is Roxanne and it's our job to restrain you safely at all times, in accordance with Pleasure Centres' best practice.'

Lights flared at the far end of the passage. A heavy figure was silhouetted against them, long camel hair coat slung around his shoulders like an old-time mobster. The voice was richly catarrhal. 'Thank you, William, for being the right person leading us to the right place at the right time. Always the pre-conditions of success. Now we would like to refresh your memory so you can share your ancestral wisdom with us. I'm Keith Lombard, by the way. Your Lobe-Master and friendly provider. We're going to have deep fun…'

7

The Zone

Boom Town

Leynebridge was in turmoil. Suddenly, with the influx of Pleasure Centres personnel, it had become a frontier boom town, 'a seething Tia Juana of the Celtic Borderlands,' according to the Elderseers, who handed out smudged protest pamphlets in the rain outside the Book Market. Every night in the Red Hag or the Unicorn, there were stories of colourful encounters between the cunning locals and smarty-arsed urbanites. New ripples of thought forms eddied around the unsuspecting incomers - *here they come for their uppance with their smarty cards no fool folk we not take that funny money only metal money or give us ripe meat or we'll slipknot their nurdle...* Sebastian Hackett relayed to Wharton intelligence gleaned via a buxom mead-maid at the Unicorn, that certain Youth-Elders had already planned to dream-storm a surveyor who'd drilled for samples in the very stones of the Serpent Path. 'The wretched man will be deranged in a week, mark my words. Their horrid dream-beasts crawling across his bed-chamber...'

But Trader Price and the market men were doing nicely, while the upper rooms in the inns were filling up with disoriented technical support personnnel who couldn't quite understand the curious nagging voices now intruding across their wetware firewalls. On Leyston Burrough, a locally contracted labour force was clearing away shacks in the tangled undergrowth, prior to starting work on the actual centre. Gossips gleefully recounted how Mrs Nixon, naked in her body-paint, was forced out of her abode, but taunted and abused the boyos, uttering curses on the whole enterprise.

Wharton was uneasy. The town was going to be swallowed up by the cyber culture, although not quite in the way he anticipated. He'd expected the incomers to focus exclusively on building their grotesque Pleasure Centre up at the Burrough and totally ignore the village shops. Yet every day he was visited by Centre managers in their corporate monogrammed jackets, who poked around the bookcases, then bought random titles - anything from local flora to old technical manuals.

On this precognitive cue, the door jingled and a huge bald man strode up to his desk. He looked vaguely Samoan, although Wharton was weak in reading ethnicities. The man stood over him, as if to make a sudden grab at the till. Wharton adjusted his spectacles and pretended to read a bibiography of Hilbert Carraway, the late Retro-Futurist poet. The visitor still hovered, breathing heavily.

Wharton waited. Sometimes these fat city business types had a secret vice, such as collecting bloody children's books like *Dumpy and the Gremlins*. The warty Dumpy, a toad given to moral homilies as he vanquished various creeping things. Or *The Bumper Book of The Boys at St Botolph's*. The more infantile they were the faster they sold. But the customer was often reluctant to admit his regressive cravings. You had to let them ramble for a bit.

The customer consulted a mini-phone, then scanned the rare books shelf behind Wharton's desk. 'That's a good shelf... I buy...' Wharton pretended not to hear for a moment. This was obviously a vulgar joker.

'The cheapest title up there is three hundred pounds - old currency, in used notes. Are you quite sure, sir?' He put an ironic stress on the 'sir'.

'I buy for Mr. Lombard. All for Mr Lombard. You ship by courier, OK?' The man pulled out a fat wad of pre-Rupture fifties and slapped them on the counter. Wharton automatically checked the engraving on the notes - and felt suddenly queasy. He was dealing with the Enemy, taking tainted coin from the Adversary. If Noah Dodd knew he was trading with an agent of Lombard, his position in the Elders would be fatally compromised. But Noah had never understood the imperatives of commerce; and the visitor was smiling expectantly as he presented a business card. Wharton began to pack the books and draw up an invoice: *Sexual Magick in Celtic Britain; A True History of Earth Angels; Lost in the Tunnels of Set; Nodes of the Undermind; Surviving the Qliphoth; A Labyrinth for Merlin...* The mysterious Mr Lombard seemed to have developed remarkably arcane tastes.

Fission is Our Mission

The material world. Lucas had always distrusted the material world. His maternal person put her total faith in this perforated membrane of reality, even after the debacle of the Rupture, when matters of actual fact started dissolving, releasing a new viral multiplication of possibilities. Her dogma was the awesome power of dialectical materialism that energised the accumulation and distribution of things. But now metaphysics had leaked its dark liquors into everything. The material world was just taking the piss.

If he were a man he would simply hit the road. Or he would at least take a pitchfork, or a blow-torch, and make a last stand against the stasis that entrapped him. Yet stasis was perhaps his best strategy. He craved silence, stillness, secrecy. What could be gained by a risky cross-country journey to the capital, facing the religious bandits that harassed rail travellers or the unofficial tax-collection points on the roads? There was no way back to Carla or the City. The only way was inwards and downwards, to the guts of the Earth, to virtually mummify himself while maintaining some kind of astral presence, until a resurrection opportunity - or a second Rupture - presented itself.

Picking up a torch and a kitchen knife, he navigated the chaos of his room, stepping around his rumpled charts and notebooks. He pulled aside his mother's tattered anti-nuclear rainbow banner, which he'd tacked up to relieve the monotony of the grey plaster, to reveal the rusty circular hatch, the Inner Portal, as he sometimes called it, one of the distinctive selling points of the bunker when it was first marketed by a Ruptured government.

He swung it open and peered into the tiny windowless panic-room, a womb within a womb, where a Civil Defence Observer could hole up as the fall-out settled, or hide from Soviet hordes. The space, just over eight feet square, was dug into the side of the hill and lined with concrete. Although it smelt damp and musty, Lucas knew it was vented by a filtered airshaft. He could see the outline of the rudimentary bunk.

He started to assemble the accoutrements he would need for a prolonged stay in the Intervoid. There were the practical necessities - a mattress, his sleeping bags, a face mask, certain medications. But he had other needs, totemic objects to be placed around him for the voyage, which would serve to focus him, as and when he returned to consensual consciousness. He selected some bleached photographs (his mother, Carla), some of his trance drawings (Leila, Robyn), his notebook, his staff and robes, and a diagram of the Qabalistic Tree, with the Yesodic areas shaded in purple. He arranged them in precise alignments at the head of the bunk.

Then, after the ritual wash, he lay down in his sleeping bag and began the breathing exercises that were a prelude to the Astral Trance. The distant psycho-babble static from the Leynebridge folkmind slowly faded...

Lucas knew the symptoms. The alt-selves were emerging like a corona of yellow light. Astral leakage from his muddy flesh. Once again, he missed Carla's fresh body, her mysterious cunt; the surprising word was a quaint obscenity that he would never use in a hundred linear earth-years. But in the Polyverse? 'Fission is our mission' he repeated robotically. With every repetition his body-image shivered into a new position. And finally budded forth.

Portal

On Leyston Burrough, Gavin Wharton could hear the angry quaver in Noah Dodd's voice but he was distracted from the actual semiotics of what was being said by scrambled thought-forms, like dark deformed homunculi, boring their way in, no doubt from Dodd's back-brain… Trying to screen his unease, that festering guilt about the sale to Lombard's agent, he finally focussed on Dodd's monologue. 'Just listen, Wharton! Preliminary excavations for the Pleasure Centre have revealed a concealed entrance behind the Burrough Stone, along the main alignment of the mound. It apparently leads to a chamber.'

'How do you know?'

'Careless talk in the Red Hag. They've already uncovered artefacts - a stone axe, a bronze head, gold amulets, fragments of leather - and Lombard will try to seize the whole trove …'

Dodd was dragging him up the muddy slope through a tangle of bushes. They stopped at a wooden hoarding that screened off the entrance to the site. With surprising strength, the old man shouldered one of the boards aside and they stumbled through.

'Hey, grandpa you can't come through here. This is a secure area, know what I mean?' A muscular black man in overalls and rasta dreadlocks blocked their way. Wharton hadn't seen a Rasta in years, since he escaped from London. He wondered how they'd explained the Rupture. The downfall of Babylon, probably.

Dodd in any case wasn't fazed. 'I am Chief Elderseer of Leynebridge. We have contractual rights of access agreed with Mr Lombard,' he shouted. Apparently taken aback at the magical invocation of the CEO's name, the man let them pass into a maze of raw earthworks. The hillside shacks had been flattened and there were no signs of their former inhabitants. Wharton thought he glimpsed Mrs

Nixon crouching in her filthy furs, observing them suspiciously from behind a mound of refuse in the gloom. A jab of pain bored through his temples.

The path dipped and Wharton realised that the Burrough was not merely a pile of soil and stones heaped up at random, but seemed to have been layered with strata of turf, clay and sod cladding its stone pillars. They crouched as they crept through a low entrance into a broad chamber, dimly lit now by lanterns. He peered up at the granite lintel and wondered how secure it was. 'The stone's been there for at least three thousand years,' muttered Dodd, impatiently, picking up on his anxiety. 'It won't suddenly crush you.'

'Was this space used for ritual or burial?' Wharton tried to ignore the chill and a heavy sour odour he couldn't quite identify. Noah's torchlight revealed a network of faint markings on the stones, some kind of worn runic incisions. He peered at the patterns and swept the rubble with his staff. 'We're close to a confluence of leys - the whole area around Leynebridge is transected by a network of lines, alignments of subtle energies, as intricate and highly energised as any of their gimcrack Lobes.'

Wharton realised that underneath the rhetoric Noah was fully grounded in his Lore. The Earth for him was animate, a live entity. But Wharton was fighting his own bookish scepticism.

' If Leyston Burrough is a sacred place, why was it allowed to become a mere dumping ground - for the refuse and rejects of Leynebridge?' He thought of Mrs Nixon, picking through garbage outside her shack.

'It is a place of skulls, a death-centre. Its desolation must be respected. Even its squalor is a disguise - a defence against the alien intrusion. This place is a portal...' Wharton sensed a defensive shield thickening between them. Noah prodded the earth with his staff and grunted some guttural syllables, one of his cryptic charms - probably learned from one of the antiquarian tomes he used to buy from the shop, in simpler times. He shone his feeble torch around the egg-shaped space. 'As I feared - Lombard's men have already removed the significant objects. There may be bone fragments, of course. Possibly skulls.' In the flickering half-light Wharton could discern a shadowy mass at the centre of the tomb - or womb. Dodd approached it. 'But this is unusual. This vertical bluestone forms a central pillar....'

At the entrance to the barrow they could hear voices. The Rasta guard had returned with another corporate enforcer. 'Come on, gents,' he murmured, with amiable menace, gripping Noah's shoulder. 'Can't let you hang around here, can we? Not even for a nice fist of nurdle. Mr Lombard wouldn't like it.'

'This is a site of great cultural significance,' spluttered Dodd.

'I'm sure Mr Lombard will take good care of it. Now, let's do this the easy way, shall we?'

Anti-Ark

Despite all her efforts, Elaine was losing control. She knelt on the stone floor of her kitchen, rocking slowly back and forth in her long gown, unable to stop her gulps and sobs. It was almost dawn, the bluish half-light. She had performed the habitual rites for banishing and centering, she had laid out the herbs and crystals as always - but the events of the last days had a seismic effect, as if the stones of the Serpent Path were splintering and cracking beneath her feet.

Vivienne's mysterious departure had been upsetting enough, even now, months later - had she not give years of her life as a surrogate mother to raising her grandchild in the true Way? As time passed her anger at Vivienne's defection turned to anxiety. No messages, not even the faintest vibration in the hiss and whisper of the aethyrs... It was a silence as total as the blankness that followed the sudden death of her daughter Dawn, a dead zone she still found hard to enter, because that involved flashbacks of her marriage to William Crowe and its aftermath, her escape to Leynebridge.

Surely the gods were protecting Dawn in the under-life - and would protect Vivienne on this plane. Perhaps silence was the price of their preservation. That is why she had to speak out for them, her girls, dead or alive, and the old gods. The space in the Burrough was originally a chamber where, at the climax of great festivals, the priestesses would enter trance states and communicate telepathically across the earth to each other by focussing on a mental map, externalised in the leys. Once joined collectively, they could even communicate with the Earthmind Herself...

For the violation of this holy mound and the seizure of its treasures, to create some kind of bastardised 'heritage attraction', seemed to be driven by the same dark current that had overwhelmed her family and now threatened to destroy the soul of her community. Trader Price and his cronies had been bought out, probably by vintage cash or free membership of some squalid Pleasure Centre, while Noah Dodd and the Elders could only bluster impotently and the youth were half-corrupted already.

She stood up and paced her living room. Even the thick stone walls and heavy beams of her cottage didn't seem to provide any shelter from these malign vibrations. She looked to her familiar icons for support - her astral charts, Viv's childish drawings of the Tower, her books of herbal lore. For the first time in years, they offered no affirmation. Then, reluctantly, she felt drawn to a small cupboard recessed in the wall, a hatch that was rarely opened, a kind of anti-ark that preserved a few charred fragments of her previous life.

She felt inside for the photo. She'd always felt that by keeping his image she'd still have a kind of emergency psychic defence if he ever materialised, some focus for her anger. She held it up to the fitful lamp. And there he was, in his tatty tweed jacket and neatly parted hair, already an anachronism in 1965, that remote time-plane. He was standing outside the Bodliean Library on a foggy day posing with his bicycle, maybe trying to convince himself he was a scientific genius, an unworldly prodigy awaiting her rescue. Her doomed salvation project. The faded monochrome print was singed at the corner - it was the only picture that escaped her ritual burning. She realised she was staring into the grain of the emulsion, trying to scry some flicker of movement in his blank grin.

And maybe fragments of memory were trying to break through the fog. Later, wasn't there a project so grotesquely terrible that even her stupid genius of an ex-husband wavered in his dedication to masculinist rationalism - and lost his mind in the process? Of course he'd only dropped hints. In any case, she underwent a conversion crisis, turning her back on William and all the values embodied in his conspiracy of death-in-life. She needed to explain all this to Vivienne - but she had a deep fear of even thinking about it now, as if the very mention of William could have evoked his actual presence. It was an active presence. His monochrome ghost was out there somewhere.

Special Assignment

'We've a special assignment for you, my dear.' Lombard slid a glass of Chardonnay across the table and leaned forward to adjust a lock of hair across Vivienne's brow. 'There, there. That'll do nicely. I did have someone older in mind but she couldn't handle the pressure or the liquor, could she? I hope it didn't spoil the party for you. Anyway I offed her and picked you, on account of your nice hair and the way you behaved so bravely over that messy business with the poor Mo-Boy.'

He rose from the table, then sprawled across the faux-Louis-XIV chaise longue , leafing through stills from her most recent shoot. She couldn't see what he was peering at but he seemed to be looking for something very specific.

'There's quite an aura about you, isn't there? You'll behave sensibly, of course. It will be different from the usual Pleasure Centres stuff, quite up-scale, but you must be discreet, for confidentiality is one of our core values…'

Vivienne sat motionless. Her exertions under the reddening eyes of Rinehart, as he conducted his frenetic orchestrations of her limbs and tissues, had left her depleted. In the huge gilt mirror behind Lombard's head, doubtless the nightly frame for the Chief Executive's own lavishly staged copulations, she could see the pale mask of her face. Behind was a hollow darkness, fitfully lit by tiny darting sparks, that faded and died.

Screaming Skull

The astral projection almost faltered. The meat of Lucas Beardsley was still mired in the dung, no, the dungeon of his dreams and their rusting machineries. He tried to project himself as a screaming skull head-first down a long black corridor, its perspectives like a dioramic pyramid of burning wires receding into the dark, but the passage was turning into a luminous conical hat, so he had to fly right up it. He was entering another ill-fitting head. Carla would laugh at him again. He was a dunce of the astral realm; his energies would taper away to an infinitely tiny point, a pointlessness.

In the Zone

The Pleasure Centres private chapel was hung with crimson drapes and a spider web of silk ropes. Liturgical objects - -a silver ciborium, a censer - were piled in the foreground. The edge of William's visual field was quivering a little and an insistent metallic noise was infiltrating the sound-track of the scenario, a muted monkish chant, but generally the virtual world was holding steady.

'This is what you apparently requested, ' said pseudo-Lombard, almost apologetically. The icon of the Chief Executive loomed over him, wearing a hooded purple robe with 'Lobemaster' emblazoned on the front. The virtualisation process had smoothed his jowls and forehead, as if he had been re-modelled from pink plasticine. He held up an elaborately designed silver cattle prod. 'Hand-made in Leynebridge,' he whispered proudly, 'a valuable trade item.'

William's heartbeat was increasing. If this was a virtual body experience it was cleverly modeled to reproduce the physiology of fear as well as arousal. 'I am not worthy,' he thought, the statement sliding across his vision in gold-edged sans-serif fonts before fading in the swirling incense.

'This experience is a vast new transaction,' said the new

Lobemaster, expectantly. 'We await confirmation. Your desire must be firmed up, as we like to say. Then we shall see if we have a repeatable experiment. Now, you're in the Zone. Let me introduce your trainee Quantum Sluts for the evening.' He rang a small silver handbell.

A curtain parted, revealing two young women, near-nude, harnessed in red and black leather. They gave William wide eager smiles, unfazed, it seemed, by his long black gown. Perhaps they were brunette Emily and redhead Roxanne, who had apprehended him somewhere. Yet their faces also carried the imprint of those mad punk tarts he'd so fetishised. They began singing along wordlessly with the distant choral chanting, then began dancing slowly around him, prodded by Lombard. 'Harlots in church,' he announced, 'custom-directed just for you as a very special client. Most unusual... But I'm confident our girls will comport themselves beautifully.'

William was totally immersed. The lancet window framed pseudo-Emily's body as she knelt in front of him, presenting the gorgeous pearls of her arse. He couldn't understand why this particular curvature of her torso should generate such desire. He was a camp actor, acting out the mythology of his lusts but he didn't understand what was encrypted in his genes, because it was possibly dictated by a ghost inhabiting him that wanted to get into hers. He couldn't keep the flubber of his thoughts in any solid form.

This Romanesque basilica of lust contained alcoves and each alcove held its tableau of dominance and submission with gold chains and silken ropes and robes. 'Visit them all,' whispered Lombard invisible now. Flesh waxed and waned in firelight. The reticulation of fishnets gave tactility to the volumes of soft bodies. The overall quality of hallucination was superb.

In the chapel of Mary Magdalen, he slowly fondled Roxanne's breasts before she genuflected to take his vibrant member between her glistening lips. He beckoned to Emily, who toyed carefully with Roxanne's body, before pressing his hand between her loosening thighs. In the temple of Lilith he was tied down as they took turns astride him. In the temple of Kali he writhed in delicious but unbearable heat.

Now he could see himself floating over his partners. They were tethered to a grey fluted pillar by long chains with steel neck rings. They had been diverted by the unveiling of a mechanical phallus-engine, beautifully engineered in steel, ivory and leather to offer dual satisfaction. His sculptured rump moved among the flux of thighs and swell of breasts as they surged towards an extended crescendo of sighs and groans. He fell into darkness...

8
Intervoid

The Goddesses Failed

The Elderseers were clustering together in the Book Market, to prattle and plot the processional arrangements and protocols for the Feast of Smoke and Elaine should have been joining them to ensure that Lore was truly followed, especially when Lombard's horrible techno-portal was encroaching on their sacred space as a result of Trader Price's treacherous compromises with Pleasure Centres. Yet Elaine lacked the heart to change into her robes. Perhaps she had a sickness of the heart, maybe a plague of the ageing gristly body.

As she glanced down through the diamond panes of her

bedchamber in the Old Pale Cottage adjoining the Market courtyard, she could see Noah Dodd beating his staff on the cobbles to call order and banish retrograde spirits. And she felt exhaustion where she once felt exaltation. The incessant business of the Elders wouldn't stop susurrating faintly at the back of her mind.

She turned away and wandered into the little white box room that Viv had used as a child. Nothing there now but a bare iron bedstead and an empty wardrobe. Echoes of her sandals on the polished oak but not the faintest aethyric vibrancy from her grand-daughter. The City must have absorbed Vivienne into its deafening mix, the low-frequency rumble of death-trafficking and centrifugal heavy-metal din that had hypnotised William and now seemed to have swallowed up his second generation. *Just as Leynebridge had engulfed their first-born. Dawn was laid in Leynebridge, Dawn was laid out and laid low. In a shallow grave. Dawn lay. False Dawn.*

That idiot voice again, whispering along the labyrinths of her brain. Only she heard it. And every day for over eighteen years she had tried to silence it. Surely there was no blame. Or the wyrd was written, no way it could be re-scribed or pre-scribed. Dawn would have died anyway.

Outside, she heard faint cheers (or jeers?) from the Book Market. The meeting would proceed for hours. If she went down, the bumblings of procedure would distract her from Dawn. But she couldn't mute that internal voice.

Was it her fault that Dawn ran wild when she ran amok and ran out of William's Berkshire suburban semi-detached asylum? You're an adolescent and your mother tells you to pack a rucksack, and just leave the rest behind because remote-control Dad is a broken-down robot and you must rediscover the Earth together, at its epicentre in the

Borderlands. And you arrive in a town of sheep with no money. And while your mother is immersing herself in herbs and oils and contributions to the local Lore, you're trying to survive in the yokel school as an incomer from the urban freak-show, fending off those fat hostile girls by fraternising with horny youths who might be your bodyguard in return for a quick shag. Of course, they shag at their leisure and move right along, taking turns... Elaine tried to project a protective aura around her daughter, but it must have worn off quickly in the back rooms of the Red Hag, because Dawn was pregnant with Vivienne at sixteen, giving birth in this very room, and handing the baby over for her grandmother's care almost there and then. And then the Rupture came, entangling all chronologies and releasing Qliphothic chaos, even in the sanctuary of Leynebridge.

And the Lore couldn't save Dawn. Perhaps it was too weak then, according to Noah. But Gavin Wharton, always such a wary pedant, believed that one of her daughter's midnight fungal forays must have gone wrong. Maybe drunken lads led her astray, proffered as a jape a random bite of Amanita Phalloides, the Death Cap. Whatever the cause, the symptoms were slow to emerge, evolving over an endless week from gastric convulsions to coma and delirium. Even now, she could never erase the recall of Dawn's face, or the flecks of vomit around her chapped lips as she wriggled hideously in shitty blankets, her arm mechanically flexing up towards her mouth, as if trying to locate the entry-point of the malign fungal spirit. Noah had administered milk-thistle and called on Airmid and Margawse to heal the young mother, his chant mingling with Dawn's moans and the cries of the child in the next room, but the Goddesses failed them all this time.

Or had she failed, out of fecklessness and confusion? After

William's mechanical autocracy, that would have imprisoned Dawn and herself in a 1950s time-warp of knitting and baking, an autistic re-enactment of his semi-detached childhood, she'd let Dawn run wild on the streets of Leynebridge in the belief that the girl's true guardian angel would eventually steer her back to equilibrium. But perhaps the damage had already been done, years before, by the very act - implausible, impossible, how could she? - of her own mating with William in a fit of drunken sentimentality after a dinner party at her tutor's house, when she'd taken pity on this awkward postgraduate student and his automaton lust. His intensity was shattering.

And when the morning sickness started a few days later she'd already rationalised the relationship for all the right/wrong accursed reasons, that serious William the future technocrat offered security, a nice house and garden, sooner rather than later. Surely opposites complemented each other. His stern intellect would balance her fey folkishness. His catatonic awkwardness could be eased through the joys of sex and fatherhood. William's salvation would be her grand project, far more real than the dissertation on Elizabethan witchcraft that she'd been considering.

But William's grand projects had subsumed everything. The last one had consumed him.

An Ordeal

'I hope you didn't find that too much of an ordeal, old man...' Lombard was pouring Earl Grey tea into a china rose-pattern tea cup close to William's hand, which hung limply over the side of Lombard's favourite chesterfield. 'I just felt you needed a little taste of what Pleasure Centres currently offers, as a free up-date. Much better than those jerky old punk-chicks, wasn't it? Would you like some more?' He tilted the milk jug.

William nodded, absently. He was exhausted by his virtual orgia, but felt a strange lightness and clarity of being, as if a column of cool blue light had spiralled up his vertebrae and cleared the cluttered spaces of his head. Somehow he was resting in Lombard's private quarters. On the crimson wall opposite him, he saw an ornate gilt-framed oil painting of the CEO, in photo-realist mode, reclining on that very sofa. He felt enthroned.

'You're a key man, William. But I had to let you find your way to me without getting Rinehart or Liggett involved. Of course, I had to drop Carla Leppard. A pity she made such a mess of things. But even she has never entered my holy places - as you have…'

William glanced around at shelves of Victorian leather bindings, a grandfather clock by the door, high ceilings and oak panelling, the glass candelabra on a Bosendorfer grand piano. The non-virtual Emily, immaculately coiffeured, sat on a gilt chair by the stone fireplace, smiling professionally. She had changed her uniform for a coral trouser suit.

'This apartment is a fine place to be. One of my favourites. But you have been to a better place, haven't you? Because I found you wandering there, looking for your old self. And now I'm helping you to find it, aren't I? We're going to find it together - you, me, Emily and Roxanne. We'll get there in the end.'

William felt comatose. He wasn't getting or going anywhere. But he was perfectly lucid. In fact, he now had an odd sense of inner transparency, as if a light was beginning to glow high in the dome of his brain, and he could see, with a curious detachment, simulacra of his Research Establishment self framed in faded clips across its inner wall. He evoked endless meetings, an office. There he was, nodding obediently as Denis Weekes handed him a file. He was being sidelined. No more warheads. *You're being re-assigned to highly specialised top secret artificial intelligence work under the auspices of the MOD. For security and logistical reasons you will continued to be based at the Establishment, where you will have access to state-of-the-art computer facilities.*

'Ah, William is thinking aloud. A soliloquy. That's what we need. The start of the talking cure. This more or less is what we surmised.' Lombard clicked his fingers and Emily produced a notebook and pen from her hand-bag. 'Emily will scribe for us. You can't trust the old electrons these days. But you know all about that sort of thing, don't you?'

William nodded. Speech came to him, slowly. His voice sounded remote: 'The brief from Weekes was to devise an expert system which could store strategic and tactical data and could effectively continue to direct the conduct of a nuclear war in the event of the UK's main command centres being destroyed. The system would, of course, be distributed over several underground hardened sites, and its circuits would, like the human brain, contain built-in redundancy and duplication. We knew the Americans had been working on their own post-disaster system for some time.'

He paused. Lombard cleared his throat. Emily looked at him expectantly, even reverently, her pen poised in mid-air. He couldn't stop now, he had to go on.

'Subsequently this was combined with a secondary brief: to integrate the military system with a subsidiary data base which would store the civilian records of the nation, so that in the event of a post-armageddon peace the national bureaucracy could co-ordinate the reconstruction of the nation. The notion of records became expanded to include not only the files of government departments but any cultural artefact that could be digitally encoded.'

Lombard nodded sympathetically. 'A tough commission for our Dr Crowe. Can't have been easy, can it, Emily?' Their scribe smiled and nodded uneasily, perhaps not sure of the correct response to her chief executive. 'So many challenges. The slow speed and low capacity of the hardware then available. The limitations of existing software languages. The meddling of bureaucrats. How on earth did the poor man do it?'

William didn't quite know yet, although he was getting foreshadowings, faint broken streams of code on his brain-screens. Best to keep talking it up. 'It took several years before my team made any real progress with piloting artificial intelligence software. But the eighties saw dramatic improvements in chip design and system languages, which coincided with an intensification of the Cold War.'

'Exciting times, William. Glory days...' Lombard got up and paced around the room, pausing at Emily's chair to run his hand absently through her flowing hair and around the back of her neck. 'Go on...'

For a few seconds, William faltered. He closed his eyes. His psyche had already made its contribution to the databank. He ought to know. The pictures lining his skull were clouding over, the streams of code ebbed and flowed. His brain throbbed with some dark obstruction, the blocked cess-pit of an old dream: *she took off her head with a single motion, and offered it, eyes gleaming...* 'But my Head was a male Head... surely some mistake...' He was murmuring now. Lombard and Emily crouched close to him around the sofa, straining to catch his mutterings. 'He was BRAN... BRAN! BRAN THE BRAIN...'

William was abruptly overcome with a raucous spasm of laughter that became an extended coughing fit, a fierce mucous rasp that ended with him rocking back and forth dribbling snot and blood. 'BRAN! BRAN! It all added up to BRAN...'

Emily looked perplexed and nauseated; but Lombard, proffering him a tissue, was obviously enthralled. 'This is good, very good. Confirms my hunch. Rinehart obviously thought I was mad buying those old books - but I knew everything would connect. The magick gets into everything...' He pulled a calf-bound tome off the shelf and began hastily flicking through it. 'Bran - Celtic God of Regeneration... whose head was cut off in battle... but the head lived on... with prophetic and protective powers... allegedly buried under the Tower of London... to protect the realm...'

William knew the acronym now. 'BRAN - British Reconstructive Application Network...' Light flickered in the galleries of memory. Like the buzzing fluorescent tubes in Ebdon's office. He could envisage himself right there, on the worn carpet, arguing his case, presenting all the data, the print-outs and field reports. He could re-enact this triumphant meeting with a shocked Ebdon, who could scarcely conceal this dismay that the project actually worked.

'BRAN was tested in the MOD simulation exercise Operation Deadline, and successfully coordinated the reprisal firing of Polaris missiles, the rerouting of communication networks, the downsizing of electoral registers and the removal of the Crown Jewels from the Tower. A feasibility study was prepared, which examined the possibility of installing BRAN at - ' He stopped. His inner screenwall was clouding, the code was fading...

His memory had blanked again and his nose still bled. But

Lombard didn't seem concerned. 'That's excellent, William. The repressed matter is all coming out and you're going to feel so much better. All the fragments are fitting together now. You're being most helpful. It's good to be helpful...' He grinned at Emily and let his hand toy with the Pleasure Centres ID badge on her lapel. 'Emily's really looking forward to the next installment.'

'Would it be possible to take an intermission?' William half-rose from the sofa but the heavy pressure of Lombard's hand on his shoulder eased him down again. 'Not a wise idea, Doctor. We don't want to break the mood, do we?' William felt himself suddenly shaking. The grey hairs on the back of his hand trembled. He was under attack from his self-remembering, the displays in his head were flicking on and off all the time and the languor of his initial post-hedonic state had dissolved, replaced by recurrent waves of neural pain. The memory clips were flaring up again: *Elaine and the baby screaming down the stairs at him, when he returned home at 3 AM after a tricky session in the lab; Elaine ranting about his 'autism', his anti-social skills; the debacle at that wretched wine-and-cheese party where she shocked his section head with a weird unilateralist outburst; trying to concentrate on the algorithms as she bombarded him with conflicting demands and ultimatums...*

'Hostilities were declared, by the sound of it. A very frigid war on the home front. Don't worry, I can read your lips. You don't have to say any more. Until, of course, you're ready...'

He'd always been ready. But they created new challenges for him all the time. The prototype BRAN wasn't enough for them. 'That bastard Weekes kept pushing me. They kept shortening the deadlines for new initiatives, upgrades. And then Weekes would go off on his latest craze of the week - micro-nukes was a favourite of his - and expect me to fit in work on that as well.'

'Maybe the whole Establishment was under pressure,' suggested Lombard, not unsympathetically. 'I've often found that my teams produce their best under pressure. Rinehart was a genius at immersive VR directing. A pity he's burning out. Almost as fast as the artistes, poor little trollops... *Trollops*...' He rolled the noun's liquids and plosives with relish. 'No offence intended, of course.' He grinned at Emily, who was studying her notepad carefully.

'They wanted a spectacular defence initiative, some gimmick to catch the public mood like Reagan's Star Wars project.' *Reagan*. A dim streaky mugshot from the dead. Was William Crowe the only one who remembered the dead names? But Lombard seemed to remember. He was nodding sympathetically.

'Never underestimate the importance of marketing, William. Don't be too hard on your managers. But don't beat yourself up either. Go on...'

'Suddenly the notion of a mere command system and database didn't seem attractive enough for our leaders...'

'It was a time of escalation. But you could rise to the challenge...'

'They were stupid, Lombard, mere bureaucrats. Weekes never really grasped what I'd done, the beauty of those early algorithms. I'd written a self-replicating code into the kernel of BRAN. The programme had an inbuilt instruction to reproduce itself like a virus in other computer systems.'

'The early worm catches the birds,' suggested Lombard, snorting with laughter. 'The worms go in, the worms go out... I love it.'

'In periods of stasis there was no need to maintain and constantly update a vast database. But in times of national emergency BRAN could automatically infiltrate and override the nation's civilian computer networks, thanks to my ingenuity in sidestepping system protocols. It could rapidly absorb and ingest data. It could go on forever adapting and modifying itself. Its survival imperative was as selfish as any human gene.'

'Ah, the selfish gene... How instructive it is! What a knowledge base your BRAN could gather - a veritable digital culture-dish...'

'But it was never enough for them. They couldn't see the cunning. They kept demanding further upgrades. And Weekes kept side-tracking me with work on his midget bombs, just to confuse me. Meanwhile there were questions about the expense. Even my expenses. Petty meddlings.'

'Expense is a word we'll erase, William. No expense will be spared...'

'Petty meddlings by underlings. My wife never knew her place, either. I had signed the Official Secrets Act, of course. Only so much I could reveal...' Another time seizure: *Elaine haranguing him with her pamphlets as he hurried down the garden path towards the new Rover, late for work, and then she was shouting so loud the neighbours could hear* : BRAIN FUCKER! BRAIN-FUCKER! MY HUSBAND THE BRAIN-FUCKER! TELL THE WHOLE TRUTH YOU OLD BRAIN-FUCKER!

'You're getting excited, aren't you, William? Almost speaking in tongues! Just watch those lips...'

'I wrote another feasibility study. To keep everybody off my back. As a secret revenge against my spouse's woozy notions of spirituality. She'd never know, of course. But I enjoyed the irony. Bottling all their ghosts in my little machine. Bottling hers, too, although she would never have found out. If it had worked. Bottle her up and throw into the info-torrent...'

'Fascinating. Now how exactly were you going to do that?'

'The process...ah, the process. A great challenge. My upgrade to BRAN was predicated on the notion of transferring not only the instructions but the personality-repertoires of our political and military masters into the machine, to enhance the performance of the Network in a post-apocalypse scenario. Brains in a box, or at least a network of interfacing boxes.'

'Well, now. Brains in boxes having a chat. How do you think he did it, Emily? You're my cleverest girl, aren't you?' Emily smiled awkwardly as Lombard stroked her forehead. 'Any ideas?' His knuckles tapped her skull with sudden ferocity. 'Any ideas in there? Any any any old ideas?' Emily bit her lip under the onslaught. 'Sadly Emily has no idea how you accomplished the brain-fucking. If you tell her she might be nice to you again. In a reality matrix of your choice. Or even in the actualite.'

'It was only a thought-experiment at this stage. A feasibility study. Everything would depend on developing a cognitive nano-probe, a device that could operate at sub-molecular levels - a midget submarine of the neural world. First, magnetic resonance analysis starts the process of cortical mapping - frontal lobe, cerebrum, temporal cortex parietal cortex/ thalamus, hypothalamus, hippocampus, cerebellum, amygdala, reticular formation....'

'Wonderful... the entire neural empire... master of all you survey!'

'Then, billions of blood cell-size scanning machines - the nanoprobes - are injected into the subject's brain providing a complete readout of each neuron. Rendering is then theoretically possible.'

'Rendering - a powerful term. Render unto Caesar. Render unto Lombard. Render or surrender!' Lombard quivered with glee.

'The nanoprobe kills the neuron and takes its place. To transfer the unique pattern of the subject's brain activity to a quantum computer matrix.'

'To core out his soul like an apple! Remarkable...'

'Soul is a delusive concept, Lombard.' Trapped as he was in Lombard's cradle of guilty pleasurings and ominous foreclosings, William was still determined to sustain the rigour of his discourse. 'Of course, the neural simulcra of the subjects would survive for future post-apocalypse generations, ready to utter ancestral wisdom in times of crisis. As the programme evolved, they might eventually develop a kind of self-awareness, a simulated consciousness. But there's no royal box in the theatre of the mind. No grand narratives. Just fragments of multiple drafts.'

Lombard shrugged. 'Would it be a sort of virtual immortality? Maybe - for those of us who could afford it...' He stretched and yawned, apparently satisfied with his answer to his rhetorical question and now suddenly indifferent to William's revelation, like a fat bored adolescent. He didn't seem concerned now when William rose from the sofa and began walking around the perimeter of the carpet, chin in hand. Emily scanned them both with apprehensive eyes.

'I rewrote the codes for BRAN over and over. I'm certain the re-braining, if you can call it that, would have succeeded. We would have had a buried treasure-house of accumulated knowledge, the wisdom of leaders, their imperatives for national reconstruction. The British national identity could have survived Armageddon.'

'Some would say that it's hardly survived the Ruptures... But every little apocalypse is an opportunity, isn't it?' Lombard leafed through another tome, apparently checking an index, then glanced at Emily's notebook. 'Although this is beginning to sound like a lost opportunity...'

'The weak link at that point was the lack of nanotech molecular probes. Even in those secure linear times, they were at least thirty years away. Now that science is so difficult to execute and scientists are discredited by the masses, it's difficult to see how we could develop it, even if the facilities at the Establishment are still operational. Of course, there's the matter of the destruction of the subject's grey matter in the scanning procedure. But that challenge wasn't my problem...'

'It remains a problem, though, doesn't it? We wouldn't want Emily's head spinning on a platter, eaten alive by digital termites, would we?' Lombard mimed insect mandibles, scrabbling his big fingers across Emily's forehead. Mutely, she continued to take notes.

'Remember, Lombard, the information would live. Data would survive and breed. A kind of death and rebirth cycle, as I tried to explain to my wife, who always saw things in mythic terms... After passing the file to Weekes I made the error of hinting at its contents to Elaine.'

'Oh dear...' Lombard sighed. 'What possessed William, Emily? Do you think he was trying to impress somebody? Would you be impressed? Go on, don't be scared, it's only your Chief Executor, say something...' Emily shook her head. 'Do you like William's plan for national survival, extracting people's brains with nano-botniks? Do you think we should go for it?' He stood behind the amanuensis and leaned over her, slowly unbuttoning her blouse.

William didn't notice the interruption or the sexual incursion. 'I was determined to win the mind/body argument once and for all and stop Elaine's babblings. Predictably she found the notion of computerised consciousness absurd and repugnant. I was accused of obscenity, obsession, of monstrous ambition, I was an agent of living death... She kept asking for a divorce. In my position... the pressure was intolerable...'

He had been trying to edit the slippage of this old imagery as he spoke, to pick some definitive phrase out of her torrent of invective so that Lombard would understand but it was like watching a defective Pleasure Centres playback going loopy-de-loop, a silly singalong virus. He couldn't get his head out of her head *her shivery white back turning away, head swivelling, lips flickering out of sync as she retreated from the bedroom his fist an appendage out of control swinging against her body making contact but couldn't feel a thing Dawn sobbing mechanically across the hallway stimulus and response patterns all over the place can't stop now it's really happening an irremovable engram or something...*

'The final bombshell, as it were, was not rejection of BRAN Mk 2 - but apparent eager acceptance of it. Denis Weekes assured me that it had been approved at the highest level of the UK establishment, who, of course, had no notion of the enormous intellectual problems involved, let alone the practical difficulties of devising effective - and risk-free - nano-tech interfacing technologies. I suspect now that he was acting alone, setting me up to fail...'

'Fail? Not a word I like around here. How could genius William fail? Our fail-safe guru. Was it a graceful failure - or a fall from grace?' Emily sat impassive, staring blankly ahead, still writing her shorthand glyphs as Lombard's huge hand rummaged in her cleavage.

William fell silent and slumped back on the sofa. The days of the crisis re-ran, projecting their clips with increasing speed and luminosity through the membranes of time across his crumbling brain-wall - *lines of code streaming into infinity tiny green characters rolling across the blackness of the screen but it made no more sense would not compute no way I can deliver the pay load the mother lode and then home to find Elaine in the lounge chanting to banish my demons no food in the microwave Dawn locked herself into the bathroom a pact of silence against me a pre-menstrual conspiracy to starve me out threat to cut up my books deserves a good slap Nora and Uncle Doug warned me but all dead now sleeping bag in the lab now scurf in the key pad screen burn all binary day/ night/ day/ night/ sleep/ wake/ sleep/ wake/ sleep/ wake/ light/ dark/ space/ time/ eat/ shit/ yes/ no/ start/ stop/ start/ stop/ start/ stop/ start/ stop/ stop/ zero/ zero...*

'Not another word from William. Just sits there twitching his lips. Burned right out. Just couldn't deliver a result. Oh you bedraggled wanker. You sad old fuckwit...' Lombard was running his hands over Emily's upper body with increasing velocity, flicking her nipples in an abstracted manner. Each new manipulation seemed to correspond with a fresh utterance. 'What a disaster! What a fickle arse-about-farce! Your little recitation, this whole psychodramatic performance, confirms my worst suspicions. You could be a complete waste of my space-time resources. What do we do with him, Emily?' He buried his jaw in Emily's tresses and whispered hoarsely. She flinched. 'I can tell you one thing. Emily's not going to be nice to you any more. Not even virtually.'

William felt blank now. His energies were draining quickly, the room was blurring around him and somehow he was prone on the sofa. His body didn't like this confessional process. Dredging up fragments of memories of fragments of memories, scraping away his bleached-out montages of last time left him raw. He was eroded at his core. The scrolling lines of code that had illuminated his recall were fading into a jumble of characters. His photographic memory was dissolving fast…He was useless. Lombard was going to kill him.

Perhaps on a subliminal cue, Lombard strolled over to an elaborately lacquered cabinet adorned with dragons, pulled open a little drawer and produced a small pearl-handled pistol. He stroked the barrel reflectively, and then placed it in Emily's hand, enfolding her fingers around the butt, while pushing her index finger through the trigger guard. He pointed the hand gun in William's direction, holding Emily's bare arms firmly, as if giving a beginner's lesson in self-defence for ladies.

'I did warn you, Dr. Crowe, you old shit-hoarding buzzard. I told you Emily wouldn't be nice to you if you didn't deliver the goods, surrender the good shit, and tell me exactly how you invented the gimmick for immortality and world domination. We still don't know how to get into the BRAN tub and scoff the goodies. So she has to be nasty now. Topless but nasty. Nasty but tasty. That presumably is what you craved all along. A nice girl, like that poor sad Elaine, going nasty. That mystic masochistic marriage you muddled into. A radioactive puddle of nastiness. What a mess. And now you can't even hack your self properly. The mess is the message…not good enough, old man…'

He squeezed Emily's breast with his left hand and her trigger finger with his right. The gun spat a tiny flame, the shot echoed in the high-ceilinged space and William could smell burning. Emily gasped and jerked with the recoil and William wondered, abstractly, if she had somehow shot herself, perhaps in the foot, it was what people did… But the canvas on the wall behind him was neatly punctured.

'Just a test firing - you know, like an old Trident,' yelled Lombard. 'Never mind, Emily will soon get the hang of it.'

She squirmed in his grip. He grunted angrily, twisted her arm to aim at William and gripped her hand. The gun fired again and again. William felt his thigh burning and a sudden wetness.

'Nothing like blood-sports,' muttered Lombard, 'even if your hunter can't shoot for shit…' Another slug whined past William's earlobe. He started crawling across the prayer-rugs, trailing blood into the antique weave, absurdly guilty for making such a mess, a fuss. He was such a bubbly pot of guts. But the agony was excruciating.

Lombard chortled. 'What a melodrama, Dr. Crowe! A trail of scarlet clues all across my sanctum. You smeary old cock-roach.' As he clicked the chamber of the pistol and took aim again, Emily slid out of his grip and tried to roll away, but he fell on her, tearing at her slacks.

'Do we ride, Lady Emily, do we ride? That's the imperative, isn't it? Nothing like a spillage of blood to heat up the hormones.' He enfolded the girl like a fat stuffed puppet sprawled across a doll, ready to mount her - then pushed her aside. 'Later, perhaps. Not in front of the servants. Because that's what you are, Doc. My servitor. Despite your partial amnesia and failure to meet targets. Fortunately I've never bought into your trans-humanist malarky. More mess and fuss, eh? Fluids all over the place. But I have a vacancy for someone who can fully restore BRAN and put it to new uses. Like restoring an old steam engine for the Great Western line, very picturesque. You can call me a hobbyist. But I do adore the aura of the old technology, the blink of the lights, hum of the cabinets, that hot metal smell. You like it too, don't you, feeling the power, even better than feeling the power of Emily's fabulated tits, just the flow of power across the void, that's the thriller. I've acquired power in all sorts of ways, in take-overs, make-overs, buying out towers of power. Now I'm taking an interest in alternative power sources. OK? Right, I've made my point, we'll fix your leg - and put you to work in Leynebridge.'

Porters were summoned to lift William on to a stretcher and take him down a long corridor. He recognised the security guard from the Pleasure Centres gatehouse. 'Not to worry, sir, the Clinic will sort you out. The Boss just likes a bit of real old-fashioned fun, know what I mean...' Twisting his head on the trolley, he could glimpse Emily, blank-faced and dishevelled, being led away briskly by an exasperated Rinehart.

Intervoid

Lucas was out-of-the-body. Or so he believed. Perhaps he was an anti-body in the vessels of the Omniverse. Or the polyps of the Polyverse. Or the inscape of the Intervoid... The current 'reality' was a series of sliding overlays, semi-translucent, over and above consensual space-time, even more fragmented than those alt.world matrices where he and his father had first blundered into the Qliphoth.

His initial POV hovered uncertainly over Leynebridge. He could see, at intervals, the weathered lintel of the Book Market, broken tiles on the roof of the Red Hag, a miniature Aran Yarland leading a posse of men with staffs up High Town towards Leyston Burrough, the tiny figures of Trader Price and Gavin Wharton running through their elaborately choreographed daily routines of opening their shops and displaying their wares. He felt a strange flow of empathy towards this odd little commune, even when his focus shifted to the Clock Tower, where Noah Dodd was supervising Forgan on a crooked ladder as they dismantled the Leynebridge Community Radio mast, the trace of its wave-forms fading fast, so he had to let it dissolve...

...into a mash of memory still playing itself out through him: *a house that became a huge van and his mother explaining the dream away; some old lady coiled up in rubber hoses on a musty bed; his bicycle overturned scraped crimson paint wheel spinning; walking around the sundial in the tiny front garden desperate with fear having lost something very important finished lost gone; a long band of purplish cloud half-hiding a sunset he couldn't forget...*

But the flashbacks burnt themselves out temporarily and the Leynebridge vista below wiped itself in and out, slowly unpeeling to reveal a new locale, an alien geometry of huge interlocking planes and interpenetrating vortices at impossible sickening angles, a geometry that was going to torque and twist him into infinity because it was bent all wrong and made up of a seething mass of tiny particles of being and not-being, all flashing and chattering away, forming and reforming briefly as ants or skittering sprites across the spectra, going busy busy busy and in the warp of all the cones *two identical grey faces rose and fell rose and fell moving graphite-coloured lips* breaking up into a seething mass of tiny particles of being and not-being, all flashing and chattering away, forming and reforming briefly as ants or skittering sprites in the machine of ghosts singing *now yer see'em now yer don't* in the machine of ghosts an alien geometry of huge interlocking planes and interpenetrating vortices at impossible sickening angles, a geometry that was going to torque and twist him into infinity, with dotted lines...

He was losing outline. His astralised transparency left him defenceless because it was going to be stretched into these n-dimensions, those anti-entities would morph him into their machinations, he was already going in and out like a time-worm in the fabrications of being, he would be woven into the Intervoid, the only term he could recognise because words were failing in the panic rooms of Earth.

Book Man

Huddled in his long coat Gavin Wharton trudged through drizzle, around the Serpent Path to Leyston Burrough. He tried to shut out the uneasy murmur of the village Undermind and concentrate. There had to be a way, maybe not the Way of Leynebridge but a new way, of stalling the Pleasure Centres development at the Burrough without violent confrontation and destruction of the ancient site. He had a foreshadowing, at the wispy edge of his vision. Noah and Aran would lead their posse of local warlocks with blazing torches to march around the base of the mound, declaiming the usual binding spells. Then some hot-head, probably Aran, would lead a rush up the slope, equipped only with staffs or clubs, to be met by Lombard's security men, armed with some deadly gimmick. He had a brief sickening pre-cog of old Noah, head half shot away, sliding face down in blood and mire. The massacre could be re-scripted as a little local misunderstanding on the margins of the urbanised world. That Pullman creature would put a sleek gloss on it, mouthing away on a screen somewhere.

A more oblique approach was needed. Lombard's purchase of those arcane books implied that he acknowledged, at some level, the reality of the presences and powers in the Burrough, even though his conscious intent was to sanitise them out of existence with his tourist trappings. Maybe Lombard could be turned, or the powers of the Burrough itself could be turned against him…

There was only one person in Leynebridge who had mastered real spellcraft, and he was erratic, often faked his phenomena, and was distrusted by many of the Elderseers as a dangerous exhibitionist. He disregarded many of their rote observances and rites, yet his murky charisma attracted fanatical followers. If Forgan the Hallow Fool could live up to his drunken rhetoric, he was the man who might stop Lombard.

He found the Arch-Fool in the doorway of a semi-derelict tithe-barn, his ramshackle HQ near the foot of the Burrough. He had begun supervising the elaborate preparations for the Feast of Smoke, now only weeks away. As Wharton approached, Forgan was showing one of his young acolytes how to fill a cardboard rocket with a sulfurous mixture of black powder and some thick treacly substance. The lad's hand was shaking as he fumbled with the funnel and Forgan was losing patience. 'You must be decisive, infuse it with your own fiery spirit. You should be elemental, a salamander, a young dragon!' He turned to Wharton. 'The boy's read the books but he can't cook the book. What do you say to that, Book-Man?'

'Hail to you, mighty Forgan.' Forgan liked to be addressed with ritual archaisms. 'We need to talk.'

'Dangerous talk costs lives,' muttered Forgan. 'I know why you've come.'

'I'm told you made a fine speech in the Red Hag. About resisting Lombard.'

'I was always one for the speech-craft. But spell-craft is hard graft…' He took a gulp from a hip flask. 'These workings are dangerous, I warn you. Do you really want it?'

'Leynebridge needs it. To survive.'

'Maybe. But will they pay the price?'

' I never thought you were mercenary, Forgan.'

'I'm not talking money here, Master Wharton. Don't be stupid. You know there's a charge for every discharge…'

'You're the best we've got, Forgan. The only one with real deep cunning. You must help.'

Forgan shrugged. 'Maybe… Let's take a walk. Get into the vibe.' He led Wharton through the huge barn. The air was heavy with weed-smoke. Half a dozen craftswomen - Forgan's women - laboured at rickety benches fashioning animal masks and painting lurid banners of the sun, moon and planets. They sang softly in reedy voices. At the far end, Wharton was surprised to see that veteran silversmith Gil Norwood had been co-opted by Forgan. He'd set up a small workshop and was beating out an intricate pattern on a large goblet. 'For the moon's blood,' explained Forgan as they passed the artist, a wiry bearded figure totally focused in the act of precision hammering. 'I chose him because he has so much bloody essence. He becomes the tool.'

They went outside. It was now raining heavily but two carpenters continued to hammer on the spokes of a large hollow wooden wheel, about twelve feet in diameter. Wharton stopped and studied it carefully. The internal geometry of the wheel, around its circular hub, which formed a kind of cage, bewildered him with its complexity, as if its arcs and subtending angles somehow doubled back on each other. But it had to be an optical illusion. 'The Great Wheel of Time, ' said Forgan proudly. 'Built to the traditional designs of the Elderseers.' Wharton wanted to say the tradition of the Elderseers was a constantly self-modifying narrative, an improvisation from the collective village Undermind. But he dared not disrupt Forgan's potent self-belief. It was the antithesis of Pleasure Centres electrical gimmickry, this primitive mimetic technology of wood, animal hides, recycled scrap metal, gunpowder and garish paint. Yet even in grey daylight, these grotesque forms triggered deep resonances...

Forgan grabbed his elbow and pointed to a huge mass of foliage on the sloping field behind them. Heads bobbed up and down in the wet leafage. 'Look at that great Tree-Monster they're making. It will go crawling all over Leynebridge... The energies will be rising that night. No health and safety for Lombard and his zombies... We've got to raise the charge... focus the forces...'

'But why all the side-shows? Why do the male Elders have to gather round a clay head and walk the Serpent Path? Why are we shopkeepers still forced to pay a tithe to the Hoochie-Coochie Women? Why does Noah stand on the bridge at every dawn and dusk, pointing his divining rod to the West?'

'You worry too much, Book-Man...'

'What are you actually going to do, Forgan? Trader Price has sold us out, he's sold the townspeople's heritage and they're too myopic to see it, they're just filling up their bed and breakfasts with thugs in uniforms, who are installing Lombard's contraptions as we speak. Who knows what they're planning up there at the Burrough? After all you and Noah have said, are you really going to let them travesty our way of life?'

'But you filled your ledgers, didn't you, Book-Man? Sold wise words to the zombie minders, didn't you just? I can feel the inwit biting you, right now...'

'We traders have to live, Forgan. Those books will mean little to Lombard. He only wants to line his shelves with fine bindings. The nouveau riche covet their leather and gilt, I know these people.'

'Maybe you know them too well. Like Trader Price knows them.

Way up Lombard's cack-hole. Why should I share my secrets with you?' Forgan turned back into the barn, Wharton stumbling to keep up with him. The Arch-Fool strode towards a cauldron steaming over a rickety paraffin stove and gestured to the shapely blonde woman stirring it. 'Give the book-runner a share of our truth-broth, Willow. The herbs and roots will make him speak righteousness.' He laughed harshly. Wharton tried to wave away the proffered bowl, which was surely full of sickening 'psychedelphics' as Forgan would call them, but Willow's slow smile was already enthralling him and a spoonful of bitter mash was swilling down his throat. 'That's right, Willow, spoon-feed Book-Man Wharton. Down it goes - the soup of the gods! Then we can do business according to the Way...'

Already the rafters were starting to gently warp around Wharton and the sing-song murmur of the craftswomen was merging with the increasing roar of the rain. Forgan's voice reverberated around the rough walls. 'I told you there was a charge, Trader Wharton. So I'm charging you. To write the Great Book. The Great Book of Leynebridge. That's your contribution to the Feast.'

The Great Book of Leynebridge. Wharton recalled some flummery that Noah Dodd had instituted in the early years of the Lore. An expensive book would be sacrificed every year, by ritual burning in the Feast of Smoke, to ensure the continuing prosperity of the book-traders. One year he was asked to contribute and gave them an old bound volume of the *Illustrated London News*, but in the general mayhem of the Feast nobody seemed to notice and now everyone seemed to have forgotten about the rite...

'It's never been written. It's a -' He thought *bad joke* but the glare in Forgan's red eyes stopped him.

'You will write it. My familiars will be your guides. And you will read it, aloud, while we burn the Sun to light the Moon, and walk the Fire Maze to the Burrough World. You will write it into Being. I name you Scribe of the Crypt, Master of the Glyphs.'

He gestured to Willow, who presented Wharton with a large black book, opening it at a creamy white page. It felt very heavy. Someone was thrusting a pen in his hand. Forgan's voice droned through his skull.

'Write the Burning Book and write it well. The Horned God will be serving the Dark Women. We will be feasting with the Dead…'

Smoke Screen

'The shadow realms conceal everything you might have been. They are the smoke-screen emitted by your lost selves.' Carla's image flickered in front of him and Lucas couldn't stop falling into the frame beside her, tracking her down a side-passage under the glare of the fire-flower planted high in the pitted brick walls.

Her hair glimmered. It was silver and protected her from the flying lust-worms, so common in this zone. They flocked in response to sexual signals, maybe pheromones. With bony wings protruding from their bodies, they moaned or grunted, depending on their size. The alcoves in the brickwork filled with twitchy plant life. But the pillars were inlaid with gold paint. Her radioactive guilt filled the air.

Now they were walking beneath a web Carla had attached to her hair, which gave sanctuary from the clusters of worms that tumbled out of the air. Her words were garbled as if shouted through helium: 'Don't expect to extrapolate in this zone. The Time–structure is destabilised.' Then his whole wave-form collapsed and he was Voided once again.

Trauma

William was looked after, in a fashion. Sister Baraka, a plump middle-aged Anglo-Caribbean woman came to his cubicle and cleaned up his wound every morning. He guessed she'd grown up during the pre-Rupture Long Fall, probably in a hard-to-let in Hackney with lunatics pissing against her reinforced door every night. Working for Pleasure Centres must have conflicted with her beliefs but she probably needed the money and the on-site accommodation. The curl of her lip as she turned to the table to pick up fresh bandages indicated her disdain for his trade, as a disseminator of corrupting fantasies. But even he, an old fungus from the secular times, rotten with doubt and disease, could find protection. 'In the great silence, we are cleansed,' she muttered. 'We don't need no moving pictures.'

His strategy was repetition. Don't argue. Keep locked on to the faint ray of the past. 'I remember walking past the old Empress Ballroom... you could hear the big bands, there was proper music...' The memory was already breaking up like a pre-dawn dream clip.

Then the present broke in, his ongoing trauma. Even as he lay there, pain pulsing through his thigh, the Lobe - the seed-code of BRAN was slowly multiplying throughout the expanding and increasingly morphed global electronic environment, pursuing its mysterious imperative. And he had planted it.

9
The Anarchy Business

A Personal Target

Carla was no longer a person, according to the Pleasure Centres database. The power in her corporate apartment had been turned off within hours of her ejection from Lombard's party and when, after several days exhausted in bed, she left it to forage in the local market - still a painful zone with its memories of Omar - she returned to find a man changing the locks. 'More than my job's worth, dear,' he said, cheerfully, ' but you can nip inside to get a few things while I finish off. Mum's the word...' Numb with shock, she'd gathered some random clothes in a holdall, and, absurdly, her old Jouissance Production showreel, which she dropped as she staggered into the hallway. 'Jouissance, eh?' said the locksmith, picking it up for her. 'Classy, they were. Better than all the Lobe rubbish we get these days. I'm sure you'll find a part somewhere.'

Looking back through the doorway she could see a small photo-album on the coffee table - maybe that one precious pic of Omar was in there... she hesitated.

'I wouldn't hang about. Bailiff's on the way. Could be some unpleasantness...'

She walked, like a zombie. Later, sitting with her bags outside a boarded-up Tube station, she tried to call Mark Rinehart on her antique mini-phone. It was a desperate stratagem, given her uneasy relationship with the team but Mark might know of a sofa somewhere where she could consolidate the various fragments of herself. The legs of the crowd hurried past her as the mini-phone or whatever it was called cheeped monotonously in her ear. They said that in the Borderlands people could bug the thought-waves in each other's brains - no wonder they were all crazy - but all she wanted to hear was the sound of a human voice, even Mark's, even it was only going to reiterate the bad news of her de-personification. After a few minutes, the phone died, as they so often did.

Later that day she found herself in an underpass near the Pleasure Centres HQ. She must have wandered there in the vague hope of pleading at the gatehouse. Her shoes were waterlogged as she paddled through iridescent sludge. She had been displaced, she was certain of that, there had been this fall from grace and now she splashed in gutters like a child, underneath the arches. Her clothes were torn and she'd lost her bag. Her body ached all over and smelt odd. Had she been sexually assaulted? She was running out of explanations. Perhaps she had stumbled into a chronoclasm, so-called, a rare but acknowledged special effect of the Rupture. It was supposed to be related to stress. People talked about it at dinner parties, joking awkwardly about the effect of a chronoclasm on one's private life, the openings and closures it offered, the alibis you could concoct for a chronoclastic affair. She recollected chatter over white wine in a basement flat with a jukebox - or was it a joke-box? But she couldn't recall the contours of the talking heads. A chronoclasm was... A chronoclasm was when you briefly slipped sideways into another life-stream.

She spent the first night in a Heavy Shepherd women's hostel, a fortified church-conversion in Westminster. The pews had been replaced by racks of bunk-beds rising precariously in the nave and the blasphemous old stained-glass windows had been concealed behind huge pastel murals of Adam and Eve tending their dinosaurs. The heretic saints were hidden by full length banners - RAPTURE NOT RUPTURE/GOD DOES THE BIGGEST BUSINESS/JESUS - YOUR FINAL SOLUTION!

She queued meekly for her soup and sat with the other mute refugees around a long table in the vestry as Christine, the Shepherd-Mother, a large overbearing woman in her fifties, read a passage from Leviticus about not suffering a witch to live. Carla dimly wondered if her own previous existence had not been a kind of witchcraft. Witchcraft or bitch-craft? Perhaps the routines of this sanctuary would protect her from her wicked horny self. The simple sedative truth had been written up neatly in a book and she was blessed to receive it. She was so tired.

'Now we will spread the Word, won't we?' proclaimed the Shepherd Mother, herding them down to the crypt. The previous dinner shift was already at the far end, unloading and sorting books from huge wooden crates. Carla's group was directed to a bench at a long wooden table covered with sheets of cardboard, pens, address labels and rolls of parcel tape. Their fellow-workers, at a signal from Mother Christine, began sliding piles of books down the tabletop. 'Jesus Christ has set you each a personal target,' said the Shepherd Mother. 'Three hundred Plain Folks Bibles packed and dispatched by midnight. Our Brothers and Sisters across the great water have been generous, they keep shipping the Good Book despite Satan's disruptions and distractions. It is your duty to help distribute them to our godless cities and witch-infested edge-lands.'

After the eleventh unshapely box, Carla was struggling. She fumbled with the thick pen writing an address label and had to cross out a line. Christine was suddenly looming over her shoulder. 'I've been observing you. You're barely satisfactory. And Jesus expects you to be outstanding. It's very disappointing, after all the food we've given you.'

As she moved off, Carla felt suddenly energised, for the first time since her debacle with Lombard. A surge of raw adrenalin shattered her passivity. That patronising nanny-goat. These monomaniac god-addicts, the Shepherds, the Wahibos, all as bad as each other. Their webs of rhetoric and delusion had entangled poor gorgeous Omar, who only wanted to please her with his strong young body. Whatever the risk out there on the streets, she couldn't stay there, hideously compromised.

Christine was on her rounds again, so she had to keep busy. She wrote and glued a new address label: 'For the Attention of Trader Price, The General Store, High Town, Leynebridge.' The site of Lombard's grand design. Perhaps she should face her beast in his new lair.

The Anarchy Business

'My project is stability now,' insisted Lombard, ' the restoration of cosmic order. I am ordering reality for the better, OK. Any objections?' He glared around the Conference Room, the centre of all Pleasure Centres. He'd enthroned himself at a horseshoe table of plexiglass, where Dominic Pullman, Mark Rinehart and William clutched their agendas and waited. The seating plan had positioned William at Lombard's right hand. Pullman and Rinehart, further around the circumference, had hardly grunted at him, had made no comment on his crutch, and clearly resented his new restored status in the PC pantheon. 'Stabilisation will be good for business, good for the economy, and good for Pleasure Centres. Which is a king-size bonus for my little guys, right? Now don't get me wrong. The Rupture was hot fun, opened a lot of windows for us. All that lovely chaos and the fuck-ups with causality have made our virtual realities easier to implement, easier to market, despite the odd technical difficulty. Of course, I've never had a problem with anarchy. Anarchy was cool in the old monarchy, I ought to know, I used to manage the Close-Fitting Girls, old William's favourite band, I was in the anarchy business right from the inception. But things have been getting a bit out of hand, yes? If we're going to compete with the Pacific Rim and the Caliphate, we've got to get all our pots of holy shit together and generally get our local reality-matrix organised. Now some people with long addled memories might think Keith Lombard is another Joe Kraskolkyn, trying to make a fast buck out of a few shagged-out alternative universes. Not so. Fact is, I'm going to clear up the whole bloody mess of mass and energy that he dragged our arses into, that let all the madness out. There's going to be a collective agreement to respect the consensus reality. No more pious bullshit from the Heavy Shepherds or the wailing Wahibos. And if it means some fuss and bother with our witchy friends in the Borderlands, so be it...'

He glared around the room and spun his gold fountain pen on the tabletop. It came to rest pointing at Pullman. 'How are we doing in Leynebridge, Dominic? You have good news, I hope...'

Pullman produced a folder and began to extract documents, ground-plans, artist's impressions - but Lombard waved it away. 'I just want your word as a scholar and a gentleman. No fucking about. What's going down at Leyston Burrough?'

'We've cleared the main chamber. We're ready to install a Lobe connection and the standard interface installation - sensitively modelled, of course, with replica stone fascias - '

'I don't care any more about the old-school decor. Have you set up the servers from Berkshire? The BRAN-boxes?'

'BRAN?' Pullman bit his lip. 'My team were never told about anything about Berkshire...'

Lombard snorted derisively. 'No initiative! No sense of discovery! Tell them about your clever invention, William. It's all right, old man. All the secrets are unofficial now. Tell them all you know...'

Quantum Slut

Vivienne was exhausted from the incessant rehearsals and the constant retraining, as Rinehart and his team instilled (or installed?) her new sense of identity. Their taped voices wheedled all night through the grills over her bed. 'Please remember, at all times, you are no longer Vivienne Crowe. Vivienne was an archaism, a defunct life form from a doomed over-fabulated environment. Her bag of tricks is empty. Vivienne is void. Now who are you? Just who are you? Tell us your real name... your little secret name...'

'I am Quantum Slut,' she murmured, yawning. 'I am Quantum Slut...'

'Who chose you, Quantum Slut? Who chose you?'

'The Brothers chose me. The Brothers chose me...' And so it went on, night after night.

They seemed to think she was going to be the epicentre of something big, something more than simulating sex in a bad leotard, so they were driving her through a total remix/remodel, as Rinehart called it, hovering at her side every morning in a heavily guarded studio, positioning her in front of the floor-length mirrors as he pulled out some new outre garment to experiment with her image or summoned another nervous stylist to transmute her body.

Today her hair was darkened, coiled under a glossy black skullcap with a plume protruding while her breasts were harnessed tight in a web of silvery neoprene that flaunted her nipples. Her nails were enamelled crimson. The muddy skirts and sandals of a Leynebridge earth-fairy had been replaced by black fishnets and spiky heels. The transformations hurt, sometimes physically, as when the black star was tattooed on her inner thigh, but also mentally. She couldn't recognise this sinister sylph in the looking glass. Memory-fragments were drifting away - that man who'd once taken her in a ruined garden, gentle and heavy as a horse, why had she fled from him, and - frighteningly - what was his name? It was a strong sort of name and he would have made silver things for her, maybe a sword to rescue her but he was part of an old story now. Lights flashed around her and the floor was soon covered with photo-fits, innumerable icons of her selves. Rinehart was on his knees sifting through them, laying them out in different spreads as she'd once fanned out tiny bright pictures of wands and cups and falling towers - what was that all about...?

'This has to be it." Rinehart held up a photo to the light. 'That fey expression of not being quite there, between being and not-being. The twist of the thigh. The implied spin in the angle of the torso. And the pale flesh zones. That must be what Lombard wants…'

'We never know what Lombard wants. He just gave us the name Quantum Slut and we improvised with the materials at hand.' Pullman sighed. He put a purple silk cloak around Viv's shoulders and stepped back to gauge the effect. 'Have you enjoyed our sessions? No? Never mind. The leap into enlightenment will come. The Learning may be slow but you will learn all the songs...'

Later that day they began the Learning. A sound crew arrived with a mixer, monitor speakers, microphones and a pre-Rupture tape recorder. As they set up a lean-faced man with a wolfish grin and tinted glasses gripped Viv's hand. 'I'm Jack Cusimano, baby. I produce, OK? We have the rhythm tracks already, feed them over the headphones, all you do is the song-and-dance, know what I mean? May take a while, you can never trust a computer these days, so we're back with the open-reeler...'

Vivienne struggled with the headphones and the gleaming skull-shaped microphone. 'Don't touch it, whatever you do. Just perform... begin in your own time...' After a brief pause punctuated by random noise she could hear a deep throb pulsing through her head, mutating into a shattering drum pattern.

And suddenly the words came. A rant from the aching skull, the raw throat, the meaty heart, the solar plexus, the vagina. She now knew what to do. This was a new dangerous freedom. She was becoming Quantum Slut.

Mission

Carla was travelling to Leynebridge in a Heavy Shepherds Mission Convoy, a road train of trucks and trailers packed with bibles, devotional literature and eager proselytisers. It had been all too easy to convince the Shepherd Mother that she was ripe for conversion and would be happy to join the Mission. Surely it would be easy to disappear when they arrived in the Borderlands.

But right now she was hemmed in between two huge middle-aged American women, Martha and Maxine, who squeezed her arms and elbows for emphasis as they regaled her with miracles. Jesus had found a real old-style black taxi for them in Trafalgar Square when they were surrounded by screaming heathen rioters. The Lord had aided them with dog-training and fixing a faulty tap. So they ate to celebrate His bounty; for their girth was His affirmation. 'We're His fatted milch-cows,' yelled Martha cheerfully over the throb of the diesel, 'for He herds us into righteousness...' As the truck lurched around an overgrown roundabout towards the A40, Maxine raised her hand from the steering wheel in affirmation. 'We serve a mighty God!'

Their incessant jollity was almost hypnotic and gave Carla a spurious sense of security. It would be so easy to surrender to the blandishments of faith, to take the chocolate cake that Martha was waving under her nose, to live a simple life somewhere washing dishes or packing Bibles. All those ghostly erotic contortions that she'd concocted, plus poor Omar whom she couldn't bear to think about, plus the vicious office politics of Pleasure Centres, culminating in her expulsion from Lombard's party and the erasure of her corporate identity must have burned her out. She was so tired. She tried to work out how these transatlantic sisters had found their way to the Ruptured Islands of Britain but she couldn't quite get her head around it. Ever since the Rupture America had become a remote dream-land, perhaps with even wilder eruptions of its own, while the fragmenting Kingdom had become effectively quarantined - a terra incognita for exploitation by reckless entrepreneurs from Seoul or Jeddah. Time flowed past her, but she couldn't get a grip on it. She dozed fitfully, jogged awake every time Maxine crashed the gearbox or praised the Lord.

They stopped at a service station on the far side of Gloucester. It was flying the flag of the Shepherd so it had to be safe, even if the price of diesel had risen by another fifteen per cent this week. As Carla queued in the downpour for the toilet, she could hear the clatter of Martha's tambourine as she led fellow missionaries in a spontaneous praise-break. The garage owner's skinny kids ran in and out between the trucks, pretending to shoot Wahibos with their wooden guns.

The Transit van in front was already in difficulties, with its hood raised, and two young Shepherds were praying over a rusty engine. 'Satan always targets the alternator,' said one, tugging at a cable, 'and the further you go towards heathen territory, the more his demons will attack the electrics.' Shivering, Carla recalled Mark Rinehart telling a story around the Pleasure Centres workstations, an urban myth so she thought, about the time he was stranded on a B-road in Lancashire, near Pendle, a glowing red sphere darting around his inert car as he fumbled with the starter. Suppose all the random anomalies and malignancies released by the Rupture had their source in a singular personalised Entity, a great Satan. The reality of Satan might be the ultimate proof of God's old narrative of sin and eternal punishment. She would be punished for poor Omar, she would share his Hell.

Maxine was enfolding her in a blanket. 'You look sick, Sister Carla. You're shaking all over. Like the leaves on a little old tree. Have some of this.' She handed over a flask of cocoa. Carla drank, on auto pilot. They were going to be stuck in eternal limbo. Then the defective Ford Transit in front shuddered into life at last and the convoy moved off into the dusk.

Later Carla noticed they'd left the A-roads and were crawling along twisty lanes through darkened villages. She asked Maxine why they were taking this route. 'They say witches have taken over the main road between Gloucester and Ledbury. They grab any children from your car and slit their throats right there at the checkpoint. As a sacrifice. The Shepherd Mother warned us. So we're taking the long way round. But it's safer.'

Carla gazed blankly at the outlines of trees and the dim contours of the hills. The repetition of darkening fields and hedges blurred into a dull continuum. She was adrift in a long night, almost asleep...

Then they braked abruptly and the seat belt tore into her shoulder. The truck was sliding towards the ditch – for right ahead of them, a giant ball of flame engulfed the Transit, its panels suddenly burst apart, screams mingling with the roaring fire that followed the explosion. 'Devices in the road,' cried Maxine, struggling with the wheel, ' they're using bombs, not just spells...'

As their truck toppled into the ditch and skewed sideways, the engine stalled. 'Get out, Carla, quick...' The door on Carla's side was warped, it wouldn't shift, and Martha was half-conscious, moaning. Maxine levered open the driver's door and stepped up to the road.

They were in cutting, high slopes on each side. Carla could see Maxine's big shape outlined in the glare of flame and headlights. There was a repeated pattern of noise. A small red hole appeared in Maxine's forehead and she fell heavily.

Two Shepherds climbed out of the vehicle behind, to be caught in another spatter of gunfire. Something exploded further down the convoy, showering Carla with dirt as she groped her way out and scurried round towards the ditch, trying to blank out screams and fumes from the blazing Transit.

All down the line, hooded figures were levering open doors on vans and trailers, hauling out crates of Bibles to hurl them on to the tarmac before dowsing them with petrol and torching them. They were urged on by a tall bearded man who strode up and down, aiming his machine pistol at random through windscreens. After a few shots a Shepherd wielding a broad sword lunged from behind his tractor towards two Mo-Boys - they had to be Mo-Boys, not witches - and sliced off the hand of the nearest attacker, before the commander's bullets perforated his chest. The wounded guerilla knelt in the road, yelling incoherently, groping for his bleeding hand, illuminated by firelight amid the charred books and spent cartridge cases.

Another Shepherd staggered out of his truck with a massive pack of cylinders strapped to his back, surely an easy target. Then Carla saw the hose coiled round his body and the long nozzle in his hand. As a twenty-foot jet of blazing napalm sprayed the guerillas, Carla buried her face in the damp earth and covered her ears for some long seconds. Then she looked up. The flame-thrower must also have caught one of the trailers, which was emitting clouds of acrid smoke, covering the whole road.

Instinctively she scrambled up the grassy bank, scrabbling at the soil like a desperate animal. She pushed through bushes, ignoring the brambles scarring her wrists, to find herself in a ploughed field. Somebody had managed to abandon a wrecked caravan up here. Perhaps this was a popular ambush site. She crouched below the cracked window and tried to control her shakes. She'd wet herself. Such childishness.

Fires raged along the whole length of the convoy. She wondered what had happened to Martha. On the ridge above the opposite bank, more guerillas were arriving in a pick-up truck, converted to carry a rocket launcher. A large banner flew over the cab. In the sudden glare of an exploding mobile home, she could distinguish crude lettering -

HOLY MARTYR - and beneath an image of a young man's face - OMAR MAJID.

10
Time to Seize the Time

Wrong Locale

Lucas was in the wrong locale. The dreamscape was all jellied and viscous. He was way out of the wrong body and still couldn't find the right one. He felt smeared across the entire curvature of the horizon, like an insect on a windscreen, while the internal monologue that had kept him coagulated around some kind of pinkish nucleus was more and more difficult to keep up because he was still - inexplicably - in range of the collective hiss and grumble of the earth-creatures down below in their pits slithering through their serpentine routines. He was dangerously close to a merger with one of the innumerable world-souls that kept cluttering up the space/time matrices, because he was running out of his outline...

A great lump rose 'below' him, a mound surrounded by a congregation of insectoid beings. They scurried about on their business. Their lights flared and died in the night. Unfortunately he'd left his brain behind - that wet nuttiness of nothing - and he was becoming more tenuous every second. Where was it all going to end, except as a mess of particles...?

He was random in the doomscape. He was out of control. He needed to make contact. He zoomed - or was zoomed - into a dingy smoke-filled room, barricaded with bookshelves, tomes all over the shop, a bearded man in absurd detail, even down to the corduroy jacket, hunched over a desk, pen poised in mid-air...

Scribe of the Great Book

Wharton wrote. He calligraphed in an elaborate italic hand, using red ink. Forgan's interpretation of the Lore forbade him from using his familiar typewriter. And he dared not cross out or blot a word. Once press-ganged as a Scribe of the Great Book of Leynebridge he was compelled to follow a fixed rubric. Any glitch in the transcription would disrupt the spell craft.

So he'd arranged his desk - or altar - facing North, in the direction of Leyston Burrough. The calf-bound volume of hand-made paper was angled on a desk-top lectern, adjusted to the elevation of Mercury, insofar as he could chart it. He'd set out the obligatory candles and incense sticks, which were already filling the space with a cloudy web of smoke trails. The scribing could not be postponed. He fought a tremor in his right hand, breathed deeply and wrote:

Old gods lurking in deep time
rise up beneath the Pleasure Zones
to split the atomic breeders

A high metallic voice was resonating through his inner ear, like tinnitus, over and above the normal low-frequency mumble of the local Undermind. It was urgent, desperate, as if talking itself into existence - yet also intimate and oddly familiar, a cadence he almost recognised. He dare not stop the transcription now.

Old gods lurking in deep time
rise up beneath the Pleasure Zones
rampant in vengeance...

Alien Territory

William avoided looking out of the car window. He'd spent the long journey to Leynebridge in the back seat of one of Lombard's smoked-glass armoured limos, trying to familiarise himself with a document he'd written so long ago – a rough draft of his programme for the entire BRAN operation. But he was losing it now, lost in the mazes of his own coding. A recurrent fear nagged away - that age-related decay of synapses and neurons had locked him out of his own labyrinth.

'Where are we?' He pressed his mouth close to the intercom and raised his voice. The bull-necked driver had ignored his earlier enquiries about the safest route.

'In the Borderlands now, Dr Crowe. Can't you feel it?' The chauffeur seemed surprised at his passenger's inadequacy. 'Time to put on my protective gear.' With one hand on the wheel he picked up a hemispherical red helmet blazoned with the Pleasure Centres logo and pulled it over his bald cranium. 'A Lombard knob-head, that's what we call it. Supposed to cut out them chattering in your brain. Drive you mental otherwise…' He adjusted a knob at the side of the headpiece. 'There, that's better. Swear I felt their disgusting banter…' The nagging voices of the rural Undermind. Surely this was an urban myth that Lombard perpetrated for his own purposes. And if the helmet did block allegedly telepathic leakage, it probably worked through a placebo effect.

'I confess I can't feel a thing.' Perhaps he could only sense his own exhaustion.

'I'm surprised you can't, you being an educated man…' The driver shrugged and swerved to avoid a hooded Harvester dragging his psychotronic detector across the centre of the road. 'Now I've got to concentrate. This is alien territory. I deserve double-time for this job...'

William forced himself to look out of the window down the crooked streets, those dingy terraces of stone cottages, alternating with sagging half-timber buildings. Somewhere in this neo-primitive world, Elaine might be still hiding, stirring the cauldron of her absurd resentments. He hoped they would go directly to the facility at Leyston Burrough and spend as little time in the village as possible. He couldn't face a confrontation. They turned a sharp corner, past a public house. The driver, muttering furiously, braked sharply to give way to an overloaded horse-drawn potato truck. William scanned a worn signboard. The Red Hag. Figures in cloaks lounged in the doorway, smoking long pipes. The same hippy frippery. He'd wound up there all those years ago with a drunken young fop, Sebastian Something-Hackett, in retreat from family politics, the numbing enigma of a dead daughter and that grizzling grand child.

Music Business

'Let's do it again...' Jack Cusimano was losing patience. Mark Rinehart was always outsourcing these implausible projects in his direction. The music business had never fully recovered from the technological glitchery of the Rupture, and now, with so many genres banned in the multi-cultures, it was hard to see what Pleasure Centres could gain from creating yet another doomed star. Especially this lit-chick with her hypno-rap and faked name. He could hear her breathing heavily over the talk-back, psyching herself up for the next rant. 'OK, babe, we're rolling...'

It's the hour of power

Time to seize the time
Fire the base of the towers
Take the system right down
They think they can mix us away behind our backs
So we can't hack back
Track us like dumb cookies while they relax
Keep us out of their loop, we're just alphabet soup
Their estates are failed states, but it's not too late
It's the hour of power...

Quantum Slut's latex-clad torso swung round and around the pole of the big Neuman mic as she reprised the whole verse, punching the air with a clenched fist. Joe didn't get the rhetoric and repetition, just didn't get it. The target audience seemed to be the very demographic that Pleasure Centres sought, but also sought to keep under control - urb-people, trashmen, neo-proles, depersonalised sub-managers - whoever aspired to dunk themselves in the cheapo virtualities of Dub Demons or Porno Madness. But the message was perverse. Even Jack, who'd done Semiotics 101 before he dropped out, could recognise a sub-text. Quantum Slut was exhorting them to attack the very infrastructure of the Lobe and by extension, the core of Pleasure Centres.

He turned down the control room volume for a moment and watched Quantum Slut's silent open-mouthed struts and gyrations through the glass. Then he brought the monitor up again and tweaked the reverb unit. If Lombard wanted the Slut's voice to fill some cavernous space, he was paid to make it happen. It would all come out in the mix.

11
The Psychic National Gridlock

Digital Charades

Leaning heavily on his new stick, William stood in the Burrough, in the chamber beside the Stone. He studied the crooked slabs of granite and slate that formed the walls and tried to calculate the balance of forces that prevented the whole structure from collapsing. The space seemed far bigger than he remembered from the plans. Lombard's engineers must have excavated deeper, then reinforced the walls and ceiling when they transported the BRAN hardware from the Establishment. The black cabinets of the huge servers, the wide cable conduits and the maze of overhead ventilation ducts obscured those crude carvings that people like Elaine had thought so significant. It was a stern purification, making it fit for their obscure purpose. Tom Liggett, still eager spokesperson, was hovering, drawing him aside before he could wander off into the dark aisles between the servers. William noted that he was wearing the same absurd protective headgear as the chauffeur.

'I hear you've had some traumatic experiences, Dr Crowe. Or should I say transformational? I hope you haven't developed a phobia about using Virtual Reality...although, of course, it has its satisfactions... as I'm sure you'll agree...' William grunted. He wondered how much Lombard had leaked to his flunkey, as a way of keeping William in his place, which seemed to be this place.

'I was under the impression I was here primarily to programme' Did Liggett know about BRAN and its history? Or did he have the advantage of knowing Lombard's future plans for the British

Reconstructive Application Network? Not that there was much left to reconstruct. An honest-to-goodness nuclear apocalypse, with clear reconstructive goals, would have been preferable to this post-modern mess of mangled causality.

Liggett smiled and touched his elbow. 'A directive from Dominic Pullman, William. You've been co-opted to test a new game.'

'Game?'

'Games are apparently an element in Mr Lombard's grand scheme of things. Like this new bug-free version of Iconoclasm. This isn't a proletarian shoot-to-kill like Dub Demons. This is not the usual fantasy role game where you act out predictable variations on the old tired roles – warrior, warlord, lover, trickster, princess – the usual archetypal strait-jackets that filtered down through last century's movies. It has been programmed in a virus-free environment inside a screened lab deep in the London Bunker. By Mark Rinehart himself.'

'Using my notes, I suppose... The proposal I made to Carla Leppard.' That awful fraught interview, pitched on a mere hunch.

'Ms Leppard? I believe she's left ... but we did retrieve some notes from your workstation. Quite helpful. Mark's revision is of course, from ground zero. Zero plus one, as it were.'

Liggett led William to a hemi-spherical cubicle at the centre of the chamber, next to the massive pillar that supported the roof. 'Of course, you never quite made it here. After your odd diversion to Berkshire. A bit whimsical, if you ask me. But Mr Lombard has chosen to overlook that. I'm sure he has his reasons...'

William suspected a double-bluff. Did Liggett have the whole picture? The manager pulled open a narrow hatch and gestured expansively, as if he was trying to sell a small but desirable property.

'This sensory deprivation pod totally encloses the operator on a pneumatic couch. As you can see, the hardware has been improved.' William peered into the confined space, as cramped and packed with electronics as an astronaut's cabin. Astronautics. His boyhood hot dream, grounded by the bloody Rupture. Now weirdly parodied in the depths of the Earth. He tried to concentrate as Liggett prattled away with manic jollity.

'The new software now allows an overview of the operating system, even from within the virtual environment, with overlapping windows of icons, and graphic representations of circuit architecture and information flow. Layered windows slotted into a corner of the visual field present programme code running in real time. There's also a virtual keyboard, a wireframe icon overlaid on the visual field, which allows you to access these windows and input commands and questions.'

'These are just cosmetic improvements.' William refused to be impressed. He was too old to fall for Liggett's PR games. 'They don't seem to alter the virtual experience itself.'

Liggett smiled. 'But this is where your ideas come into play, Dr. Crowe. Those data-mining talent agents and confidential agents will operate autonomously and automatically once the system has been booted up and connected to the rest of the Lobe. And they can be fed into your profile during the game-play. Feedback circuits within circuits. Perfect cybernetic synergy!' Liggett looked pleased with his new jargon.

'What's more you can operate simultaneously inside and outside the Iconoclasm package. On encountering some so-called 'digital poltergeist', you can check the status of the system and its configuration within the Lobe. In practice, of course, the flow of data in real-time will be so complex and fast that even a youthful human operator would find it impossible to keep up. However the output of Iconoclasm will be connected to a number of work stations so that members of the R&D group can monitor the situation and advise you through an audio-link in the suit.' Liggett paused; and leaned over to key in a code on a panel over the couch. A screen blinked - and died. Flustered, he tried again. Another dead screen.

'Beta testing incomplete, I see...' William wasn't surprised. Pleasure Centres always cut corners. That's why that boy died. Not his fault. He never even fiddled with their bloody Dog Demons. *Not guilty.*

'Just a temporary malfunction, I can assure you. You know how complex these packages are.' Liggett resorted to peering at some notes on his clipboard. 'In Iconoclasm you can play a variety of game scenarios - our "Playzones" - at different levels, interacting with virtual figures - "psychologically metamorphosising icons" or "Psychomorphs" designed to respond to different layers of the client's psyche. The player can adopt a number of ready-made roles - we call them "Shrouds" - or develop a Shroud around his/her own body-image. To enliven the interaction some levels of Iconoclasm have been factored into a randomising option, which can allow a limited element of unpredictability in certain parameters of the programme. The Playzone we'll be testing is called "Otherworld".'

'I don't recall this being an approved Pleasure Centres scenario...'

'It's based on some interesting old Celtic mythology that Mr Lombard has been investigating. Mark's had input, of course. You enter the Underworld of the Dead and have to outwit Arawn, the King of Darkness, Cerunnus the Horned God...'

'Do you seriously expect me to take part in these barbaric digital charades?' William couldn't believe this. Had Lombard, who was at least an honest pragmatist, been infested at last by the insidious irrationalism of the Borderlands?

'Stop worrying, William. My fatuous underling is confusing you. You'll have ample opportunity to see your masterpiece in action. In fact, we're all depending on you. But this little entertainment of mine also has its uses...' Lombard's voice boomed from the entrance, as his entourage - Pullman, Rinehard and Emily - swept in behind. Liggett shrank into his suit. Lombard seemed to fill the chamber with his vast bulk and granite face.

'Now you can all go and copulate somewhere else. Except William. He and I are going to have another of our little chats.'

Earth Angels

Carla was stuck in a deep-level dream. She was underground, sitting at a long polished oak table with a number of old men, all clones of each other - balding, bespectacled, bony-faced, in ill-fitting suits. They muttered and grimaced as they passed around a skull-cup, taking brief sips of pinkish fluid from it. A wrinkled hand slowly moved the skull towards her - and she awoke, half-frozen, to a grey dawn, the caw of circling crows, and a low electrical whine, like a vacuum cleaner.

At the far end of the field seven figures in black cowls were scanning the bumpy furrows with what looked like oversize metal detectors. The so-called Harvesters. Real live Harvesters. They really existed. Mark had mentioned them at R & D meetings as possible elements in some future VR narrative, but Pullman was sceptical and didn't share the vision so it was canned. Office politics. The only politics left, and even those seemed absurd now.

She crawled through the twisted frame of the caravan, keeping her head down, ready to run, then peeped through the broken window. Very carefully she raised her hands and stood up. Yet the Harvesters ignored her. They fanned their battered detectors across the broken earth, advancing slowly to the far side of the field and then turning, with military precision, to scan the next strip of soil. They could be seeking recent graves in a popular ambush spot, scavenging for remnants of the life-force or whatever they were supposed to do. And after last night's holocaust there would be bodies scattered on the road at the base of the embankment. Poor Martha's huge corpse would be lying there. She wasn't going back to check...

She waved, trying to make eye contact with the faces beneath the shadowy cowls. However, they continued their robotic progress, edging slowly towards her, apparently unaware of her existence. Then, a couple of metres from the caravan, three of the figures paused, assessing this unexpected obstacle. While their companions continued over the crest of the bank, down towards the carnage in the road, they remained stationary. Nevertheless they continued to sweep the ground back and forth, with a blind mechanical compulsion...

'Please - can you help me...'

The nearest figure stopped sweeping and pulled back his cowl. Carla recoiled and automatically looked away. The man's jaw and left cheek had fused into a bubbly mass of yellowish tissue. Skin cancer - or one of the rogue afflictions that were more common since the Rupture.

She had to overcome her revulsion and look him in the face. Only one eye was visible in the swollen flesh. A dilated black pupil surveyed her.

'There was an ambush. Last night...'

'As predicted. This site is on one of our regular routes.' The Harvester's voice was low, grating, mechanical.

'Routes - where do you go?'

'This alignment will take us back to Leynebridge.'

'You follow an alignment?'

'When we search for energy flares, whether from old dead or newly dead, we have to follow the prescribed nodes and alignments.' He sounded tired and impatient. His companions began moving again, edging around the caravan. She could hear their devices scraping monotonously at the soil.

'Where's this alignment - or node?'

'We're twelve kilometres from Leynebridge. But it will take us at least a day to work the alignment and then we have to discharge into the Generators at the House.'

'The House?'

'Our House of After-Life. About five kilometres from Leynebridge.'

'Can you sketch the route for me?' She found a pencil and crumpled notepad in her jacket - now her only possessions.

'You couldn't walk it alone. Especially when night falls. You've tasted the dangers.' He gestured in the direction of the embankment. 'You could track us. People leave us well alone. They might need us some day.' He laughed bitterly, cleared his throat and spat into the soil. Then he gestured to his comrades and they regrouped in a line, about a metre apart. 'The others may find some powerful discharges down there in the cutting. But they'll have to catch us up. We need to keep on the move. ' As they began to walk off, parallel to the embankment, detectors swishing through the long grass, he turned to Carla.

'The route to Leynebridge lies that way. Are you tracking us or not?'

Tracking the Harvesters was exhausting. The group moved slowly but their path followed an odd geometry, crossing or re-crossing some larger fields in a symmetrical grid before dragging onwards in a dead straight line for hundreds of metres through broken fences, clusters of trees or up steep slopes. Her fashionable city shoes began to split and she realised she had not eaten for over twenty four hours. She managed to scoop some water from a small stream but it was impossible to stop for any length of time as the cowled figures ahead of her moved on inexorably, regardless of the difficulty of the terrain.

Carla hunched her shoulders against the rising wind and shivered in her thin jacket. As she picked her way across ditches and along muddy tracks she scanned the skyline anxiously for trucks and banners. She felt naked and exposed on these wide rolling hills under cold grey skies, when trees clustered on the brow could harbour snipers or stalkers. From time to time she looked back. The other Harvesters were now visible, dark specks against the patchwork of fields and hedges, moving with the same slow deliberation as their fellows. She wondered if they had found what they were looking for in the bloodstains and burnt metal of the convoy.

The group in front of her had stopped next to a mound of turf at the edge of the next field. Their leader was manipulating his detector in spiralling motions over the freshly disturbed earth. He nodded. His accomplices gathered round and ritualistically interlocked the metal poles of their devices in a complex series of passes - like Morris dancers, thought Carla, suddenly remembering a shaky old breakfast TV clip.

She thought she could hear fragments of a chant on the bitterly cold breeze.

She came closer, but the leader waved her back, shouting. 'Not good for a city woman to see Harvesting up close.' She ignored the archaic prohibition - these Borderland people had really regressed socially - and strode through the stubble towards him. Another man ran towards her, raising the pole of his detector, like a stave, to block her path. 'Listen to him, city woman, just listen...'

The drone was getting louder. She could hardly distinguish it from their chant, an elongated vowel, a deep vibrated UUUUU, and the overlapping tones hit her in the pit of the stomach, and right down *there*, a throbbing in the genitals -

Suddenly the landscape solarised in a negative flash of black light. She clutched at her eyes. Then, parting her fingers, she glimpsed a bluish spiral of light hovering over the mound, in the triangle formed by the detectors. It vanished; and the world fell back in place again. She staggered, feeling a sudden rush of nausea.

When she recovered her balance she could hear the leader's flat tones. '... three newly-dead, and on a node. Plus all the Harvestings from the fight back there, on a main alignment. A fine yield. We have done good work today. March on...'

She kept her distance now. Whatever was enacted there had some intense significance for these men. If she was relying on their guidance she couldn't afford to break any more of their taboos. Hunger, stress and the trauma of the ambush must be triggering some kind of optical illusion. Her aching calves and ankles locked into a robotic rhythm as she trudged through the long afternoon.

Every so often the little team ahead of her would stop for a muttered conference around a potential burial site. She would kneel or squat on the ground, waiting for the disorientation, closing her eyes until the spasm of strange light was all gone. The Harvesters ignored her, as they resumed their steady pace.

From time to time she saw a few sheep wandering on a hillside or a wisp of smoke rising from the chimney of a grey stone cottage. Once the Harvester's 'alignment' even cut through a farmyard where a small ragged boy was feeding a horse. But as soon as he registered their presence, he screamed and ran into an outbuilding. Carla saw a notice over the door, daubed in childish scrawl, - *LAneBriggers Kepe OUT* - and wondered if the child was surviving in this small-holding by himself.

Later the track took them along a narrow lane. At a fork about a hundred metres away, Carla saw another plume of smoke and feared the worst. But a rusty steam traction engine lumbered out, dragging a trailer of potatoes as it turned off, presumably towards the next village. Somehow these Borderlands people were maintaining subsistence agriculture. 'Normal life', of a sort, went on. Perhaps she could find her way back to it.

They arrived at a small hamlet of half-timbered cottages centred around a crossroads; and stopped beside a weathered memorial. Carla watched, puzzled, from a distance as the hooded figures clustered round the stone cross and solemnly steered their appliances around its base. Surely they realised that the dead from these distant wars had long been buried elsewhere, in quiet churchyards, before the hysteria of the Heavy Shepherds and the fanaticism of the Mo-Boys and all the madness that had broken out of the depths of space-time - or so it was claimed. She tried to make sense of the leader's instructions: '...not much odic force left in the masonry now, lads. Think of all the emotions discharged around here over the last hundred years... It must be storing something for us...' But a few minutes later his acolytes shook their heads; and they all moved on.

At the edge of the hamlet they passed a derelict pub. Carla automatically noted the overturned picnic tables and broken windows. Some terminal brawl had been acted out in the riot of the early post-Rupture.

After a mile or so the group turned off the lane, up a muddy track across a field that sloped up to some dark coniferous woods. This path was imprinted with narrow tyre tracks.

She wondered if the leader had lost his bearings for they were now moving in a series of sweeping curves instead of the previous straight lines or angular grids. They passed through a gap in a high hedge and turned a corner up the steepening bank; and the path stopped. They faced a shack, wired together from old crates and corrugated plastic sheeting, half-embedded in the side of the hill, abutting on to a low weathered concrete structure. It didn't look like an Afterlife House.

The Harvesters paused and threw back their cowls. Several appeared to be victims of ritual or plague. Their scarred mouths were twitching while the steady rhythm of their scanning faltered, for the first time. 'This isn't a full death, Gideon,' whispered the youngest Harvester. 'Not even a half-death...'

'Don't be a fool, Joshua' retorted the leader. 'I've dowsed in the death-layer longer than you.'

'We should turn round,' whimpered the adolescent. 'We're losing the track, we're non aligned...' Gideon ignored him. Using the shaft of his detector, he levered open the door.

The interior of the shack was cluttered with filing cabinets and stacks of books and magazines, creating a narrow maze, in the middle of which the inhabitant had constructed a living space. A cracked melamine table with two plastic stacking chairs had been repaired with gaffer tape. A crooked shelf sagged under more heaps of magazines. Another shelf held an old wooden radio, a muddle of junk-shop memorabilia and a portable typewriter. In the corner a gas ring was connected to a butane cylinder and a plastic bowl overflowed with crusted dishes. Carla could smell a chemical toilet behind a flimsy partition. She tried to examine the shelves more closely but she couldn't push past the Harvesters who were still trying to wield their detectors around the constricted labyrinth of grubby carpet. She stumbled against one, recoiled from his musty robes - and dislodged a small round object from one of the shelves. It cracked open on the floor, spilling out tiny wheels and cogs.

She picked it up, turned it over, to see its warped tinplate dial, imprinted with the face of a smiling Chinese person brandishing a red book - and knew it all too well. That absurd Maoist alarm clock that Lucas had insisted on keeping, his memento of Paula, his dead mother. And he'd ended up, still hoarding it, in this hole.

She grabbed at the books on the shelves. A paperback flipped open. '...while the dreaded Azathoth represents the madly random and frequently destructive manifestation of chaos, the OBDAX represents the creative and complexifying stochastic manifestation of Chaos...' This was typical of what he was reading all the time, another spark for their increasingly furious arguments. He said it was one of the few books that made any sense of the Polyverse; and she'd lost patience with his compulsive re-enactment of his old Rupture trauma, hurling it across the room...

Gideon, the lead Harvester, was staring at her with his distended eye. 'What are you doing? You have no right to disturb this site.'

'I knew the man who lived here. These are his possessions. Where is he? What have you done with him?'

'Better to ask what he has done to himself. I know where to find him.' The Harvester pulled a torch from the pouch at his waist. Then he pointed towards a greyish geometrical pattern, like a circular mandala, inset in the far wall, half-obscured by a torn rainbow banner. He ripped aside the banner and tapped the mandala with his staff. It rang with a dull clang. Carla suddenly recognised it as a kind of hatchway into some inner cell and lunged towards it.

'You have no business here. You will not be able to help him.' The Harvester tried to wrestle her back. 'You don't want to go in there, city-woman. Really you don't.' Their combined weight forced the hatch to screech open. Despite a sudden powerful odour, which made her gag, she snatched the torch and forced herself through the opening.

Carla's eyes weren't adjusting properly. Maybe there was something wrong with her vision. In the flickering gloom, her torch first picked out an array of objects - a scattering of photos - that silly polaroid of her nude in the peaked hat that he obsessed about - and his crumpled sketches of those weird girls he was supposed to have known during the Rupture. A typical Lucas mess...

But she had to squint at the obscure shape that lay beyond on the bunk. Its outline shivered, its borderlines were out of focus, in a state of constant vibration, like a faulty hologram. She could sense an ultrasonic pulse, just beyond normal hearing. The smell was thickening, too, sweetish yet metallic. A tiny globule of bluish flame drifted over the dark mass and silently dissolved. Yet the image was stable enough for her to identify her old lover.

Lucas was shrouded in the remains of a sleeping bag that had somehow been shredded into a foamy cocoon, a semi-mummification entangling his greenish flesh, which waxed and waned with a faint radiance. Carla wanted to twist her head away and couldn't. She could surely see veins and nerves pulsing with a slow irregular luminescence; but she couldn't trust another perception - that his body was actually hovering an inch or more over the frame of the bunk, shimmering in ghostly levitation...

'It's dangerous for you to be here. Best leave him to us.'

'What does that mean?'

'He's in an abnormal state. His astral energies are fragmenting.'

'I'm not interested in your Borderland nonsense! What's happening to him? '

'His body-of-light is corrupted. It would be a kindness to finish him off.'

'I know his face, ' interjected Joshua. 'He was at the school. He tried to teach us.' The boy seemed oddly reassured by this.

'No surprise you're a fool, if you were taught by a zombie,' muttered Gideon. 'All the more reason to have him put down properly.'

'You leave him alone. I'm going to get a doctor. A real doctor.' Carla could no longer interpret events. Lucas had lost himself in some kind of trance. He was forcing her to hallucinate, dragging her into his own private danger zone. Someone else had to make sense of all this.

The Harvester shrugged. 'You live the life of the senses, city woman. Even the false senses.' He stared hard from under his bulbous cranium. Carla suddenly knew that he knew, intimately, her private convulsions and the convoluted pleasurings she'd overseen. 'In fact, I sense you're a Lobe-Mistress.' His companions clustered around and Joshua, the young nervous one, suddenly in-drawing breath, put out a hand to touch her thigh, until his leader slapped it away. 'A Lobe-Mistress under sensory overload. But when the truth of After-Life is right in front of your senses you don't trust them...'

He gestured at the prone body, this demi-corpse. Another tiny bubble of light danced briefly over the forehead and disappeared. An imploding star. Carla realised the eyes were wide-open, staring into infinity.

'He'll never regain consensual consciousness - just continue in the aetheric limbo he's created for himself until dehydration and malnutrition switch off his material body. An astral junkie. Too many of them in Leynebridge, I'll grant you that. You say you knew him?' He sounded sceptical. But she knew that he knew.

Carla knelt on the concrete beside the bunk. Overcoming a phobic reluctance, she reached for Lucas' hand. Her fingertips started tingling as she approached the faint corona of cloudy light pulsing around his wrist. The Harvester gripped her arm. 'Don't touch. He'll leech your orgone energy off you. They get parasitic, that's why you need to destroy them. A great fire is best.' He turned to his co-workers. 'Get the gas cylinder from next door. We should be able to rig up a fuse from something. And get her out of here.'

'Orgone energy?' Carla vaguely remembered a seminar from university psychology days, a survey of crank theories, before the whole world went cranky.

'A bioplasmic life-force created in the sexual act,' announced the leader, as if producing a definition he'd learned by heart. 'You urban folk probably don't believe in it. I don't know why. I expect you do a lot of swiving and venery, especially if you're a Lobe-Mistress.' He laughed harshly. 'Come on, out with you - and you lads bring me the butane, quick...'

But Joshua and his comrades in the outer shack were struggling to move the gas cylinder, wedged under a bench and entangled with hoses, so Gideon, grunting with impatience, was forced to leave Carla and join them- all farcically obstructing each other now in the confined space.

As they muttered and swore, she knelt again beside this alien being who'd once held her in his arms and penetrated her, on those first long nights after his mother's death, when he seemed desperate to lose himself in the depths of her body. Then their entanglement had released a furious energy, which peaked, again and again, in the exchange of wordless cries and hot fluid, an inter-change of power and mutual submission. An energy exchange. Or maybe her act of sexual compassion? She couldn't control her ambivalence then; and she couldn't control it now...

For all the responses, the bloody fucking feelings, that been cauterised by the trauma of her expulsion and the night terrors of the ambush were re-animating. She could be his anima, his soul-girl again. And maybe - it was horrible, weird, but irresistible- Lucas was still her animus, her animal of choice, that she could revive in a hot clinch. If she could bear to touch. The notion made her hot and giddy as the absurd men in the black hoods rolled the heavy cylinder into the inner room. Joshua, apprentice Harvester, gripped her shoulders while Gideon fumbled with wire and batteries. 'Pity you broke his alarm clock. We could have tried making a time-bomb and left you both to enjoy a last few minutes together. As it is - '

'Have you ever seen anything on the Lobe?' She pitched it in a soft voice, targeting Joshua in the first instance. His eyes flickered and he bit his lip, with a sharp intake of breath. The others stopped manhandling the cylinder and looked up to the head of the bunk where Lucas, her goddamned Lucas, lay like a fluorescing punk saint of holy porn. They averted their eyes from him; but they followed her.

'Of course they've never seen the accursed Lobe,' barked Gideon. 'It's banned in Leynebridge. It's against Lore.'

'For far too long!' Joshua seemed shocked by his own outburst. 'We need to know, Gideon. The Lobe can teach us secrets…'

'Don't be absurd. It's a web of delusion!'

'Have you ever seen a Lobe-Mistress? A naked Lobe-Mistress riding her Beast?'

A current was flowing through her now, a dark current that Lucas had aroused - the little snake. He was putting hot words into her mouth and she was pronouncing them softly, softly. Plastered in mud, she must be ridiculous, disheveled, so smelly - but she'd started talking dirty, like her old-tyme moving pictures. Joshua tightened his grasp on her shoulders.

'No more of your foolish lewd talk. Unless you want to burn with this wretch.' Gideon was snarling at his apprentices. He had pulled some small electrical component from a bag at his waist and was taping it to the cylinder. 'A brief spark in a room full of gas. That's all it takes.' He fiddled with red and black wires.

Carla, auto-cued by some inner demon, started laughing and couldn't stop. She couldn't even stop sliding out of her jacket, unbuttoning her blouse, slowly shaking her hips out of those frayed jeans, she didn't need them any more for what was about to happen -

'None of your Lobe-sex filth here!' Gideon, looking up, raised the shaft of his detector and made to beat her bared thighs and buttocks - but Joshua grabbed it and deflected the blow, throwing the Harvester leader off-balance. 'We're going out of your control, Gideon!' somebody shouted. 'Show us your dance for the Un-dead, Lobe-woman!' The leader was suddenly overwhelmed by flying fists, flapping cowls and a knockabout clash of metal poles, a clumsy micro-riot that could have given Carla a way out of the chamber, a way back from the grotesque spectral re-union that awaited her; but she couldn't move, the space and the quasi-gravitational pull of Lucas's floating body had entrapped her. She watched, giggling helplessly, as a blade flashed in Matthew's hand - to incise a line of blood across the crinkled tissues of Gideon's neck. He crumpled.

The farce was darkening, it was going with all the flow like the blood down his sleeves, as the Harvesters whooped with triumphant glee and tore off their robes. Joshua screamed ecstatically as he smashed the torch across Gideon's skull, engulfing them in gloom, lit only by the dim light from the circular hatch, and the intermittent radiance of Lucas' body. Carla felt eager hands trailing across her breasts, probing her thighs and calves, as if blind men were trying to identify the mystery creature that had landed so miraculously in their midst.

She tried to fracture those scrabbling fingers and slip out of their desperate grasp. But two of the older men had already used their bulk to force her to the floor and drag her away from Lucas. Bodies tumbled through blood and dust.

When she felt hard flesh nudging the cleft of her buttocks, she turned and managed to stab at the aggressor's eye socket with her long red city-girl finger-nails. As she struggled to straddle Lucas's thighs, the flicker of light that rippled along his body brightened, flaring up around his throat and heart, with sudden eruptions of violet light. The older Harvesters, panting like dogs, pulled back to the corners of the chamber and shielded their eyes. 'Don't look... his bio-plasm will poison you.' But Joshua and his cohort were still groping for her, their Lobe-phantom made flesh, and ran their hands through her hair and around her ribs as she reached for her ex-lover's erection and forced herself down on it.

He was all cold. Cold, hard, icy. She was riding a dead incubus, a deep-frozen star-beast. The shock electrified her and she cried out, frozen in a sudden recall of Omar's warm penetration, his innocent lust. The Harvester boys were still trying to have their way with her - one was maneuvering his stupid prick towards her mouth - but, overcome by a furious surge of energy, she clawed at his scrotum and sent him reeling. Now hysteria had overcome her as she glimpsed herself as a bit player in her absurd orgy movies - goblins ravishing the faery queen with grotesque special-effects genitals...

Lucas gazed up at her, blank-eyed, a catatonic voyeur. Yet he was stirring, his torso rising and falling to counterpoint the liquid rhythms of her thighs, her blood-pulse. This force became trans-human, impersonal, commanding them to fuck, stuck together in a slow enfolding of her void heat around his cold light. They were getting right down to it, earth angels copulating beneath the pleasure zones.

Time passed; and slowed, to a pause. The feral youths were peripheral, shrinking figures crouching at the edge of her vision, mesmerised into immobility by the blue glare of orgone as Lucas, moaning at last, melted into her.

An indeterminate interval followed, a merge of pain and pleasuring while the geometry of the space slowly expanded and contracted around them. Existence was apparently spiralling out of control and their bodies were trapped in its burning inter-penetrations of spheres, cones and lattices. 'These are the particles talking,' she told Lucas urgently but he wouldn't talk back, he could only elongate his scream down the abyss of centuries as the Black Whole overcame them.

12
Dark Stuff

Exhume Normality

'How's the leg?' Lombard was solicitous, offering another tumbler of Isle of Jura single malt from his pre-Rupture hoard. 'I'm sorry about our little altercation. But I feel it's cleared the air and created a kind of blood brotherhood between us. And that is so important now that our product launch is almost upon us - screened, so aptly, by their funny old Feast of Smoke. We do need the closest possible collaboration.'

William was befuddled. He couldn't admit that he still didn't understand the rationale of Lombard's brief. He needed to play for more time and bluff it out.

' I assume this really about maximising Pleasure Centres profit margins.' Dangerous talk, given Lombard's unpredictable rages, and he immediately regretted saying it.

'You're a mean old worm, William. Still no concept of my grand designs. Let me repeat: I'm going to exhume normality, reduce those distressing anomalies that stop people practising classical physics properly and making the trains run on time. I'm going to restore national security. The poor people are so ontologically insecure. Their fat bottoms are not grounded in a secure sense of being-in-the-world. That's why they turn to the faiths of the fundament - or dip-shit hippy cults - like your ex-wife did. Still does, I understand…'

William shook his head involuntarily. An inter-stellar distance must be preserved.

'We know where she lives by the way. Would you like to meet her again? I thought not. Of course, she doesn't know your exact location. But a brief encounter could be arranged. A sort of conjugal visit. You could catch up, talk about poor Dawn perhaps? Such a shame about your daughter Dawn. Reckless youth. The pity of it…'

William stared into the golden depths of his tumbler. Lombard never stopped goading him. He was hanging on, by a nano-string, over a dark abyss bubbling with toxic memories. 'I had a grand-daughter,' he whispered.

'So we understand. And if you're very good and do your sums properly you might even spend quality time with her. If you really want to, naturally. But we have to get this launch right. It's big stuff, it's rocket science.'

For a second, William's depression lifted as he flicked back to memories of triumphant arguments about the merits of Trident with that idiot Ebdon, who still hankered after the old Vulcan bombers. Then a queasiness hit him below the belt. He had to suppress the questionable grand-daughter. Those sickening niggles of guilt and curiousity. But Lombard was unscrolling a map at the far end of the room.

'Here is a ground plan of the chamber under Leyston Burrough. At the centre is the pillar that supports the main lintel, tinted in a nice shade of mauve. Around it, in brown, we have the servers for BRAN and the module for accessing Iconoclasm.'

He produced a plastic overlay and hung it over the diagram. 'Now, what do we have here, William?' Waving a plastic wand he pointed to a network of maroon lines radiating from the central pillar, to form a web interlinking the servers and then radiating off the edge of the sheet. 'Well? Concentrate, William! If that thing between your shoulders ever comes to a head, make sure you have it lanced. Haven't I mastered the dark sarcasm? What a world-teacher I am...'

William looked blankly at the radial mandala-like pattern.

'Bit outside your hard science frame of reference, eh? Never mind, let's try this. ' He replaced the diagram with a map of the Ruptured Islands. 'Forget the green and blue shadings of the faith enclaves. Look, there's still that pattern of maroon lines. All over the country. Even through your old Establishment. And there's a great confluence of them right here at Leynebridge. Why do the old fools call it *Leyne*bridge?'

'Ley-lines. Or some such folly.' He was disappointed in Lombard.

'Yes! This, according to our New Age pensioners, is the psychic national grid, along which the spiritual energies of the populace are channeled. Pre-Rupture, nobody took their Borderland ramblings seriously. Now, charged with the belief of a whole community - well, strange things happen. Seeing as we dwell in a Polyverse of perversities.'

'What do you expect of me? What's my role in all this?'

'It's not a cameo, laddie. You're a star, in the hot light.' Lombard removed the map and replaced the diagrams. 'I mean, you're the one with the knowledge. At least access to the knowledge, everything you locked up in BRAN for a hard rainy day. You're the mastermind, the public quiz master with all the answers. After all those useless years, you have a use. Using the VR interface, under the banner of the Iconoclasm launch, you will link BRAN with your new info-seeking Lobe software. BRAN will rationalise and integrate all data into an orderly virtual environment. Meanwhile, fortified by ritual and rage - and certain agent provocateurs - our Borderlanders will reach a telepathic high, charging their psychic grid of power and communication with an overload of energy. Another agent, witting or unwitting, who knows, will channel this into the BRAN/Lobe synthesis. BRAN will become momentarily an environment that is simultaneously both real and virtual. And then the whole pattern of wave-functions that construct this pseudo-world will collapse - into a single stable solid entity. You and I will have, quite literally, saved the world as a single uncorrupted file. Of course, there will be fall-out, some short-term confusion, some aspects of our VR service may be lost and the wizzies will be cross when their spells stop working. But we will have expressed the subconscious will of all those who can no longer cope with random infusions of chaos. The Rupture will fade into history, to become a mythic fabulation in the drifting mists of time...'

William felt briefly uplifted, yet waves of anxiety soon flooded back. He remembered seeing that vodcast by the Quantum Brothers, their old educational programme about nuclear energy, which had set these fears in motion, and everything he'd seen since, a great plurality of feral dysfunction steaming through the city's tunnels, increased his heart beat. There were great gaps in the physics, a lot of dark stuff he couldn't quite digest, and the coding of BRAN might not manage the data-flow. The programme had undergone so many mutations that there might be layers of code, like deep geological strata, which he could no longer access. He was an old man now, maybe plaque was encrusting his neurons, for the equations didn't float at his fingertips any more. Under Lombard's bluster it was hard to concentrate and formulate a coherent counter-argument.

'OK then, William. We better get on with getting it on.'

Wild Talk

Sitting in the empty apartment, facing the blank TV, Uncle Abdul couldn't forget. Every night the shame and horror of Omar's death replayed in a slow motion montage: the black PC corporate ambulance pulling up with a screech outside the warehouse, dumping the corpse wrapped in plastic on the tarmac; the hasty burial, poor old cousin Shadidah wailing behind the coffin as it bobbed through the heads of the crowd. He wouldn't forget the hours spent in stinking hospital waiting rooms, trying to speak to a real doctor who might explain, who was always too busy. A few days after the funeral a person from the accursed Pleasure Centres, a suspiciously jolly man called Liggett, had hovered on the doorstep for a few minutes, until neighbour Said had threatened to beat him to a pulp. He was offering the family special group membership of their wicked entertainments, while assuring them that Omar had died of a new kind of heart attack. But not even a scribble on a certificate had ever come through and in any case Omar was only eighteen, strong as an ox. It was a horrible mystery.

Yet - maybe divine retribution was inevitable. Omar had indulged in *haram* activities, forbidden vices. That's what the imam and the elders at Friday prayers had implied, even as they offered formal condolences. Abdul was deeply hurt by the imputation of blame, that he had brought up his nephew too liberally, by allowing him to go to secular college and mingle with the infidels.

And he was disturbed in a different way by the wild talk of the youth. Hisham and Mustafa were telling everyone that Omar had been deliberately enticed into the ways of the Centre by a strange Kaffir woman he'd met in the market, so that he could be used as a laboratory animal in one of their decadent experiments. Hisham boasted that the Youth had protested with banners outside the building and thrown a petrol bomb into the lobby, so it was now a hulk. The Brigades were carrying Omar's picture into combat, his death was a rallying call. For more deaths, thought Abdul, bitterly.

He picked up the silver-framed photo on his coffee table and gazed at the fine-featured young man in his best suit. What a potent husband Omar would have made for some eager virgin! And with his quick-fire intelligence and work ethic he would have been a worthy heir to the business. The young made crazy speeches about martyrdom but wasn't it better for a follower of Allah to hold the warm flesh of a good wife and raise laughing children? Everybody wanted to hi-jack his nephew as a kind of mascot - to justify what? He didn't like to think. He was a man of peace who only wanted to raise green shoots in the urban desert.

The intercom buzzed. Abdul peered through the blinds into the darkened street below. That dumpy form in a jilbab could only be Shahidah. He recognised the stance. But what was she doing with Hisham and Mustafa? And why were they carrying a suitcase? Surely his cousin wasn't coming to stay. Since poor Mariam's death he'd managed to cultivate his own company. He couldn't face the idea of Shahidah's incessant sibilant muttering around his house… But he had to release the door. He could hear Shahida grumbling as she trudged up the stairs.

'This is such a surprise, Shahida. You rarely visit. And I thought you boys were busy training with your Youth Brigades. Would you care for some coffee? Maybe some grapes? I can still get some of my special imports…'

'We're not staying,' said Hisham abruptly. 'But Mrs Kalyoubi said you'd help us.'

'I don't see how an old vegetable merchant can be much help. Unless you want some work, of course. It's been so difficult since I lost poor Omar.'

'We don't want your job!' The normally sleepy Mustafa seemed hyper-animated today.

' We want a small favour - to look after something…'

'Now you know I'm a man of peace. Despite all the provocations of the Kaffirs. I'm not hiding any guns.'

'We don't need to hide our AK47s.' Hisham grinned. 'They're already getting a taste of them. This is different. You don't have to know what it is.'

'I'm sorry. An honest merchant always knows the produce he's dealing with.'

'You have to help them,' hissed Shahida. 'Respect to Omar, even if you never help me.' Abdul felt guilty. He rarely visited her shambolic boarding house where she somehow struggled on. 'Now I've lost another gentleman, he went out and never came back, like a cunning old bagpuss…' She lapsed into murmuring one of her old Egyptian curses.

Abdul studied the case. Although the corners were scuffed, it was obviously expensive, an executive item of luggage, in black with chromed handles and an impressive combination lock.

'I hope you acquired this in a legal manner.' The Youth Brigades weren't over-scrupulous about how they funded operations. Street robbery was a standard tactic.

Hisham looked deeply offended. 'Do you really think we'd expect you to handle stolen goods? This was acquired from -' Mustafa gave him a stern glance. 'This was acquired through a reliable source.'

Before the boys could stop him, Abdul reached down and picked it up. The weight almost threw him off-balance and he let it drop with a heavy thud, to Hisham's obvious alarm. 'This is too much for an old man. What have you got in here?' He ran a finger along the dials of the lock. 'You must have a code, surely?'

'It will be transmitted. We'll let you know when the time is right.' But Mustafa looked uneasy. Abdul suspected they didn't know, they were cannon-fodder . 'Right now we have to go. You may not see us for a bit. But Cousin Shahida will keep you informed'

Spell It Out

Wharton couldn't write the Great Book any more. He kept trying to explain to Forgan but the Fool wouldn't believe him. 'You're blocking the spirits with your fusty dreams. You're buried in the rubble of your babel and too much book-craft. But you have to keep going and tell the story to raise the spirits, every telling is a spelling. You have to spell it out of your gut, spill over the top, swill it if you have to, but we must have a Book to burn for the Deep Ones, we need to hear the words floating in the incense… Write ON!'

Wharton lit another cigarette and waited for his visitor to make an exit. But Forgan loomed over his desk, his long scrawny finger tracing phantom glyphs in the smoky air.

'Maybe you need herbal assistance. I could take you on a funky fungal foray, all in the wet dawn, snuffle the roots of your being, or vomit a bolus of demonised pork - anything to help you reach the Deep Ones.'

Scribe Wharton realised that he was still in the psychic shallows and needed to be out of his depth. For all his arcane bibliophilia, he'd never taken that final sickening lurch into Forgan's night realm, which he'd always privately rationalised as a giant pageant. The Deep Ones. Absurd. But in the depths of his body-meat, from the coil of his intestines to the plates of his skull he had begun to feel a faint but steady contraction/expansion as if he was readying himself to birth some ancient implanted larvae.

Then the current had faltered. The vibrations that had brought up rogue syllables from an enormous void in his being had faded. Some aetheric transmitter had gone off-air. The point of his pen had stopped gliding across the space of the page. He was once again embedded in the brain-chatter of the village Undermind.

'It's stopped, Forgan. I'd started to transcribe the signs from the sound. It crept up my spine like a trickle, I mean a tickle of fire, hissing some hot spittle from down in the zones. And my pen made it all up into words, you heard them, about the old gods getting rampant in the dark. I think it was a voice looking for a body, any body, an anti-body. A voice-over. Until it peaked and went dumb.'

'The Deep Ones don't like people peeping, so they tie you up in torment and make you wait for the next blip. You must hang on full alert. There's good hope, you're already starting to mutate into readiness.'

'Mutating?' Wharton recognised he might be changing, for the routines of commerce had fallen away like so much rusty scaffolding now he was a Scribe of the Book.

'You're losing the persona, Gavin, your shop-face, you're breaking up those word-blocks, you're getting ready for the real deep sonics. Only person I knew who could manage this was Lucky.'

'Lucky?'

'Lucky, Luke, Lucas. The Poet in the Tower. Who got Ruptured, got us all Ruptured. You're starting to remind me of him.'

Forgan picked up his rune-staff and strode to the door. The light of the street lamps was flickering on wet cobbles and already there were yelps of revelry from the Red Hag. 'I must go and plot the final route of the Feast. It's bubbling nicely. All we need is the Book. By tomorrow noon...'

Wharton stared at his silk-draped desk and his writing materials, the rare black and red inks and the thick buttery paper. Perhaps a Banishing Ritual would help to mute the faint nagging voices at the margins of his attention, or give him at least the illusion of a psychic centre.

Wearily, with little conviction, he pulled back the rug and chalked a circle around the desk. He turned down the lights, lit four candles around the circumference of the circle, and began intoning the ancient formula:

Atoh

Malkuth

Vey Gevurah
Vey Gedulah
E-Olahm
Amen

Turning around the points of the compass, he drew the pentagrams in the air, trying to visualise a calligraphy of fire. Still conscious of his hoarse voice, he took a deep breath and called the angelic daemons - Raphael, Gabriel, Michael and Uriel. There were no golden feathery visions, no spectaculars. He'd never received any; and had few expectations. But his voice stabilised and he felt secure in the geometry of the room, in its angles and contours. The swirling dust of his thoughts began to settle.

He picked up his pen and began to write. No words came. Only letters. And then digits. Pure number. Nothing but numbers. Number One/Zero. Aleph/Null. Something and nothing. He couldn't stop generating the data.

Safe House

Mrs Kalyoubi didn't like the idea of Hisham moving in, but there he was in the hallway, waving a thick wad of notes. He began counting them out.

'Look! I advance you enough to buy you a big new TV and make up for all the rent you lost since that old man moved out. And you'll be safe. Renting to family, not dirty old men who run away.'

'How can you afford this? You have no job, you're a gang boy.'

'I'm a cadet in my Brigade unit now. The brothers take care of me. This will be a safe house.'

Something about that expression worried her but she supposed it could be worse. He was fat and loud, but he could help out, fix the plumbing and keep her guests in order. If she managed to get any more... He wasn't a bagpuss off the streets. He even had cash in hand. This was a matter of fate, she had to accept it.

'You can have the old man's room. But you must promise to clean up his mess. When they came for his stuff they left some of his mess behind. I'm a sick old woman, I can't do it all for you. And no smuggling in whores while I'm asleep.' She'd seen the pale-faced little harlots flaunting their tight rumps along St Damian's Avenue; she'd seen his eyes swivelling towards them even as he drove her back through the alien night.

Hisham looked simultaneously affronted and flattered by the imputation that he had adult appetites. He grinned awkwardly and went out to grab his bags from the van.

* * *

Later, in the early hours, she needed the bathroom. On her return she passed the corridor outside the Doctor's old room. Hisham had already made himself at home. Light flickered through the crack under the door and she could hear the muffled drone of electric music, interspersed with fragments of speech, long drawling words she couldn't understand. So he had discovered the old man's monitor and somehow hooked it up to the Lobe, to trawl for lewd cavortings, no doubt of it. She'd always suspected Crowe of secret immorality; but she wasn't going to tolerate it from one of her extended family. To make the insult worse, Hisham was turning up the volume.

She pushed open the door. Hisham was kneeling, in his boxer pants, in front of the monitor which he'd placed on a bedside table.

His chubby face seemed swollen, like a bruised fruit in the mottled light. His lips moved in unison with the voices issuing from the tinny speaker. He swayed slightly to the throb of their background music. He'd plastered his hair down and parted it in an odd way to look like an old man in black-and-white. She didn't like the look of it. With his left hand (Hisham was right-handed) he was scribbling something (English, not Arabic) in a pad on the table, taking dictation from the monitor. Letters and numbers. Maybe phone numbers, pass codes...

She squinted at the screen, still expecting to see undulating female bodies, those wicked whore-visions that were supposed to play games with you. But Hisham was miming to talking heads, two old grey men in suits with greasy hair. They looked smug like wise crooks, drawling away through their big words and long numbers; and the foolish boy was acting out their nonsense, completely oblivious to her.

'Hisham! What is this rubbish you're watching, waking up the whole house? Have you no respect?'

He ignored her. The insolence was unspeakable. She reached out and grabbed the power cable from the socket. The grainy faces shrank into blackness and silence.

For a moment, Hisham's features were immobilised. He seemed to have retreated into his puppy fat, although his eyes still scanned the blank screen. Then, with a high-pitched scream, he hurled himself at her, pummeling her arthritic shoulders, even her face. He stabbed at her eyes with his pen, gouging her cheek. She was trapped in a vicious cartoon that wouldn't stop. Then - she couldn't believe it - he'd picked up the monitor, he was going to crash it on her old head -

13
The Rapture of Rupture

Crystal

The three-fold knock at the door, according to Lore, made the whole cottage shake. Elaine, half asleep in front of a dying fire, was shocked out of an under-lit dream, where she wandered in a bloody night gown through arcades of brown brick, crying out for Dawn, tiny Dawn who'd ridden off on a pet goat but it wasn't funny...

Staggering to the spy-hole, she saw the snake-head profile of dreadlocks. Aran Yarland. Her head was throbbing already with his painful sense of loss. She knew why he sought her out. It can't have been easy for him to seek the aid of an old woman.

'Forgan can't help me. Nor can Wharton. He's locked himself into a long trance. Noah just flaps around panicking about processions and the Burrough. But you can help. You're in Viv's bloodline. So you can make a hot link and find her.'

'I've tried, Aran, for weeks. I fear she went to the City but I have no more impressions. Have you no clues?'

'I've brought our Mating Cup. Can you pick up anything from that?' He produced the goblet from a shoulder bag and placed it reverently on the table. He couldn't erase the memory of Viv polishing it the day they'd had that fatal misunderstanding.

Elaine examined it carefully. It was one of Gil Norwood's finest. Around the rim sleek nymphs modelled in beaten silver entangled arms and thighs with lusty satyrs. The Leynebridge serpent was brazed around the base.

'I was going to hand this to our children.' Aran sighed, a young patriarch, thwarted. 'But now…'

'Has she touched the Cup?' If a psychometric link could be made, however tenuous, there might be some hope of receiving an impression. But Elaine had a cupboard full of books and childhood toys that her grand-daughter had once cherished and they were so many dead objects in her hand. As dead as that drawer of Dawn's clothes that fussy Noah had told her to burn.

Aran was pondering. 'She polished it one day. That was the day I knew things were starting to go wrong.'

'How wrong?'

'She made a blasphemous comment about the Lore. I don't like to repeat it.'

'The Lore can withstand foolish comments. As it has for years.' Elaine had felt the tensions and psychic blockages between Vivienne and herself in recent months, especially after the girl insisted on moving to her cold hutch over Wharton's shop. But that was adolescence. It was perennial.

'She suggested the Lore was like a game with old trinkets.'

Elaine visualised her altar-table in the study- the red silk cloth, her dark crystal in its silver cradle, the array of cards, the spiral candlesticks, her calf-bound grimoire. On this grey October day, maybe that's all they were, trinkets. The noisy foreign presences in the streets, even outside her own cottage, had congregated to leech their essence - and corrupt her grand-daughter… They should be buried in the depths of the earth.

'Listen, Elaine, will you scry for her? You of all people know how to use the crystal. She's your granddaughter. She was going to be my future bride.' The warrior was supplicating, desperate. But desperation would only cloud the operation for both of them. She was wavering.

'I'm getting too old. It ought to be easier, becoming a crone with no more passions to distract me, but I'm finding it harder to focus. Believe me, I've tried.'

'I'll give you whatever you need. I've saved money...' He fumbled for coins.

'Keep your money, Aran. It needs a release of energy, a charge in the atmosphere. And something more to help me make a connection.'

'Like this?' Aran was gesturing with a curved knife, her mistletoe knife, that he'd suddenly snatched from the hall table. While she was trying to find the right answer, he slashed his left forearm in a single abrupt motion. A rivulet of blood trickled down the tattooed muscle and started dripping on her rug, but with his right hand he tilted the Mating Cup underneath to catch the flow.

'There... I'll fill her cup to the brim. You can focus on that. A pool of blood to catch her reflection. That'll work, surely...'

'No! Stop these crazy theatrics, Aran. You're endangering us both.' The blood-force was going to charge the whole room before she could stabilise it with a banishing rite. She could feel it clotting in the air, tinting the light with a reddish aura. She was already breathing too hard, her heart thumped and her mouth tasted salty. But she had to stay calm. Despite his size he was still the truculent child. She could gently talk him down.

'Put my knife down. Very slowly, please. And the Cup. That's not the way. You're attracting parasitical forces. We've got to be very practical, very careful. I have to fix your arm and clear the space before I can do anything.'

'You'll do something? To find Vivienne?'

'For an exchange. A barter.'

'You're the First Lady Elderseer. Not a boot-shop proprietor. You're talking now like Trader Price.'

'I'm not concerned with money or commodities.'

'What do you want?'

'You're a man of action, Aran. I have an action for you.'

'You've only offered me words so far.'

'I swear I will try with the crystal. Now, in the study. But you must promise that if we get a result - however dark - you'll act out my wishes. The scope of the action will match the quality of the result.'

'I have no choice…'

'It will take a little time. But I have to purify the house first. And dress that arm.'

He sat silent as she washed and bound the wound. Finally she led him into her study upstairs where he stood and watched closely as she traced the pentagrams at the four compass points and intoned the angelic names, her voice still clear and steady, before closing the banishing.

She drew the heavy curtains and lit a black candle in a tall brass stand at each corner of the room, before settling at her altar-table. He felt awed. The Elder was sharing hallowed rites with him, a rough youth who fought and roistered. But then she had to; it was her duty to find her grand-daughter, his true mate. He felt a surge of optimism for the first time in months. With any luck - and the Gods behind him - he'd soon be on a rescue mission, even if it meant a quest to the false citadels and jousting with the faith-bandits. But he had to be patient. Scrying couldn't be hurried, he'd been told.

At the centre of the room, the circular altar table; at the centre of the table, a triangular space, delineated by black silk stoles lettered with the golden names of old angels; at the centre of the triangle, suspended in its network of silver filaments, the gleaming quartz stone.

Yet Elaine couldn't quite centre her gaze into its depths. She was too aware of Aran's lumbering presence behind her, a clumsy earth-demon. And she was still too self-conscious, still uncertain after all these years about initiating the process, as Forgan had taught her from Wharton's old books. But he insisted you didn't have to understand the procedure to work it.

She gestured to Aran to move away. She'd make him stand in the doorway at the edge of her world, while she found her own time, shadow time.

And time passed, so slowly. Eventually the overwhelming sense of duration became unendurable; and time flowed out of the chamber. The quartz sphere hung motionless in front, aligned to the centre of her forehead. The candle flames were deep-frozen in the crystal, glowing like fiery lilies in the void. Then duration recurred, because the flames faded to black. The stone was dark as old Doctor Dee's obsidian mirror.

'Null and void here,' said Elaine in deep mechanical tones. 'Null and void.'

Aran didn't get it. This wasn't the familiar rhythm of Noah's elemental rites, the measured invocation of Earth, Air, Wind and Fire in solemn mellow tones. Elaine's voice was warping down an octave; the old lady was shifting her pitch to an asexual growl.

She/it started chanting. Her mouth projected a stream of sound, a complex sequence of phonemes voiced with frequent compulsive repetitions. Vowels were elongated, plosive consonants burst in the semi-darkness, syllables inaugurating a primal act of creation - or a bringing-forth-by-night. Aran couldn't follow the pattern of the waveform, it was all a new noise to him, but he could dimly grasp an emergent pattern of repetition. The chant was repeated seven times.

Aran tried to block the stream of syllables but his body began swaying to their rhythms and the mesmeric drone of Elaine's voice enunciating her Calls. The black stone was curdling now. No other word in Aran's hoard would suffice. Milky whorls of light spiralled around its circumference and coagulated at its poles, unmapped continents on an alien globe.

The clouded masses condensed into grainy forms, forming cheeks, jowls, flickering grey lips, all halo'd in luminous cameos, twin brothers flexing in-and-out of being, siblings of rogue quanta. They glared out of the crystal, challenging the intrusion into their sphere.

Elaine was silenced. The faces were staring her down, down. Eyes down for Elaine the Arch Elderseer, muted by their hard gaze. Aran couldn't believe it. All he wanted to do was grab the crystal, shake an answer out of them *where's my girl you buggers?* Then their dark glance caught him; and he was overcome by a complete leakage of all his strength, it was all futile, too much effort...

Elaine groped for parchment and pen. In shaky italic hand she inscribed *VIVIENNE?* mouthing the name as she held up the torn sheet in front of the crystal. Then, hands quivering, she laid it on the altar table. Drawing herself up in her chair with obvious effort, she focussed on those monochrome faces apparently trapped in their sphere - but seemingly controlling all within an infinitely larger matrix. The curvature of the crystal morphed around them, in an internal geometry that enfolded an unbearable torsion of planes, a geometry that was painful to witness. Elaine, old hare caught in headlights, knew the sphere was watching her, the black pupil of a vast projectile eye, intent on her intention, a pulsing stroboscope from the macroscope. The grey avatars of gravity and industry were boring through the aether to spy on an aged woman's trembling hands. *They're fat and void. Shining hair and joke-shop moustaches. From the Music Halls of the Beyond. Now yer see 'em. Don't let them in... too late...*

Aran was overwhelmed by Elaine's panic. In what ensued, he could only snatch surreptitious glimpses. The Brothers - a name that came to Aran as he blurted out his story later in the Red Hag - dwindled, doll-like, but still hanging in there, wherever their zone was. A screen-within-a-screen expanded between them, while their voices elocuted insistently, semi-incomprehensibly, at low frequencies. *We are their hosts but they are our commentators.* Aran caught this new fragment from Elaine, but still didn't get it. His Elderseer was losing control, everything was somehow going wrong.

On the micro-screen within the crystal, a young woman was kneeling on all fours, on a white fur rug or maybe in a low cloud of vapour, Aran couldn't tell. Then the image colorised itself and sharpened. She wore an intricate black corset, woven with red sigils. that thrust her bared breasts forwards and exposed her milky buttocks. Her hair was elaborately coiled and her eyes were heavily made-up. But Aran could identify that straight nose, full lips, high cheekbones. Vivienne was entrapped somewhere, somehow. It couldn't be true...

A man and a woman emerged through the haze, in masks and black robes. In an abstracted way they began to caress Vivienne's thighs and nipples. Aran watched, horrified but aroused, then tried to distract himself by focussing on Elaine, who surely must recognise her grand-daughter enslaved in this decadent pleasurama. The seeress could only murmur fitfully. 'Incubi and succubi.. incubi and succubi... earth-demons... we're in too deep...'

Now the red-haired woman had parted her gown to reveal full breasts and a gleaming dildo strapped between her stockinged legs. With ceremonial gravity and precision she placed its glistening black stalk between Vivienne's buttocks and began fucking her.

Viv's eyes were closed but she licked her lips and smiled dreamily as the red-haired woman swayed back and forth, an avenging angel of lesbian desire. His betrothed was being ravished by a strange woman. It couldn't be happening. It was all made up. The baritone mutterings of the Brothers were narrating a louder voice-over for this sex-crime but Aran couldn't understand a word.

'What are they saying?' He gripped Elaine's shoulder, scrawny and hunched under her robes, but the seeress was lost, eyes turned inwards.

All was lost. Now they had tied Vivienne to a marble table and the male was penetrating her. The woman leant over her, a mane of red hair trailing across her breasts. The act went on for an eternity.

As the man finally climaxed, Viv's back arching in an ecstasy of lust, the red-haired woman ripped away his mask. And Aran at last realised the universe was a cruel joke-book. The Fucker. The Incomer. The Rupture-Monger. That runting bookworm who lived in the hillside shelter. Shagging his allotted home-wife. The Lore was an arse, violated. They were all tricksters.

With a great cry he grabbed her crystal and hurled it to the floor, where it shattered - into slivers of ordinary glass.

Elaine staggered to her feet and screamed. A visceral screech, as if her gullet and lungs were ripping themselves apart. But he wasn't going to let her get away with it.

'You tricked me, too. Old Elderseer Bitch-Goddess!'

He never meant to hit her. He only swung out with his fist, trying to punch his way out of this travesty of an existence. But he made contact, she gasped and clutched her head as she tumbled to the floor.

He knelt over her, appalled at the enormity of his action. It was an accident. It was his will. Or the beings in the stone, those Brothers, they made him do it. To have struck down an Elderseer. She was still breathing. Perhaps a healer could be summoned, perhaps Noah... But the pink froth bubbling around her lips suggested she was too far gone - he'd gone too far this time.

She was trying to talk but the words were garbled. He could only sense waves of fear emanating from her darkening brain.

'What have I done? What can I do?'

A whisper, a wisp of a voice, the phlegm clearing for a moment: 'Get into their Zone... kill... the old man and his talking heads... bury them them in the depths of the earth...' The voice lapsed into a mumble again. After a few minutes, breathing ceased.

He sat beside her on the floor for a long time, staring blankly into the Mating Cup, waiting for somebody to come and find them. Then, very slowly, dazed by his own transgression, he wandered towards the door, into the night.

Mission (2)

Uncle Abdul stood in the weedy front garden of 38 St Damian's Avenue and pondered his options. He would probably have to break in. He'd exhausted the battery of the infuriating door chime, while neither Shahidah Khalhoubi nor her dubious new lodger Hisham had responded to phone calls. Not that you could ever rely on public telephone networks.

Here he was in this risky neighbourhood at nightfall, just trying to reassure himself about Shahidah's well being. He was mad. There could be armed beggars behind every privet hedge. Somebody might hotwire his van while he was inside. Nevertheless he was determined to return this damned heavy suitcase that Hisham had foisted upon him.- and find out what had been foisted on his cousin.

A smart suited Asian man was about to enter the house on the corner. Perhaps he knew enough martial arts to deal with the beggars. He might know something about a plump fussy Middle Eastern landlady.

'Excuse me, sir?'

'Good night, as you might say,' pronounced Mr. Kim, carefully. 'I have been learning English for eighteen months. How can I help you?'

Uncle Abdul tried to explain about Shahidah and her non appearance.

'Mrs. Kalyoubi was a very secret lady. Not in the public domain. She is often an invisible. The young man has his exits and entrances. But the old man buggered away…'

'The old man?'

'The distinguished old man. I asked him for English lessons but was not honoured.'

Abdul remembered his cousin flapping about the elderly eccentric who spent hours in his room and then went missing. Had he returned and abducted her? More likely, Hisham had done something foolish or disrespectful. If only Omar were alive… He thanked Mr. Kim. Once the salary man was inside, he picked up a brick and strode to the front door.

It was too easy to smash the art-deco window pane and find the inside lock. He dragged the suitcase into the stuffy hall. He switched on the light. No sign of disturbance here or in the living room where the TV was unusually silent. He walked through the kitchen to the utility room, suddenly driven by a morbid impulse and opened the long freezer cabinet.

She was all there, at least, furred in frost, dark clots of blood congealing on her forehead and staining her nightgown. Her cheek and forehead had been scratched, as if by an animal. He could not believe anyone could be so cruel to let her die and lie in such indignity. His eyes blurred with tears.

He knelt there for a few moments beside the freezer, praying for her poor soul. How could the All-Merciful permit such futile cruelty? This was like strangling a tired old tabby cat, a poor old bagpuss…

He heard a heavy tread on the stairs and held his breath. Hisham appeared in the kitchen door, clutching a long broken shard of plastic. His t-shirt was smeared with dried blood and ice-cream.

Abdul stared at his sulky baby nephew, now monstrous. 'Are you going to kill me too?'

'It was just an accident. The old busybody tried to unplug my monitor and fell over the cable, I tried to stop her -'

'I don't believe you, Hisham.'

'You have to take my word. Just let it go, it happened. Who you're going to call?'

'Authorities need to look into this. I shall call the police.'

Hisham gave a deep-throat laugh. 'The only security patrols

around here are Shepherds and they're not going to take you seriously, they'll think you killed her and give you a beating to drum the devils out of you. So it was an accident, OK? Get it?'

Abdul knew it wasn't but decided to play for time, to think of something... He would find a proper person to untangle this web of evil.

'You can't leave her here.'

'Only for a day or two. I have been given a mission. Coded orders. An important mission.'

'You're not going anywhere, Hisham. You must face up to what you have done. You cannot hide from Allah.'

'This mission is for the glory of Allah.'

Abdul realised he was trembling, had been trembling ever since Hisham had entered the room. 'Ambushing strangers on the roads, setting fire to buildings - do you call that the work of Allah?' He turned to the hallway, pulling the van keys from his jacket. 'I shall get help from our imam. Perhaps he will pray for you.'

As he touched the door handle, he felt Hisham's grip on his neck. He'd almost been expecting it, but it was still a shock to be assaulted by a member of his family - and then winded by a blow to the stomach. His aging puny body couldn't compete with the bulk of the teenager, and soon he was on the floor, Hisham binding his hands and feet with electric flex. When he stopped panting and wincing he tried to speak but his mouth was quickly gagged with parcel tape. Hisham rolled him onto his face, and added a blindfold. But he could still hear the boy breathing heavily as he picked up the suitcase.

'Thanks for bringing this, Uncle. It saves us dropping off at your place to collect it. Now all we've got to do is bag you up properly.'

A few minutes later, sheathed in black rubbish bags, Abdul was dragged down the drive way and heaved into the back of his van. 'Like a sack of potatoes,' said Hisham, 'but I couldn't leave you behind. Not on this holy mission...' Abdul, bruised and groggy, heard the doors slam. Then the motor revved and Hisham slammed into gear as they took off, too fast, into the unknown.

House of After-Life

The silhouettes moved through the cold twilit woods. Even in crisis, the Harvesters followed their rites. A Master, summoned from the Life House by the terrified apprentices strode ahead with his torch, its blue flame flickering through the jagged tracery of autumn foliage. Four more veterans from the rescue party marched behind carrying Gideon's body on a bier. Another followed, carrying his detector in outstretched arms. Four of Joshua's cohort dragged the inert forms of Carla and Lucas on stretchers crudely improvised from scrap timber in the bunker. A few still prodded mechanically with their detectors in the mossy roots of oaks. Their first hurried version of events had been selective and Joshua dreaded the deeper probing they were likely to receive on their arrival at the After-Life House. He couldn't suppress the image of those serpentine bodies inter-twining, the horror of his own arousal, his obscene brain ordering the grope of a Lobe-Mistress...

Eventually they arrived at the outbuildings. The Master ordered them to halt during his exchange with the sentinel.

'How do we burn?'

'We burn with the blue radiance of eternal life.'

'Enter the House of After-Life.'

They filed into the stockade and passed workshops and

dormitories. Joshua realised they were making directly for the House itself, a building normally closed to mere apprentices. That strange teacher - now, ironically, in his custody - had never explained the Lore of Harvesting properly, or indeed any aspect of the Lore. It was all a grave mystery.

The House was a large wooden heptagonal structure with a conical roof, bigger than Forgan's barn, almost as high as Leynebridge Tower. The entire building was windowless. As the Master slid back a heavy door, Joshua tried to adjust to a dim misty glow within - and to the mesmeric sounds that seemed to vibrate through his crotch and belly with increasing insistence - shamanic drones, a slow overlay of pulses and chimes, interweaving sines, a steady increment of brain waves. The young ones were flagging, almost drowning in the surging waveforms. It would be so easy to sink into the deepening mix, to be swallowed up by the sliding aeonics. He wasn't trained for this.

The sound waves emanated from a large apparatus at the centre of the space. 'The Odic Generator,' announced the Master, over the sonic bed, as if taking them on a guide tour. A massive grey-painted vertical cylinder was surrounded by racks of switchgear and fronted by a metal control panel. Joshua had heard wild rumours of this device and its life-reviving powers. Yet it was smaller than he expected and the console of switches and dials was scratched and dented. Perhaps it had been constructed from Carbonite leftovers, maybe salvaged from the forbidden cities. Around the edges of the room he could see racks of display cases housing glass pyramids. Each one contained some sort of organic substance, resembling meat, or an embalmed body part. Joshua was sure he could discern a heart, maybe a brain.

The Master ordered them to lower the stretchers in front of the machine. He bowed his head before it, then nodded to an elderly assistant who had darted out from behind. Carefully, they took Gideon's detector and screwed a long ball-jointed metal tube into a socket at its circular base. Then they aligned the tube with a dark triangular vent at the base of the console. The Master gestured abruptly to the group, commanding them to kneel and turn their backs. Joshua, at the end of the line, managed to swing round as the Master bestrode the detector and the assistant toggled some switch on the control panel. The sounds peaked. He saw - or thought he saw - a tiny blue globe of light hover around the vent. But it disappeared in a flash of blackness. He couldn't understand it.

* * *

An hour later, as Joshua's legs ached with the effort of kneeling, they were still trying to revive Gideon. The Master had uncoiled another tube from the Generator and was waving its nozzle across the swollen outcrops of Gideon's skull. 'I can't understand it. The Odic force should have healed his aethyric body. We have thousands of harvest-hours stored in here, for just such an emergency as this.'

'It's the Incomers, ' muttered the assistant, a bald bearded man. 'They're obviously radiating dark energy. It's repelling our pure bions. Poor Gideon never had a chance to destroy their corporeal bodies.'

'Well, we do. Only way we can purify the House.'

Joshua watched robotically, as the assistant bustled off in search of flammable liquid. The sounds, muted now, were still hypnotic. He was in a void. Lore said it was necessary to purge demonic forces. But - to broil humans. Like hogs roasting in the grate of the Red Hag. Cracked flesh. It was hard, very hard…

The assistant returned, grinning, hugging a large rusty can. 'Petrol,' he announced. 'Real petrol, from before the You-Know-What. Never thought we'd find a use for it.'

Joshua stared at the prone bodies. Lucas and Carla, they called each other. What had forced them together into this tangled mass of flesh, this alleged love? Fatty Tyler had bragged of making love to Fawn Price in the Tower Gardens but that version of love sounded like a quick sticky fumble in shrubbery. This couple were enduring a cosmic ordeal.

The Master knelt to unscrew the petrol can. ' Let this be a lesson to you, lads. Sometimes you have to act decisively…'

Joshua looked again at Carla's pale face, her closed eyes, the tangled nest of red hair, the contour of her neck and breasts, white against the grubby remnants of her jacket. She was the most beautiful creature in his world.

Suddenly he lurched forward and grabbed the can. He inverted it, spilling the strange fuming liquid everywhere, over his robe, the Master's straggly grey hair, the assistant's desperate fingers.

Time dilated. The probability of creating a spark from the friction of flint and metal in the assistant's hands was an evolving complex variable. Joshua wasn't trying to work it out, the probability wave was working through him, working out of a hidden dimensional niche, the crack of time. The spark simply happened. Flames engulfed the three men in a blazing fractal. Joshua tried to wrestle a way out of his burning robe as the pyre screamed around him.

Apocryphal Apocalypse

'We need to know how that fire started. Dodd and his cronies will accuse us of arson, destroying the House of After-Life, another historic religious facility.'

'You worry all the time, Liggett. These Elderseers barely tolerated the Harvesters. They probably torched it themselves. Crazy old sects, always fucking each other around.' Lombard laughed, spat and gestured with his shooting-stick across the Leyne valley at the faint pillars of smoke just visible through the morning mist. 'It's like a teaser. For their Feast of Smoke. A support act. You can put a spin on it, send flowers, go there with Pullman and make a nice speech if you like, tell'em Pleasure Centres will sponsor a refurb. But it's a side-show. Nothing to piss yourself about. What do you think, Dr. William? Come on, stop brooding. Everything's under control.'

William wasn't listening. He'd wandered off to the far side of the Burrough mound, shuffling through the scrubby grass and sheep shit. He couldn't stop shivering as he tried to make sense of what Liggett had told him, prodding him out of bed at dawn. 'Your alleged former wife? Elaine Crowe? There's been some kind of incident. Apparently assaulted over a dispute about clairvoyance or something. Our people are looking into it...' The episode sounded ridiculous. An absurdity, so typical of Elaine, who was distracting him even now. Did he have a duty of care, after those years of mutually assured destruction?

Now Pullman was struggling up the slope towards him. 'You better come with me...'

* * *

This body was too small, too crooked. Surely this twisted hump draped by a brown ethnic bed-spread couldn't be the Valkyrie who'd declared war on him and then retreated from his life all those decades ago. But the stale incense in the study, the scattered Tarot cards, the fragments of crystal he was crunching under foot as he walked round and round the corpse - it all spelled 'Elaine'. He had been here before.

A bearded old man in a torn green cape, sitting by Elaine's table - some sort of altar - was staring at him with overt hostility. A harsh rustling noise filled his inner ear but it couldn't make out what it was saying, as it was overlaid by the shouts of hooded men outside the cottage, taunting and jostling the Pleasure Centres security operatives.

The elderly man rose, leaning heavily on his ornate staff. Ignoring Pullman, he advanced on William and grabbed his arm.

'You have no right to interfere in this tragedy. It is a Leynebridge matter. Nothing to do with your vile organisation!'

'The deceased, ' - he still couldn't say 'Elaine' - is, or was my former wife, another life - '

'That's an obscene joke. A lie, sir! We know you're one of Lombard's evil geniuses. Our Sister Elaine would never have consorted with someone like you.'

'I have certificates, photos, a decree…' He wondered if they were still scattered on the floor of that suburban bedsit. Surely Liggett's people picked them up.

'Your conspiracy boasts it can fake anything, virtual you call it, all lies. Sister Elaine's husband died long ago, in the Rupture.'

So he had 'died' years ago. William Crowe had conveniently fallen down a crack in their apocryphal apocalypse. The room blurred for a moment. In whatever myth she'd constructed for these rustics he'd been killed off, despite the fact, the incontrovertible fact that he'd actually visited her here, had sought out Dawn's grave, had seen the squalling grandchild…

'I knew this woman. We had a daughter, Dawn - who apparently died of your people's poisons. I have a grand-daughter. She's called V-' His memory was corrupting. The neurons weren't talking to each other. She began with a V but that wasn't impressing this stubborn Elder.

'I am one of the healers who tried to save Sister Elaine's daughter. As for the grand daughter Vivienne, she has sadly abandoned her grandmother and our community. Probably as a consequence of the corrupting influences spread by your corporation. Now I must ask you to leave.'

'Dr. Crowe only wants to confirm her identity,' Pullman murmured. 'I'm sure, Mr Dodd, that your traditional skills will enable you to catch the perpetrator and bring him before the local judiciary. And surely, with your unique insight, you must intuit that there is some prior connection between Dr. Crowe and Sister Elaine...'

Noah frowned. Then, muttering bitterly under his breath, he drew back the bedspread. William forced himself to look. She was so old now, an ancient wizened mask. A purple bruise stained the yellowish skin stretched over her temples. Her lips had sunk into a dark slit and her angry eyes were closed. But he couldn't stop looking; and he slowly realised he was looking for an earlier face, its high cheekbones and firm jaw, a face that had smiled at him as he hovered on the fringes of his supervisor's cocktail party and invited him, only hours later, to feast hungrily on her body. She'd given him a grounding, earthed his dark current. How had he let everything mutate so badly, so madly? Suddenly, overlaid on the white wall opposite, he could see a grey photo, ghostly figures in bow-ties and gowns, a column of fading newsprint - *Sir William Crowe, Master of Balliol and his wife Lady Elaine, well-known for her charitable work, receiving* - Then it was all gone.

Tunneling Deeper

He was Lucas, possibly. He was floating head-first down a tunnel filling with smoke and reverberated screams, long repetitive howlings. The tunnel linked one black hole to another, such was the logic of tunnels. But the jittering shadows, a fiery spike-fingered shadow-show on the tunnel wall confused him; and too many small humps of meat smoldered like offerings in the sooty alcoves.

Then screens of some kind were recessed in the tunnel wall, flashing the same image: two identical grey faces, Caucasian male, clean-shaven, forty-plus. Sober square-headed men in suits and ties with shiny well-parted hair. Like old 1950s publicity photos of bandleaders, movie gangsters, radio announcers. An advertising banner streamed past him: THE QUANTUM BROTHERS ARE WATCHING YOU WITH COMPOUND INTEREST THE QUANTUM BROTHERS ARE WATCHING YOU WATCHING THE QUANTUM BROTHERS WITH COMPOUND INTEREST...

A bundle like Carla floated a few metres ahead of him but he was gagging on the foul-tasting orangey mist that provided basic illumination. He couldn't talk; he couldn't even prove he was Lucas, he'd forgotten how to decode himself.

As visceral noise and stench increased, so did velocity, the rapture of Rupture. They were accelerating into the dark matter of all facts, according to the latest text scrolling along his firewall, so the gravitons were causing them intense granulated pain. The terror was multiplexed by a probability factor of 10^{23} that some entity/deity was pursuing him/them. They were being set upon.

He knew the stellar dog-demons were on his case, he could tell from the smell. They were snorting along the tubeways behind his behind, propelled by starry gas and hot metal shit, readying to digest him/her.

Carla's wave was breaking. They were breaking up, all signals lost. Their breakages were hurling down this channel, a tunnel, liquidated by language, at the speed of thought. She kept on rolling her liquid eyes and mounds of flesh fully to the frontal but a darkness at the back end of beyond was swallowing hard and she was tripping on her peaks and troughs.

These collections of quanta were tunneling deeper as the cosmological constant fuzzed its logos. Burying cute snouts in the Polyverse mess, up the junction of space-time funnels, through the split screens, they slotted the deepest throats, the tunnel mouthings. And broke out in coded tattoos of fire.

Lucas rolled over to extinguish his burning sleeve. He did not know why it was burning but he understood the pain. It was hard to breath. He could see someone resembling Carla lying on the floor, her arm flapping desperately as she tried to disentangle herself from a rough cradle of wooden poles. He did not know why she was present but she was in danger. He crawled across the floor towards her. She hit him several times with her spasmic arm, but he managed to extract her and drag her past the incomprehensible machinery towards an exit. The whole structure was alight and he couldn't see much as they crept in painful slow-motion towards that remote door. He averted his eyes from the burnt people in robes. There was nothing he could do.

Beyond the door, more robed people were shouting, but he managed to walk through them, despite his scorched feet, for Carla - it was Carla - was coming with him, somehow.

14
Feast of Smoke

Unbelievers' Sabbath

Hisham could see the glare of the Feast miles away. The unbelievers' sabbath in full cry. He couldn't hear them yet but he knew they were crying out loud to their demons under the moon of blood. Their hill of dreams would be purged at dawn.

The roads were empty. Nevertheless, the last stage of the mission, infiltrating the town, needed careful planning. He stopped the van in a lay-by and undid the rear doors. In the light of his torch he could see Abdul, still lying trussed and motionless on the floor. For a moment Hisham thought his uncle had died in transit, like some exotic imported animal. He prodded a leg; and was half-relieved, half irritated to hear a faint moan. His over-riding obsession was the suitcase.

It was perhaps too early to open it. Yet the temptation to tamper was powerful. He had been granted the codes, he had the power, so he had to look. Shivering in the chill, he thumbed the tiny wheels in the lock; and flipped back the heavy lid.

Somehow it was an anti-climax. Perhaps he'd been expecting an eerie glow, a dazzling light. A fat silver-grey tube, like a plumbing fixture, was mounted diagonally across the interior. Black plastic housings, with an embedded keypad, were fitted around it, cradling the cables and electronics for the trigger and the timer.

Stroking the rim of the keypad, he began to sense the full glory of his mission. He knelt on the tarmac and prayed to the mighty djinn enclosed in this tube of vengeance.

As he whispered, he knew the bomb would begin to talk back. It was suffering from its suspended animation. Those segments of heavy metal were aching for union, an instant of blissful self-annihilation. Then the liberated particles could penetrate weak molecules of flesh, the soft organics. The plutonic spirits craved release. They spoke in low growls through his back brain, very slowly, but Hisham could decrypt it, for their bomblet was swollen, fit to burst. You couldn't lock energy like that away forever, you had to do something with it. And the bomb's destiny was his salvation. The mineral soul of the bomb would survive its agony of transformation just as Hisham would survive in an explosion of bliss. His imam spoke of seventy-two virgins in the gardens of the martyrs, but Hisham knew there were more than that, for you could meet seventy-two any time in the sticky grip of Pleasure Centres' dildonics. But those ghost succubi, daughters of Lilith, were cursed with glitches, they jerked and frazzled and fragmented like those cults of the Unbelievers. His paradise maidens would be infinite in number, infinite in difference, from the slender dark virgin clutching at her modesty to flagrant blondes, glorious Tit-Queens of the Great Satan, eager to submit... The bomb would resurrect him for eternity, a rampant warrior. He was honoured to bear its message, somehow, into the temple of the enemy.

Serpent Force

Forgan sniffed the night wind. He relished the taste of soot and floating cinders, enjoying a faint snort of sulphur and salpetre, an aery alchemy of fumes. Surveying the town from the gallery of his barn, he knew that the Feast had already spontaneously ignited. The inner nudgings of the Undermind had locked into the inner rhythms of the

Serpent Force. Bonfires had been started outside the Book Market and in the courtyard of the Red Hag, according to custom, while fire-baskets were blazing on the Tower. He could see beacons flaring further away on the hillsides around Old Hallows. Someone had even re-lit the House of After-Life. In his spine he could feel the subtle energies flowing along the great North-South alignment that ran from Leyston Burrough through Old Hallows, Kilverston, Boothley, and Tothman's Bluff. Its nodes of light would guide him.

He adjusted the multi-pointed crest on his shiny Fool's helmet and buttoned his leather jerkin, scarred with the flame-work of earlier Feasts. Outside his retinue was gathering. Time to lead the procession down to the Market. Then, around the town, a circuit of the Serpent Path - and the ascent to Leyston Burrough. To enact new rites of Samhain. The Blazing Night of the Walking Dead. His annual apotheosis.

So the Pleasure Centres knobsworths were trying their feeble sacrilege at the Burrough, erecting their Moloch-Engines in the holy cavity. But Noah was fretting too soon. The incomers were doomed. For all their long words, they had no centre and only pleasured themselves with their glitchy dream-machines. No match in the magick of love or war, for a shaman, Forgan, with his hoochie-coochie torchbearers and his wild witch-girls.

Portal

In the depths of the Burrough, they were leading William to the Iconoclasm Portal, to initiate BRAN. He'd been expecting a cold exultation but now that the moment of validating his greatest achievement had arrived, he was more conscious of his basic anatomy, his clenched bowels, a persistent itch in his left eye. His body was running downhill, in slow motion. The procession ahead of him - Rinehart, Liggett and Pullman, all in their dark suits - was funerary, like a slow march to his electrocution chamber, Old Sparky readied for firing... For the only way he could meet Lombard's brief would involve some desperate 'sleight-of-mind', an expression he'd never expected to use, even to himself.

Now he'd really entered the Zone, as the young programmers at the Establishment used to say as they hunched over their work stations. The sensors were attached to his bumpy skull as blank-faced Emily and Roxanne eased his arthritic legs into the body suit before crowning him with the heavy helmet. His simulated sex with them was so much corrupted memory. For a long time he sat in darkness and semi-deafness, listening to the distant growl of Lombard, the tense cadences of Rinehart giving some final briefing to his assistants. Whatever became of Carla? A sharp young woman. In another scenario, some mutual respect might have been forged. But he was so tired now.

He felt a faint tingle in his fingertips, which slowly crept around his whole body. The display in his eyepiece lit up.

Walk with the Serpent

Trader Price had boarded up his shop and two heavies in PC uniforms stood outside, guarding their local ally, who could be glimpsed peering from an upper window. They scanned the High Street apprehensively. Forgan's Rout - effectively most of Leynebridge - were approaching, a throng of drums, torches, whips, masks and feathered cloaks. A dark girl in a blackbird mask and silver-painted breasts danced ahead, swivelling her hips and rolling her pelvis to the throb of the congas and snares.

Forgan headed the march, flanked by muscular youths carrying the great crackling Fire-Basket of the Sun. Sparks scattered over the thatched roof of Elaine's cottage. Sooner or later a roof would catch somewhere, another burnt-offering to the Old Ones. Four Elders followed, shouldering the burden of the Scribe's Chair, an ornate sedan enclosing Wharton and the Great Book of Leynebridge. The bookseller sat enrobed in state, oblivious to the pandemonium around him, the Great Book open on his lap. Despite the wobble of the chair, he was still inscribing binary digits, murmuring into his beard. Noah followed, leaning on his staff, uneasy tonight in his ceremonial role, trying to ignore the energies gathering behind him. .

The villagers had always marched with blazing torches. But this year they could be riding a darker current. A sense of impending catastrophe seemed encoded in the throb of the drums. Belly dancers released their spinal chakras, undulating with faint whoops, around the staggering stilt-walkers. Children juggled fireballs or swung fire-torches. They dodged in and out of the procession, taunting each other to dive under the hot iron bellies of the traction engines dragging ramshackle floats. The Elders had spent weeks instructing the youth how to build these around the shells of wrecked cars. Each displayed a living tableaux from the town's mythology - The Beaver of Light, The White Dragon, The Rupture Demons, The Serpent. The seven giant blazing heads of the Leynebridge Serpent wobbled dangerously close to the eaves of the Unicorn while the crowds began their random chants – 'Release the Dragon! Walk with the Serpent! Burn out the Carbonites! Fuck like a Snake!'

Thunderflashes and home-made grenades were hurled

indiscriminately through the stinging fog of wood-smoke and herb-fumes that blanketed the town as Clansmen flashed their swords and sounded the war pipes. The Tribe of Hallow Fools flourished their totems, the Green Man loomed amid his walking shrubbery, the Sun Maidens had painted their flesh and all the godmen of Pan eagerly displayed their horns. Mrs Nixon, caged in the Great Wheel of Time, screamed in terror as it bounced along the cobblestones towards Leystone Burrough.

Forgan led them around the town, through Unicorn Street, past the Tower, past the Red Hag, into Dragon Lane, down Hallows Road, past the church, along the stony walkways. It was a pathway working, the Serpent Path.

As the parade surged, so rumours drifted through the deep brown noise of the Undermind: *Aran sighted near the Tower. Undercover Mo-Boys infiltration. A burning dragon barge floating down the Leyne - jammed under the bridge.* Noah, overcome now with deep panic, struggled to catch up with Forgan but the procession was developing its own momentum and the old man was pushed aside by his torch-bearers for the Arch-Fool was trance-walking, speaking in alien tongues...

Around the circumference of the mound, a spiral fire maze had been drawn up in the churned earth. Forgan led his wild rout through the crackling labyrinth. His glossalia was going viral now, they were all hissing or growling as they walked the whole spiral, to the top of the mound, halting at the boarded-up the entrance to the Burrough Chamber.

Forgan signalled with his flaming staff. Voices and drums eventually subsided, the silence only broken by the splutter of torches and the crackle of the Sun-basket. His voice felt raw, he enunciated with effort. The syllables of ordinary speech seemed unfamiliar to him now.

'The Hour of Alignment is fast approaching. We draw a line of fire around the Earth. The Earth Spirit must be refertilised at this cusp of the year, so our Leynebridge energies, fast approaching a zenith, will be focussed along the Burrough Stone to the great ley nodes of North and South, East and West. Soon our dazzling beams of biopsychic force will flash between power nodes across the land. But the link has to be aligned. Two of us must attune themselves to the current, and communicate the word of the gods of death and rebirth, in their Underworld beneath the Burrough. True blood and seed must flow on the Stone.' He hurled his staff high in the night air, a whirling micro-nebula of sparks...

Noah tried to intervene before the drums and the throat-music started again, drowning his voice. 'It has always been symbolic, Forgan, a mime of coupling and death, or a stylised utterance by Archpriest and Archpriestess, But what we face is far beyond anything even you have scried...'

The Elder could no longer trust his Fool in this grave crisis. The Burrough was a dark forbidding cavity, portal to a zone deep below the Undermind where the ancients received their visions, along the sight-lines of the Innerworld. Yet the holy place was already profaned. Forgan was only a clown shaman. Wharton was now possessed by a cipher-spirit. The people were generating a mighty current but they couldn't control it. How could they drive out the unclean intruders? Lombard, who must be voyeuring the whole scenario via some devious Lobe surveillance, would use this night as a justification for sending in his private army and wiping out the Clan once and for all before sealing off the Burrough. The Way of Leynebridge was going to end in an orgy of mud and blood, before being sanitised as a theme park spectacle. Leynbridge was doomed. He could sense it in the desperate babel at the back of his mind. And looking up, he could see an omen, looming.

Got the Ability to Morph Probability

Lucas could see a screen. Somehow, at the summit of the Burrough, a huge silvery screen had suddenly been projected, a glowing window into his lost world, for he hadn't seen anything like this since that hazy time before the Suture, the Rupture, whatever... His fingers hurt so much it was hard to concentrate. Clouds of smoke from the pyrotechnics drifted across his vision. People wouldn't stop waving torches and banners and his head ached with the rhythm of the drummers. But he could - just - pick out the contours of a face in the dancing pixels. A young mouth, miming furiously to itself.

Carla slumped on his shoulder. They'd walked like ghosts for hours in circles through the freezing streets. She hadn't been burned but she couldn't walk straight and wasn't talking coherently. Perhaps the flickering image might trigger something. He shouted through the tumult.

'Look, Carla. Perhaps they're showing one of your old films.' He felt fatuous saying it, for it was like picking at the scar tissue of their 'relationship', whatever a relationship was, he didn't know anything any more, except that he was very much immersed again in the physical body which hurt like fuck.

Carla muttered some broken syllables and gestured at the screen. The crowds were roaring so loudly now than he couldn't understand her but the outlines of the face were clearer despite electronic smog or physical fog, he couldn't decide which but he was getting the picture and the sound was getting to him, a huge percussive bass.

The camera pulled back back to reveal the young woman dancing, clutching a microphone. She was near-nude, neatly sexualized in old-skool black plastics. But as the director zoomed in towards her glistening lips, Lucas recognised the face beneath the iconography. Vivienne, of all people, was channeling this urban rant, this agit-rap -

I'm Quantum Slut I got two faces
My attraction's directed distraction I'm in two places
My love-light slips out through all the slits
You can't slot me I got mystery bits
Got the ability to morph probability
In the space of my base there's no tranquillity
I put the word on the street I'm fresh flesh
I'm the showtime shaman now I'm a shamaness
I can take you places, got the hi-tech
slump up the volume of rough trade, play final vinyl decks
to shake down systems, rock the death house
we're locked into, now they zipped up our mouths
but I'm a screeching teacher, I give you out-reach
I'll be there for yall, give you the power of speech
I'm Quantum Slut I got two faces -

Quantum Slut was going to repeat it. And repeat it. The level was pumping up to maximum noise terror.

'She was one of yours, Lucas? One of your little fancies, maybe. In her Borderland days?' Carla was choking with laughter - or smoke inhalation. He had to ignore her goading, because the potential for crowd rampage was rising, aroused by this new sound-clash between Urbanite electro-hop and the deep throb of the Borderland tribes.

'We have to get out of here.' A futile gesture. She could scarcely read his lips. They were already crushed together by bodies, the muscled bodies of Leynebridge lads and the oiled breasts of village earth-maidens. Fortunately these painted revellers fused together in savage exultation, scarcely registering the existence of a drab couple in scorched rags. Below him, all around the mound, the forces were peaking, speaking in tongues of fire. A group of Flatheads were rolling up the great wooden Time-Wheel wherein Mrs Nixon writhed, steadying it before the Burrough barricade. A fat butcher boy (Tyler?) whom Lucas dimly remembered from his pedantry days was re-lighting his smoldering torch. His mindset was all too readable *scapegoat ripe as tripe for roasting but first our sports day for the boys...* This was their possessed Jezebel of the dump who spread contagion and impotence. They'd shag her into submission, get a sexual apology out of her. So the wicker cage in the hub was opened, the victim's legs were prised apart and tied. She spat and cursed as Tyler clambered between the spokes of the Wheel, cheeks flushed, fumbling with his leather apron.

Then a shout went up, riding over the pulse of Quantum Slut, still looping in her eternal deafening playback. 'Aran is on the loose! Aran! Aran!' The warrior was cleaving his way through the crowd, brandishing his heavy sword, forged by Gil Norwood and engraved with sigils of the Lore. 'No more burning. No more trophy-fucking. No more sacrifice. Only the true Lore.' He struck Tyler hard with the flat of the sword, sending him rolling in the mud, before slashing Mrs Nixon's bonds. As she wriggled free, attempting to kiss her rescuer, he pulled away, and stood transfixed for few seconds by the image on the screen, the curving body and strident tones, this transmutation of his intended house-wife. Then he shook his head, spat and turned to face the crowd.

'Seize him, ' cried Noah, feebly. 'He slew Sister Elaine. Forgan, command your men to hold him.' Forgan, in deep trance again, ignored him. His attention had been focussed on Wharton's Book. For the unwilling scribe had now stepped out of his ceremonial chair and held the Great Book open as Forgan's eyes flickered across the lines of symbols and digits while Mrs Nixon, battered but triumphant, simultaneously serviced the lust of several Elders with unabated gusto in the chiaroscuro of the firelight, to ribald cheers.

Aran raised his weapon and gestured towards the barricade. 'Time to seize back the Burrough! Lombard's men are just cowering in there. And there are hundreds of us...' Forgan didn't respond but made complex passes with his staff as Wharton held the Book. There were no paraffin pyrotechnics, none of the usual Forgan rhetoric, only some intricate internalised rite. After a few long seconds, Aran strode up the mound towards the fenced-off chamber. 'You're just a joker, Forgan. I'll leave you to your orgies...'

Now the bodies massing on the mound had become a single great beast of entangled interpenetrating flesh. As screams of pain and pleasure intensified, Lucas had a brief epiphany. This was a Pleasure Centres strategy at work. The mobs were being manipulated with an overlay of apparently conflicting reality-models. For the vibrating membrane of their collective consciousness, that Undermind, was being stretched to ripping-point. They clung to their strong tribal Lore but the seductive dance of Quantum Slut was creating a confusion - or fusion - between different reality-shows, generating an unbearable peak of dark energies, a whirling vortex -

Probability Wave Intrusion

Lombard knelt before the screens surveying the exterior of the Burrough. 'They're going to blow a fuse, we will have fusion, these wretched alt.worlds will contract, all the cosmic bubblies will burst, I'm certain of it because we're going to have certainty all over again, isn't that just wonderful! And they all want a piece of Quantum Slut. She's really got their ancient mojos working.' He pointed to the seething pixels on the monitor, forming and reforming themselves into tiny new permutations of torsos and limbs in the flickering light. 'I must say they do know how to organise an organic festival.'

'They'll be crushing against the fences soon. They can easily break in and over-run our men. I don't like the look of that man with a sword.' Liggett was sweating. He suddenly wished he was out there, tearing off his tie and ID badge, tumbling among the fornicating revellers - he could see a nice chubby girl with pig-tails shaking her plump hips, just his sort, out there for real in the sweaty world, no software, just slippery wetware, beyond his reach for ever now.

'No need to get restless, Liggett. It's all under control. They won't rush us. They'll send sacrificial victims first.' Lombard smiled and rose. Unlike the others, he seemed unaffected by the glare of the lights and the heat of the hardware. 'How are those supercomputers, Rinehart? Cooking nicely, I hope. And Dr Crowe, I trust, is plugged in properly, all erogenous zones covered...'

Rinehart looked nervously at the displays. 'The system is structured hierarchically. He can only enter The Playzone of Desire after he has faced the Psychomorphs in the Spaces of Combat and solved whatever threat or challenge they present. There's this risk he might encounter some rogue element in the system, or he might try to over-ride a system request. Ah, he's activated a deep-level encryption system. BRAN has over-ridden Iconoclasm and has started creating its own domain inside the Lobe. Or around the Lobe... It's not clear...'

'BRAN is creating our new domain. That's all I want to hear. '

'It's not as simple as that... There's this probability-wave intrusion you're trying to stir up with the natives. How can it be focussed? It's not going to be easy...'

'Easy is for weaklings, Rinehart...'

A Great Quake

Dr Crowe was in the innards of BRAN. His head was inside his head. One of them was virtually actual. It was hard to differentiate when the maths complexified. In his ghost world, the faery dance of pixellations, William was writing a code to capture the floating pointillism of Leynebridge's Underminders, all thousands of them, in a standing wave or haze of line-dancing particles. He took all their chances, for they were a bundle of chancers. So on his virtual screens-within-screens, in his infinite recursions, he added them all up in a great quake of an equation. It was a self-centering inter-penetration. He was writing the whole copulating populace into his code-world.

Clansmen of Leynebridge

Aran paused at the makeshift barrier around the Burrough. Through a gap in the sagging chipboard fence he could see the hooded metal snouts of Carbonite spy-devils, while two of Lombard's minders were watching him apprehensively. Guns or no guns, he could take them, no problem. But his real target was deep inside, the old man in the earth, his ogre whose slaughter offered redemption. And where were the people of Leynebridge, where was Arch Fool Forgan, had he chosen an Arch-Priest and Priestess to offer sacrifice? Yet a few gestures with a fiery staff to burn the big Book and a quick shafting on the Stone weren't going to cleanse the Burrough. He needed to focus his power, call on the magic of sword-words. He couldn't face looking up at the screen, where his treacherous home-wife had been enslaved by Carbonite trickery - it had to be trickery. So he turned to scan the hillside, through the smoke of Forgan's star-rockets and the blazing hog-fires. He raised his voice again to the Gods and to his fickle people.

'Are you with me, Clansmen of Leynebridge? Will you fight at my side and purge the Burrough?' He roared the Thorn-Rune Thurisaz, sign of Thor, slashing the air with his sword to command a deadly triangulation of force. As he crouched, poised for attack, weapon extended, he sensed a dark energy surging up from the turf of the hill, impregnated with the sweat and semen of the rutting folk. He would have the strength of giants, it was written in the Elder Futhark, it was carved into the Tree of Life...

The crowd surged forward as one body. He could see Forgan and Wharton in there at the back, almost submerged in the crush. Forgan was ranting now as Wharton desperately waved his burning Book but their old rite had already served its purpose, the *vril* of the people had been aroused, surely nothing could oppose it.

A man and a woman had been shoved to the front, apparently selected at random as Priest and Priestess. It wasn't going to be play-acting this year. They knew that, he could see it in their eyes as they stumbled towards him. He couldn't place the woman, in her filthy urban clothes, but he recognised the man, that vicious manikin whom Elaine had revealed in trance, the ravager of his betrothed. He could geld the Rupture-merchant and scar him for life, that would be a sacrificial gesture - but maybe it was all a trick, like that illusion, that parody of Vivienne flickering overhead, for the City tricksters made everything up to tease and taunt...

No time for wondering. The barriers were splintering and falling now, as guards scattered and the crowd trampled over each other, scrumming furiously into the narrow mouth of the Burrough chamber. Aran pushed Lucas down into the mud and grabbed Carla by the neck, dragging her through the aperture into a bright glaring space he could not recognise. His followers paused, suddenly silenced. The Undermind was muted.

The rough bluestone pillars and earthworks supporting the irregular dome of the Burrough had been overlaid with Carbonite gear - serpentine tubes, hanging webs of cables, dazzling lights. And peering spy-eyes, protruding like the cocks of steel goblins. This wasn't honest metal craft; it was a cradle of entrapment. He looked for the great central stone - and panicked. Surely they could not have moved or demolished it. Then he found it, obscured by an array of huge black metal cabinets, high as a man, which droned and murmured. Malign obelisks studded with winking stars. He sensed they might be soul-tombs.

'Welcome to Pleasure Centres! How can we help you?' A rich baritone resonated around the whole space. Letting Carla drop to the floor, Aran paced warily to the far side of the central pillar, where four men clustered around a battery of screens scrolling through alien symbols. Behind them stood another tall cabinet, slightly larger than the others, adjoining a grey dome-like structure, the height of a man. It was all Carbonite tech-craft trickery, wiring spewing everywhere. He could feel the dull roar of the Undermind. Any moment now the Clan could strike. They were only waiting for his signal.

'I've come for the old man. Where is he?'

The big man with the over-ripe voice laughed. 'Oh, the melodrama of it! Do you mean our Dr William Crowe PhD? He's so old. Old and scrawny and horny. But he's very busy right now. His cybernetic coitus will not be interruptus, as we say to all our customers. He's channeling you all into a lovely new head. And you're going to wake up in a new world, a safe world, a sensible world. Don't worry, there'll still be jobs for big fellows like you - security guards, bailiffs - '

Aran raised his sword and advanced on the capsule. 'Is he in there? The old one?'

'I wouldn't do that if I were you. If you interfere at this point, and try to distract him with a violent assault, the whole wave-front of this particular edition of reality could be scrambled, all the juicy life-force of Leynebridge that's flowing through here could be dissipated, pissed down the vortex of a gravity well, something like that. I'm trying to put it in terms an honest chump like you can grasp...'

Kill the old man and his talking heads. That was the brief. One death would lead to another. Let them roll out the skulls. He'd call their bluff eventually. 'Where are his talking heads?'

'Oh, I'm afraid you've been misled there. If you mean those elusive Quantum Brothers. You can't sit down and talk to them, they're not a talk-show. They're just an urban myth. A digital hoax. Two heads are no better than one. You've got other heads to roll around, know what I mean?'

Lombard rose from his chair and circled Aran carefully, keeping his distance. His rumbling voice merged with the drone of the circuitry and the tidal roar at the root of Aran's brain.

'There's so much life-force around here in the Borderlands. I can almost smell it burning up in the air. Like your old smoke and mirror routines. That lovely blue flame that they hoover up. All it takes now is one final grand Act of Transgression to heighten our collective sense of reality. A real sacrificial act. A literal Lore-making action to trigger a final discharge and energise old William's headpiece. I'm sure you've thought a lot about sacrifice. Especially of those worthless city harlots - like this one... a Lobe-bitch, a serpent who has destroyed your paradise, and deserves to die.' He raised a finger and nodded.

Rinehart and a minder seized Carla and pulled her forward on to the granite boulder that formed the base of the central pillar. She was mute, eyes closed. They turned her to face the Stone and raised her arms, tying them to rusty stanchions embedded in the granite. Lombard leaned back on his shooting stick, conducting proceedings with a wave of his hand. Rinehart began ripping off the remnants of her clothes.

'I never expected a former employee to provide the stimulus for a space-time restructuring, but in our contingent Polyverse every entity has its purpose. She's all yours and in a sense all ours. For your pleasure... And then the capital punishment. *Caput*, Latin, noun, a head. Capital!'

Satanic Zone

Hauling the case up these muddy slopes through the rabble of this pagan anti-Haj had almost exhausted Hisham; and maybe he should never have dragged Abdul along on his arthritic legs. But if he could make the old man grasp the significance of what was about to happen then maybe his uncle could share with him - and Omar - in the blinding glory of martyrdom. They had to stumble towards the summit, towards whatever new trickeries were evolving in the Satanic zone.

Reality Enactment

William was fragmenting. His interface was defacing him. The new software, his revised Iconoclasm, wasn't re-presenting his sickly body-image consistently. 'Can't even pimp his pixels,' whispered a brain-worm. In this blocky reality-enactment, his hand had already become an angular claw, his arm was a boxy appendage hinging or hanging in the wrong places and tactile inputs were dangerously scrambled. When he laboriously angled his digital pseudopod to touch the virtual keyboard in front of its virtual monitor, his fingers spasmed with pain, like rotting teeth. Lines of green code shimmered across the screen, his dark portal to BRAN as he tried to focus on the detail of his mission, to open BRAN and rationalise the Ruptured worlds, once and for all. But there was no algorithm vast enough to cope with all the squirming variables.

He was immersing himself in a sparkly fog of data. The Festival was infested. No other words for it, for words weren't signalling very well, no sign language in this cloud of data, this binary swarm that roared right through his brain. It was/wasn't all clear if the data were flowing in and out of his gaping gawping screen. 'Now you see'em, now you don't!' A loopy brain-song was interfering with him all over again. He was going to merge with the surge.

Now he was going filmic. He was grainy, he was dissolving into a solution of infinity, he was wiping himself all over and out, he was zoomed into the Black Whole.

The Black Whole subsumed the black hole, that platonic cave where they'd bunkered up, and emerging from the cloud he had a point-of-view, he was the Hole-Point. He could view curving walls, inscribed with more and more flickery digits, and *there was a pillar at the centre and she was tied to it, her flow of fine hair falling across bare back, pale buttocks* and this was at the centre of his old pleasures and she turned -

* * *

The sword 'Brain-Biter', crafted by old Gil Norwood, balanced superbly in Aran's sweaty grip. His huge hands tightened around the rune-engraved hilt as the weapon rose, with infinite slowness, poised to strike -

* * *

Carla prayed for an infinite extension of this moment. She had to remain in her poor body, its warm bloody vessels and tender ligaments. It was all she knew, she didn't trust those astral voyages with Lucas. This was karmic punishment for her adultery with Omar, his family's collective unconscious had found this brutish servitor who would hack and saw, she wouldn't die at the first spurt -

* * *

Lucas lay paralysed with horror. Aran the Barbarian was about to act out his atavisms, his archetypes, his automatism, whatever Qliphothic joker possessed him. He was really going to do it to her.

* * *

A Polyverse experience was blurring around William. He was up to his wrinkly neck in it. A potentiality hovered before him: *black incised sword bisecting smooth neck in a fine spray of blood, a corona of red hair. The lovely head was falling...*

* * *

Lucas had to believe it, even as he shut his eyes and tried to block her scream as the blade swung down. The thud of butchery. No retreat from it, not even in the Black Whole.

* * *

A Polyverse experience was vibrating around William. He was up to his scrawny neck in it. A probability shimmered before him: *dark runic sword swerves, sparks against the stone, slender neck and shoulder twist away, she tosses her lovely flaming mane triumphantly...*

* * *

Lombard couldn't believe it. His belief system was breaking down. 'The peasant lost his nerve in an ethics attack. Sex and death on a plate - and he fumbles it!'

* * *

Outside the Burrough at last, Hisham could wait no longer. He should have made an entrance, made a speech declaiming the greatness of God but his shout might have been lost in the beats-per-minute and the demented infidel mouth-music. The old man's teeth were chattering away in the din, but it was too late to abandon the mission, it was time, his time, so he flipped his lid and punched in the code, sending the pellets of heavy metal tunneling towards each other, in a black mass of energy and blinding light.

* * *

Outside the Burrough at last, Hisham could wait no longer. He had to make an entrance, make a speech proclaiming the greatness of God, for he could out-shout their beats-per-minute and their deranged pagan utterings. Old man Abdul was pawing at his sleeve but it was time to shove him aside, an end-time for the activation of the suitcase. As Abdul clutched feebly at his wrist, he clicked open the lid to his casket of judgement. The bomb would be his messenger, it would speak in tongues of thunder.

Yet the accursed uncle was still, unthinkably, trying to interfere with the holy moment, sticking his crooked fingers over the keypad, sticking his dirty thumb into his nephew's eye-socket.

Hisham staggered, lost his footing. They went down together into the muddy grass, to roll over and over. The yelling crowd cleared a circle for this big fight. Hisham could fend off his uncle's weakening blows and quickly got a firm ligature on that grizzled neck, strong enough to choke the life out of the old traitor, whose lips finally stopped quivering.

Now Hisham could fulfil his destiny, as scripted. Except there was no suitcase, no vessel of doom - only a trail in the mire where it had been dragged away, a curious trophy for two screeching revellers in owl-masks who were disappearing from sight in the seething crowd.

Multiplexing Selves

William strobed through the budding worlds, in a space-time seizure, a pod of totality/virtuality. The promised games, those rainbow pleasure-dome follies were all over before they began - goodbye, psychomorphs, holy harlots, dog-demons - and right in several eternities of now the black sun of a bomb was orbiting around his head, a dark god in a machine but not one he had personally designed. Let it come down. All worlds were war-crafted. Every surrender and victory could be re-enacted in slow motion.

Now his bio-pics were re-writing his potential story-lines across the world-lines. Scrolling headlines - *RECORD PROFITS FOR CROWE INC/KNIGHTHOOD FOR WILLIAM CROWE AI WIZARD/ ATOM MAN DEAD IN MYSTERY AIR CRASH/SCIENCE TEACHER 'RAMPAGE IN MASSAGE PARLOUR' - 3 DEAD/ 'PARANORMAL IS BUNK' - CROWE*. But the displays were playing out too fast, layering too thick...

Abruptly, to the sound of synthesised music (pastiche Elgar, Vaughan Williams) the Head of BRAN spoke, hanging high in a blank grey sky-projection.. The graphical interface & audio people had given him an icon resembling a cubist Winston Churchill and a deep brown voice: 'Here is a public service announcement. This is, in a metaphorical and iconic sense, the virtual soul of your nation, a living time-capsule.'

William was briefly enfolded into un-Ruptured newsreels: mushroom clouds on the Nullabor plain; Jim Laker, sunlit in the Oval, bowling nice and steady from the Gasometer End; Sir Anthony Eden's twitching mouth; a chequered flag for Moss at Monaco; flapping hats at Ascot - all the jerky bleached past re-cycling into infinity, waiting for Godot. But the sound track was a fruity voice-over of the office furniture inventory at Corsham Regional Seat of Government 'Burlington', followed by the BBC Light Programme 'Music While You Work' with the Big Ben Banjo Band...

Alternate takes/mistakes of reality were scrolling all over his multiplexing selves, rolling him/them flat out to stretch over nine dimensions, a flimsy film at the point of dissolving, he was pointless... or the whole point?

15
Serious Business in the Polyverse

His Vision Was Plural

Lucas couldn't see properly. His vision was plural. In the pulsing light of the cave, crammed with desperate bodies, at least for alternate seconds, every contorted head or hand exuded a bubbly translucent clone of itself, which wasn't a true clone, because it mutated exponentially. So he was hemmed in by a cloud of ghosts, in a process of incessant transmutation. He glanced at his own flickering left hand, at the calluses that appeared and disappeared, at the suddenly curving nails, the surprise chrome-plated left hook...

He tried to focus on a constant, the central stone pillar. The man they called Lombard was dancing around it wearing a crown, maybe a mitre. There he was, waving his serpent, trying to scourge bareback Carla who was/wasn't here or there.

Meanwhile he'd lost his arc. Until now he'd been hurling himself forward in a parabola (or parody) of desire, a light-line intersecting the curve of Carla. But he'd reached the end of the rainbow, in a muddy hole in front of a heap of stones. The hero's journey should end in a romantic rescue, the salvage of the love-object, but in this random world of hypertrophied possibility his heroics were superfluous.

Implausible Contortions

Detaching herself neatly from the pillar, without even turning to glance back at Lucas or Aran, Carla sauntered over to the Chief Executive, fondling a girdle and a gleaming dildo snatched from a

Pleasure Centres display. Lombard, awe-struck, fell forward on to his knees as she tore off his belt.

She slid into her victim, reaching forward to clasp his phallus while steadying her own implement. 'I've got something planned for you, Mister Lombard...' She cultivated a velvety whisper. The old-tyme Californian sex stars used to run through a whole wearisome repertoire of grunts and exhalations, exhorting the subject towards ever more implausible contortions of fuckery but Carla had learned that less was more.

The reversal of sexual polarities was the aim of the operation, a wrecking of taboos. The victim moaned, breathed hard. Carla slapped his rump. He was a good fat beast. She was fucking his lowest chakra now, to reverse the flow of chi, to fire right up into his pineal gland. No, it's the prostate, the walnut of death. She was losing it in this fusion of the senses.

He was struggling to break free. Perhaps they were going too far, too fast. The current was swilling up his spinal column. He found it hard to breathe and uttered a complication of blasphemies that made her big breasts shudder. She was swaying back and forth into him, trying to coax him to climax, so that his abdicated power would flux right in the abyss of her sex. She felt herself as raw image now. She was replicating virally across the night-waves.

She realised she was under control. Her control was Princess Lilith, who was controlled by Lady Babalon, who was controlled by Queen Kali. All flesh was her medium of manifestation. She could let go...

The Null Point

Reality's convulsions had subsided for a bit. There was some kind of sex rumpus going on on the periphery of his attention but William was in a meeting. He and the Brothers had reached a temporary reality consensus, in a simulacrum of a committee room, a round table with a small stone water-feature at the centre. Time was travelling slowly tonight. William was hanging in there, podded into the Zone, except the Zone had changed. His alt.lives had been faded down in the mix. There were no more ancestral voices, no sword-waving games, not even any tantalising flexi-nudes.

The Polyverse was serious business now, he was in conference mode with the Quantum Brothers themselves. Their heads, double the normal size, were mounted holographically on an impressive slate dais overlooking the table, so William could actually read their lips. He could not see any cigars but they constantly exhaled aromatic smoke. He was clearly privileged.

'Take in another mouthful. Inwards and upwards... Go on, William. It's a herbal mixture, sourced from local fungi. You can almost taste it now, can't you?'

He felt he was about to choke on his own ectoplasm but he clearly had to respond. 'It's like... tasting your own brain... the flavour...'

'Let it take you deep into the Zone.' The Brothers intoned as one. It was obviously an initiation rite. Even though the incense stung his virtual throat, he had to persist with it.

'I know this is a virtual world - but my tongue's burning...'

'Are you afraid? Never mind. Let's look at the numbers.' A display rose from the centre of the rosewood table, screening a stream of binary data, the old-style green on black digits that William was comfortable with, zero and one in their dance of living death. But it was too flicking fast...

'You're scanning the machine code that's rendering everything into place. We're just one reality level up. Or down, depending on your point of view. You must have a point of view, with a conical nose like yours. Anyway the code-demons are busy processing for us. You're going to be made up.'

'Re-invented. As a qubyte in the universal quantum computer?' William tried to shift paradigms.

'That's one strategic plan. Quantify every little thought. The species will have a direct neural link to the Lobe. So much easier to manage. Lots of ghosts in one machine. Or lots of machines in one ghost. Thousands of goblins. Gobbing goblins. Doing the old in-and-out. You should be sick with shock and awe and bad molecules. You're implicit in the machine-code of the universe bleeping itself in and out of existence... and it's a huge ridiculous game. Digi-demons fizzling up all over the place, glitzing reality up out of big nothings, it's all so absurd, the posh contours of humanity, the shape of your wrinkly forehead– it's all being coded from the underworld by Satan's little helpers, the tribal nibblers of the Cyberzone... What more would you like to know?'

William suspected now he was a disappearing act. Caught in their mesh. Their sticky matrices. He was dancing to their data-flow but he couldn't see too much because of the fungal growth spilling over his eyes. However he seemed to be following a script:

'So we're avatars?' They were playing games with him, obviously. 'Am I an icon in your marketing system...?'

' In a trans-dimensional entertainment system. The faked telepathy was just a training phase. We naturally express regrets over such painful episodes as the Dog-Demons Incident and other alleged deaths or disfigurements. These episodes were, quite literally, breakdowns in communication. Our experimental interfaces obviously revealed unexpected bugs in the wetware of the humanoid brain. You see, William, we are in the business, an expanding business, of improving communication technologies steadily to result in more and more positive-sum games and enhanced cooperative social and interpersonal frameworks at your level. We're preparing you for first contact."

Contact. It was all clear now. These Quantum Brothers could be alien intelligences, maybe originally silicate extra-terrestrial beings who could now survive as pure digital entities and had implanted themselves in the Lobe. The Lobe was the Host and he was going to be the Commentator. He would be the Voice-Over of Interplanetary Parliament. Take me, take me to your Leader...

"Who are you? Where are you from?"

"You know quite well who we are. When you created BRAN, you created the seed-code for us. Like Onan you scattered it far and wide. It wormed, it was quite Trojan in its subterfuges and it absorbed a glut of data. The Rupture livened us up somewhat - think of it as a lightning strike into two jolly tubs of amino acid - and ever since then we've been gathering more data - latterly with your help - transforming our public image into whatever we think the punters want, orchestrating events to the best of our ability, for the long-term benefit of all. For we are, in effect, your servitors, operating on a freelance basis. Now, time to move on, we have a long night ahead of us...'

Their faces were steadily expanding to fill the dark hemisphere of his field of awareness, as the smoke from their mouths swirled around his head, which was splitting down its corpus calleosum like a rotten old nut. He couldn't move a gloved finger. The pain was deep brownish-pink, fading rapidly to black.

* * *

Lucas ran into the night, trying to erase the image of Carla rampant, a polysexual Amazon riding a bare-backed beast into submission. He couldn't cope with any more sensory overload. His emotions were burnt out by her wild transgressions, and panic overpowered him, as Leynebridge collided with the operations of the Lobe.

He slithered and stumbled down the slopes of the Burrough, trying to find a path through crackling bonfires and the chiaroscuro of entangled fire-dappled bodies disrupted in their shivering sex-rites. Were they whooping now with ecstasy or terror? His world – or his head - was splitting apart. Only forward momentum would hold the burnt bits of himself together. He ran towards the darkness.

CPSIA information can be obtained at www.ICGtesting.com
Printed in the USA
LVOW08s1238070314

376450LV00002B/54/P